THE FIRST BOOK OF THE SMALL GODS

WHEN SHADOWS FALL

BRUCE BLAKE

When Shadows Fall

Fall

The First Book of the Small Gods

Bruce Blake

Comments?

Contact Bruce at: bruce@bruceblake.net

ISBN 978-1-927687-10-9

Prologue

*I*T RAINED FIRE THE *day the Small Gods fled.*

"Watch out!" the priestess Rak'bana shouted, ducking behind Love—one of the granite Pillars of Life.

A ball of flame hammered into the earth with a spray of dirt and the stench of burnt grass. She covered her head, waiting for the ground to cease shaking before she peeked out from behind her arm to find her twin brother. Ine'vesi peered back at her from around the corner of the next column in the row of nine—Trust.

"Are you alright?" he asked.

The crackle of flames all but kept his voice from her ears, but they were well enough connected she knew what he'd ask without needing to hear. She nodded in response and he crept out from behind the column, the roll of parchment in his hand.

"Time is short, Vesi," she said. "The Goddess is angry."

Ine'vesi made no effort to hide the sneer upon his lips as he hurried across the ruined garden to her side. Before he opened his mouth to spill out the blaspheme imprinted upon his brow, she raised her hand and gestured with her fingers. A thick stream of water the height of five men rose from the river and flowed across the air. It splashed into the newly lit fire with a hiss of doused flames and white steam billowing toward the sky. Another ball of fire crashed into the top edge of the nearest wall, sending chunks of stone tumbling to the ground. The twin siblings ducked their heads.

"We have to go," she urged.

"Out of the city." Ine'vesi brandished the roll of parchment. "Once we have inscribed the scroll, it will not be safe here. The wrong hands will find it."

A fiery ball crashed into the base of a towering pine, its flames leaping up the trunk, spreading through its branches, jumping to the next tree like a playful squirrel, then skipping to the next. Rak'bana raised her hand again, intending to call the river and extinguish the fire to save her garden, but Ine'vesi caught her by the wrist.

"Let it burn, Bana. Let it be a testament to the unjust wrath of a jealous Goddess."

The priestess' eyes widened and she shook her head, unable to comprehend why he'd speak such blasphemous words. She pulled her hand free of his grip and faltered back a step toward the river.

"You are a priest, Vesi. You know as well as I that we have brought this on ourselves. Righteous anger falls from the sky, not jealousy. The Goddess gives what is deserved."

"The—"

Another ball slammed into the pine. The great tree leaned with a creak of wood, bending slowly at first, then the trunk split with a crack louder than thunder, and the tree that had grown in the courtyard for a dozen hundred seasons toppled, spilling flame across the dry grass. The fire raced toward the siblings, fueled by a swirling fireball, then another. A third pelted the ground, the closest yet, and the impact threw Ine'vesi into his sister, his momentum carrying them both into the river.

The frigid water clung to Rak'bana as she clutched her brother, and the red rage of the Goddess' flames shone through the shimmering river. She understood that, if they surfaced, the fire would hunt them mercilessly, never giving up until the blaze consumed them. Deserving of the Goddess' wrath or not, the priestess could not let that happen before they'd completed their task.

She held Ine'vesi tight to her chest and swirled her free hand, ma-nipulating the water around them to increase the river's current. It bore them away from the garden, away from the courtyard, but the red and orange glow above them brightened and the water grew warmer, heated by the anger of the Goddess. Worry burned in Rak'bana's chest along with her held breath—if they didn't leave their warning, this would all happen again. They'd both seen it in their dreams.

The water shivered around them as the Pillars of Life toppled, thumping to the ground. Ine'vesi jerked in her grasp, fighting the current and the heat, but she held him and gestured again. The river flowed faster, carrying them along like autumn leaves fallen from a dying tree, dragging them on until the light disappeared.

They'd entered the channel beneath the temple.

The river cooled again, but Rak'bana held them under, allowing the raging to current carry them deep into the heart of the temple and away from the Goddess' fury. Only when her breath threatened to explode in her lungs did she allow the river to bear them to the surface. Ine'vesi's head emerged from the water and he gasped a ragged, angry breath.

"Are you trying to aid the Goddess in killing me?"

"I saved you, ingrate." The priestess stroked toward the side of the channel, pulling her brother along behind. "You should thank me for not letting you burn."

"Hmph."

They reached the side and she hooked her arm over the edge, pulled Ine'vesi close to allow him to do the same. No light penetrated so far into the tunnel, leaving them in utter darkness, but she knew the door to be directly in front of them; she sensed it as surely as she sensed her brother at her side.

"One way or another, you were going to get me here, weren't you?" he said, pulling himself out of the water to stand on the narrow stone path beside the channel.

"You know it must be here." She climbed up alongside him, rested the palm of her hand against the door.

"It won't be safe here, Bana. The scroll might fall into any hands. It must go to Teva Stavoklis."

Rak'bana hesitated before opening the door. They'd had this discussion and thought they'd decided the matter, but it appeared Ine'vesi remained unconvinced. Her mouth opened to argue the point, but the stone of the tunnel shook minutely with an impact to the building above them, stopping her.

"Come," she said instead, and pushed the door open.

The pristine chamber beyond gleamed, its white marble walls and soaring granite pillars flickering with the orange light shining through the high windows. Rak'bana hurried into the room and down the three steps to the floor, sparing a brief glimpse for the massive suits of armor standing guard beside each of the four columns.

"Hurry," she said as she swept across the chamber toward her goal at the far end: a marble lectern that sprang up out of the floor as though carved of the same block of stone.

Droplets of water fell from her hair and dress, spattering on the smooth marble. The air in the room smelled old and unused, as well it should; no one had entered this room since the building of the temple. Thousands upon thousands of times the sun had risen and set, shining its light through the high windows, and the Sek'bala had stood watch beside the gray and white flecked granite columns, but no foot had touched the floor until Rak'bana's. The immensity of it was not lost on her but, with fire falling from the sky to spread the Goddess' punishment, no time for emotion and awe remained.

She reached the podium and glanced back across the room at her brother near the entrance. Ine'vesi stood motionless, staring at the imposing guards with their horned helmets and gleaming weapons.

"Vesi," she cried, waving for him to join her. "Bring the parchment."

He set one foot in front of the other and crossed the room slowly without tearing his gaze away from the Sek'bala. Outside the sanctuary, something rumbled. Rak'bana raised her eyes to the high windows, the flicker of flames shining through the narrow frames. Vesi had paused halfway to her, the roll of paper dripping as he held it out toward her.

Time is running short.

The priestess came around the lectern and jumped down the three stairs to the floor, her sandals slapping wetly on the white marble. The time for waiting and marveling had passed.

"Give it to me, Vesi." She held out her hand, expectant. "We must speak the words to prevent this from happening again."

Her fingers brushed the edge of the paper, felt its roughness, its power, but then it disappeared. Ine'vesi pulled it away and glared at her, his brows drawn together.

"Prevent it?" he asked, incredulous. The priest shook his head without removing his gaze from her eyes. "We must take this to Teva Stavoklis and leave instructions how to bring us back."

Rak'bana's mouth fell open. How did she not see this coming? She'd heard his words bordering on sacrilege, seen his disdain toward the Goddess in this time of judgment. But her sight had been clouded by the dreams, her mind filled with visions of the gray man, the Mother, the man from across the sea. She'd neglected to think for a moment that her twin brother—the man with whom she shared the priesthood and trusted more than anyone short of the Goddess herself—could have anything but the same goal as her.

How wrong she'd been.

"We can't let this happen again, Vesi." She despised the desperation creeping into her voice. "The generations that come after us must know."

Another rumble echoed through the chamber, this one louder than the last. Ine'vesi sneered. "We are in agreement, sister. This cannot happen again. The Goddess cannot be allowed to treat her loyal subjects in this manner. They must be given a way to prevent it, and bringing us back is the way."

"No. We deserve it. The Goddess never intended us to live this way. We—"

The priest took a step back and her gaze fell to the parchment he held in his right hand, out of her reach. The visions that visited her dreams meant nothing if she did not set them to words on the scroll, left them to be found when the time they were needed came. If she didn't, she'd have failed the Goddess.

"The scroll will go to Teva Stavoklis, to be used when the Goddess again over-steps her bounds. To ensure her subjects are never again punished for being human."

Rak'bana narrowed her eyes. "We are no longer human, Vesi."

"No, I suppose not," he conceded and took another step back. "We are closer to gods, aren't we? Small gods, perhaps."

She bit down hard and fought against the oncoming tears choking her throat. A louder rumble, and this time the walls trembled. The long pike of one of the Sek'bala warriors shivered in its hand, the metal shaft rattling against its gauntleted fingers. Rak'bana directed her gaze toward the massive suit of plate, lowered her chin and raised her hand. She wiggled her fingers the way she did when she called the water to her bidding and her brother realized her intent. Ine'vesi's head snapped to the side, eyes wide as he looked to the Sek'bala, expecting it to come to life.

Rak'bana leaped toward him and snatched at the roll of parchment, her fingers grasping the edge. It took only an instant for Ine'vesi to realize she'd tricked him. The priest danced back two steps, but she'd gotten a grip on the scroll and it unrolled between them. They both stared at its blank surface as another ball of fire struck the building and a shower of sparks spilled through one of the high windows.

They raised their heads; their eyes met.

"Bana," he said, voice calm and even, though his eyes reflected different emotions. "Don't do—"

"*When days of peace approach their end.*"

"Rak'bana."

"*And wounds inflicted are too deep to mend.*" Fear and disappointment surged through her, but she forced herself to speak clearly, drawing out the words to their full power, ensuring the parchment heard what her over the reverberating impacts shuddering the walls. "*A sign shall come, a lock with no key.*"

"Stop, Bana!"

"*Borne by a man from across the sea.*"

The wavering light of the flames licking the world flashed on Ine'vesi's blade. Rak'bana had an instant to recognize the slender knife before he jerked her toward him and plunged the tip between her ribs.

The wicked point tore through her flesh, found its way between the bones, and pressed against her heart. The agony of the wound stole her breath, but the anguish of her brother's betrayal crushed her soul. He pulled her close, the loose parchment folding between them, and a fresh wave of pain crashed through her, transported along her veins to the tips of her fingers.

"I am sorry, Bana, but it must be this way" he said, his tone quiet amongst the thunder of the Goddess' judgment. "We *are* gods."

Unable to do anything more, she stared, open-mouthed, at her twin brother, the priest to her priestess, the man for whom she'd always thought she'd give her life if necessary, and now he'd taken it.

Ine'vesi pressed harder on the stiletto and the point pricked her heart. The priestess gasped; her skin went cold as hoarfrost. Her brother pulled the knife out and jerked away, attempting to wrench the parchment's edge from her grasp, but her fingers held fast. The paper stretched, then tore, the sound of it ripping echoing through the marble chamber. Ine'vesi stumbled back, caught his balance, and advanced on her, his expression pulled into an angry shape that made him nearly unrecognizable to her.

Another fireball struck the temple. Then another, and another. The armor of the Sek'bala shivered and rattled, their weapons clattered in their grips. Ine'vesi glanced away from his sister at the towering guards, the sparks cascading through the high widows, and stopped, the anger on his face melting to fear.

He brandished the half of the parchment he still held. "This is all I need," he said, backing toward the door.

"Vesi." Rak'bana reached her hand out toward her brother. "Please."

The priest stopped short of the doorway, gazed back at his sister. For a second, his expression appeared regretful, and she thought he might return to her, help her complete what must be done. Instead, he shook his head.

"This wasn't what I dreamed, Bana. I saw a world where we can be what we are, and not be judged by a jealous Goddess. I dreamed of becoming the Small Gods we are meant to be."

He hesitated a second before disappearing through the doorway and into the channel beneath the temple. Rak'bana stared after him, her belly clenching at the thought of losing him, but soon, it would no longer matter. Soon, they'd all be gone, but she had one last task to perform before the end.

She glanced at the red stain spreading across the front of her dress, the droplets falling to the white marble floor, running along its veins, filling them. The temple shuddered under the Goddess' wrath and the priestess raised her head, gazed toward the lectern.

It seemed so far away.

Rak'bana put her left hand on the wound in her chest, felt her life force pulsing out of it, making her fingers sticky. With careful, plodding steps, she crossed the smooth floor, smearing her blood behind her as she went. It spread out along the stone, coloring it red; the Sek'bala watched, unconcerned.

A few paces from the goal, the fingers of her left hand tingled briefly, and then she lost feeling in them. The tingling climbed up her arm, racing toward her chest. Her breath shortened, cold sweat fell like winter dew on her brow, her knees trembled. She stumbled the last few steps, caught herself on the lectern's edge before her legs gave way and spilled her to the floor.

The priestess spread the parchment across the podium, holding one edge with shaking fingers, weighing the other down with her dead hand. The blood of her heart smeared across the paper, sticking in its texture. Thunder shook the walls, lightning flashed, tears streaked paths along her cheeks. Rak'bana drew her dry tongue across her icy lips and spoke the words given her by the Goddess in her dreams.

"When days of peace approach their end,
And wounds inflicted are too deep to mend,
A sign shall come, a lock with no key,
Borne by a man from across the sea.
A barren Mother, the seed of life,
Living statue, treacherous knife.
To raise the Small Gods, a Small God must die,
When the stars go out, the end is nigh."

She paused to draw a weak breath and watched her blood etching the cursive lines of her words across the paper. The walls shook and she raised her gaze for an instant to see the marble had gone red with the life dripping from her heart. She returned her attention to the final stanza required on the scroll.

"One must die to raise them all,
Should Small Gods rise, man will fall.
One can stop them, on darken'd wing,
The firstborn child of the rightful king."

As the last word crossed her lips, a wind carrying swirling flames howled through the high windows. Rak'bana tilted her head back, watched the fire snake toward her and closed her eyes, waiting for the Goddess to cleanse her and free her from her sorrow and pain.

And the flames consumed her.

Ine'vesi stumbled out of the tunnel into what had once been a picturesque courtyard filled with gardens for prayer and fountains for bathing. Now, instead of a place of beauty, it was a conflagration. The water for washing billowed from the fountains in clouds of white steam, the flowers and trees were ash, all but one of the Pillars of Life had fallen, and the river itself boiled and bubbled in the heat of the inferno.

The priest raised his arm to his face, protecting himself from the blaze as he fell to his knees, the roll of parchment pressed to his chest. His nostrils flared at the stench of his own hair melting, the stink sickening him, but he ignored it, thankful he'd paused in the channel to set the words of his dreams on the paper.

He lowered his arm and held the scroll on his lap, closed his eyes. Flames licked at the sleeves of his robe, crackled in the grass on which he knelt. It singed his flesh, but he'd prepared his entire life to concentrate on the task that needed his attention to the exclusion of everything else, including himself.

Ine'vesi ran his reddening fingers along the surface of the rolled parchment. Its coarse texture instilled hope in him and he brought to mind the solemn, sparse temple in Teva Stavoklis. He imagined each grain in the wood of its posts and beams, every rock and pebble strewn across its dirt floor. Bundles of protection herbs hung on spikes protruding from the walls; greasy smoke snaked up from tallow candles. He breathed deeply and, instead of scenting the blazing gardens, he inhaled the unsavory odor of the burning fat.

The priest opened his eyes and found himself in the temple. He rose to his feet, knees creaking and vague pain crawling across the surface of his flesh, but he ignored it, concentrating on the table set in the middle of the room.

When he took a step toward it, pain shot up his spine. Ine'vesi gritted his teeth and pressed on, covering the distance with a stumbling gait. He reached the table and leaned against its edge, raised his hand to place the scroll upon it. Flames flickered along his sleeve, and he fought the urge to shake his arm to extinguish them. They'd not be put out.

With greater effort than expected, he extended his arm and set the roll of parchment down. The flames on his sleeve leaped to his hair and he released his grip on the scroll lest the blaze make its way to the paper. As soon as his fingertips left the surface of the scroll, the humble place of worship disappeared. Fire filled the priest's vision and the stink of burning flesh replaced the scent of protection herbs and melting tallow.

He stumbled back, his foot teetering on the edge of the boiling river. A bolt of lighting rode a thunderclap down from the sky, striking the base of the last of the nine Pillars of Life: Faith. The column tumbled, and Ine'vesi watched it fall toward him. He raised his flaming hands and an instant later, the heavy stone crushed him.

On the last day the Small Gods walked the land, fire fell like rain from the sky.

I - Horace - God and Devil

*T*HE DAY LAY UPON the sea like death, without breath nor pulse, movement nor care. The sky ran into the ocean with a drunken sailor's grace, and even the gulls wasn't takin' to the air for fear the heat'd bear them down to be swallowed by the depths. His Imperial Grace's Ship, *Devil o' the Deep*, languished upon the idle water more'n a hundred leagues from the turn, and she weren't gettin' none closer on days like this one.

First Man Horace Seaman squinted out across the smooth and shinin' sea, watchin' it stretch to the horizon and prob'ly beyond, like a metal sheet awaitin' the first strike o' the smith's hammer to dimple it. He scanned the green depths, wishin' for a single wave to break and bring hopes of a windy gust along with it, or at least desirin' to glimpse a fish jumpin', its splash relievin' his boredom, but there weren't nothin'. A sweaty bead ran off his nose and caught itself in the thick stubble growin' above his lip, collectin' with all the other drops o' sweat. He wiped the moisture away with a cloth he carried for no other purpose and wrung it out o'er the side, addin' his salt to the sea's.

Despite the name and profession given him by his lineage, Horace didn't have no love for floatin' atop the water, less so on this sort o' voyage. It weren't the dearth o' wind what increased Seaman's discomfort, but the trip itself. Any time a boat took the turn, it put the crew too near the Green, in Horace's estimation. Even sailin' as far offshore as a seafarin' man dared, with the jagged coast nothin' but a mirage on the horizon, that land still crouched there like an animal waitin' to pounce. Somethin' 'bout the place were enough to make a man's staff shrivel and his ball sack claw itself back up inside.

If that weren't enough to make a sailor's tackle shrink, they was on this most damnable boat, too. Who with a good thought in their head named a boat *Devil o' the Deep*? It seemed to Horace more'n a bit like temptin' fate, and he weren't the only swingin' dick what thought so. The *Devil* didn't have neither her own crew nor a perm'nent skipper, 'cause no one wanted to spend time on a vessel what were surely destined to get itself ate. Thrice Horace Seaman sailed on the *Devil* and thrice survived, but the absence o' wind and the sun's oppression made him suspect trip number four might've been askin' too much from the poor, o'er-worked possum tail stuck in his breech's front pocket for the purpose o' bringin' good luck.

The trip'd be faster crossin' the Inland Sea, but tension with the Water Kingdom meant no ships was makin' the excursion, 'cept them what were good at skulkin', and skulkin' weren't hardly the *Devil's* specialty. Even so, he figured sneakin' across still might be safer'n gettin' close to the Green.

Horace snorted and spat o'er the wale, not partic'larly able to spare the saliva, but desperate to set the water movin'. He watched ripples race away from the floatin' snot glob, some tiny waves washin' against the boat and dyin' without givin' aid to pushin' the *Devil* closer to her goal, others headin' for the horizon like they stood a chance o' reachin' it. Horace watched 'em as if it were his job, 'cause what else were a man to do on a day dead as today?

"What ya doin', Hory?"

But one man called him Hory, and he wondered for an instant whether ignorin' the voice might make it go away. The answer were no. Horace'd tried payin' the feller no mind before with the result o' makin' the questions multiply and come out more absurd. He heaved a breath, the air hotter'n it had any right to be, and answered without facin' the man.

"I'm fixin' to work up to shittin' a gold block, Dunal. What's it look like?"

"Har, har. It looks like you ain't doin' nothin', Hory, that's what."

Horace got the eye rollin' outta the way first so Dunal wouldn't see, then rotated slow, feelin' akin to a ground hen skewered and cranked on the rotisserie o'er a bed o' red hot coals. Difference were, the ground hen got to be dead when it got cooked.

The smile on Dunal's gob made Horace either wanna laugh out loud or punch the swab in the face, but he couldn't spare the air to do the one and the other'd get him tossed in the brig. See, Dunal were not only head swabbie for this turn on the *Devil*, but cousin to the skipper's wife, or some such thing, and a simpleton on the top. The o'ersized child possessed an eye which pointed off at nothin', a head o' thick, straw-colored hair to match the mop he carried with him ev'rywhere he went, and the self-proclaimed ability to fuck a woman for half-a-day without rest. Course, weren't no women willin' to confirm the claim, though Horace'd heard rumors a good few goats and other farm beasts knew the truth.

"Ya caught me, Dunal. I'm starin' off at the water wishin' to throw myself in and drown, is all."

The simpleton's eyes went wide and worried. "Don't do it, Hory. The skip needs you."

Horace shook his head, loosenin' a fat drop o' sweat outta his hair to spill along his neck and onto his back. He shivered, but whether from the hot water rollin' down his spine, or the thought o' Dunal fuckin' a sheep for a half-a-day, anyone's guess'd be good as another.

"I'm just havin' at ya, Dunal, what you be doin'?"

"I'm swabbin', Hory."

He held up the mop and shook it with more enthusiasm'n Horace could've found for anythin' on a day as hot and shite as this one. Dried chunks he'd prefer not to identify flew outta the ragged mophead, a few findin' their way to the jumbled hair perched on Dunal's head, likely never to be see again.

Horace shuffle-stepped to the right to see past the simpleton, peekin' at the deck behind him. Not a drop o' water to be seen nowhere on the wood, 'cause Dunal'd forgot to fill the mop bucket again. Seaman laughed despite himself and shook his head, then looked up, seein' more'n just the planks beyond the big oaf for the first time.

The sun beatin' on the flat water were blindin' on the shoreward side o' the boat, so Horace squinted and held his hand to his forehead, blockin' out the glare. More sweat ran offa the spot he touched, stingin' his eye and drawin' a curse to his lips. He blinked the salt away and stared out o'er the wale, stretchin' and standin' up on his toes as though it'd make him see farther.

"Whatcha starin' at, Hory?" Dunal asked spinnin' 'round to join him in lookin', the dry mop head slappin' Horace square in his high, sunburned forehead.

Horace brushed the stinkin' strings away and shook his head to get the dirt outta his sweat-damp hair, then gazed out across the water again. He pushed his lips tight together and stared, hopin' Dunal'd stay the fuck quiet and give him time to concentrate.

"Nothin', Dunal." He took one step away from his post on the ship's seaward side, movin' toward the shoreward wale. "Fuck me dead, I don't see nothin'."

His boot heels hammered the planks, hurryin' him to lean o'er the side, hopin' to be wrong, but knowin' he weren't. Too many miles o' sea'd passed beneath Horace Seaman's feet for him not to locate the shoreline quicker'n he'd find his own cock.

"The tide got us," he said o'er his shoulder, knowin' Dunal'd followed him. He faced the swabbie. "We drifted. You gotta run and tell the skip."

The head swabbie stared at him with the blank expression he got most times anyone talked in his direction. His one eye stared somewhere up into the sky and his mouth hung open, waitin' to catch a bug. Another time, Horace woulda stopped and walked Dunal through 'til he understood, but a matter o' life and death didn't leave the time. Rather'n explainin', he grabbed the lad's sweaty shirt front and gave him a hard shake.

"The shore, you simple, thunderin' oaf! We can't see the shore."

Dunal cranked his head 'round to gawk o'er the wale; his sausage-thick fingers opened and the mop hit the deck with a clunk before the swabbie began shriekin' like one o' them goats which preferred not to be fucked for half-a-day.

"The shore! The shore, skip!"

The simpleton took off for the aft end o' the ship, where the *Devil's* skipper'd be hidin' in his cabin, avoidin' honest work and the burnin' sun, but Horace Seaman didn't have the time nor the care for the man to give two shits. He raced back across the deck to his post, the sweat streamin' from his forehead caused more by fear'n it were by heat.

He leaned against the wale and gazed out at the same monotonous stretch o' water what he'd stared at for hours and hours before the oaf took him from his duties to stab him through the heart with a lance o' panic.

"Three fuckin' trips on the *Devil*," he muttered, gaze roamin' the horizon and the expanse o' glistenin' sea between it and the boat. "Shoulda never signed up for number four."

In all his time floatin' on the damnable sea, in this boat or any other, he'd never been outside sight o' the shore. Not when the day wilted and drooped the way it did today, and not when storms threw the ship 'round with the malice of an angry child tryin' to break his toys. In near thirty-five turns o' the seasons, the water ain't never surrounded him the way it were right now.

Horace gulped down air hotter'n what he exhaled, pantin' and wipin' his brow with his hand to keep sweat from fuckin' up his vision, the cloth stuffed in his back pocket for no other purpose forgotten.

For a hundred or more racin' heartbeats, nothin' changed. The sea lay unmovin', uncarin', unknowin' 'bout the *Devil's* presence, and Horace thought the rowers might get oars in the water before it were too late. If it stayed calm for the little bit o' time it'd take them to get their asses on the rowin' seats, they might have a chance.

Before the first oar head came pokin' through its hole, the bubbles started, and First Man Horace Seaman's heart shriveled up no bigger'n a grape left to dry on the vine.

For near thirty-five turns o' the seasons livin' a life he never wanted to live, Horace'd laughed off the stories told in ev'ry tavern along the coast, and he'd been in enough to know the tales. Ev'ry time he set foot on a ship, he told himself they was yarns spun by old-wives and older seamen, but down inside, he knew them the truth, even if he'd never seen none of it himself.

"There!" Horace shouted and pointed. "Keep them fuckin' oars outta the water!"

If he hadn't seen nothin', they'd already be pullin' hard on them paddles, as if their lives depended on it, not slowin' until they saw the shore again. Them what weren't rowin'd either be prayin' or gettin' in a last fuck in case they didn't make it. But with the sea a-bubblin', they didn't dare touch oar blades to water for fear they'd attract somethin' they didn't wanna meet and find themselves another tale told in ev'ry tavern along the coast. Until the disturbance stopped, no one'd be doin' more'n holdin' their breath and hopin'.

Thirty man-lengths off the bow, the bubbles roiled and built, as if someone'd stuck a reed in the sea and blew angry breath through it, stirrin' up the ocean when it didn't wanna be stirred up. Water spilled o'er itself, mountin' up to half a man's height. Horace's lips formed 'round the approximation of a prayer he'd heard once before but never said himself, prob'ly fuckin' it up right bad, but his lips gave it a go anyways, in case such things might help his feet find shore just one more time. If the prayer worked, he swore then and there, on the grave o' ev'ry Seaman what come before him, his scabby, callused feet'd never touch a ship's deck again, so long as he lived.

The commotion stopped quick as it begun, and with it the whole world paused. An indignant sun glared down on ev'ry swingin' dick aboard ship, each one starin' at the low waves rollin' across the water from where the bubbles was. Each and ev'ry man joined the world in holdin' their wind, just like it'd been doin' these last days to get 'em into this shithole situation.

The hard wood o' the wale went slick under Horace's sweatin' palms, but he didn't move 'em, just kept leanin' and watchin' until the first wave lapped up against the side o' the ship. He let out a breath, slow and quiet, and drew another, hopin' this one weren't his last, neither. A chunk o' shocked air caught in his throat when the thing bobbed to the surface.

Too much water lay in between to see clear, but it didn't appear big enough to be what the stories told at ev'ry tavern along the coast talked 'bout. A white patch, maybe red, too. It didn't look much bigger'n...

A man.

First Man Horace Seaman gave his head a shake and leaned farther out o'er the side, findin' it more'n a might difficult to believe his own eyes. But there it were, right before him: a white-shirt-and-red-pants-wearin' man floatin' atop a sea what a few minutes before'd been smooth as a lookin' glass. And now it belched up the impossible.

"What is it?"

Dunal!

The bubbles stoppin' didn't mean they was past danger—far from past it. The tales told at ev'ry tavern along the coast never said nothin' 'bout a man floatin' in the sea, and Horace didn't know what to make of it. He felt ev'ry sailor on board waitin' with him and hoped the lead swabbie'd follow what his mates were doin' by shuttin' the fuck up. Might as well've hoped for a giant to appear outta the thin, hot air and sneeze into the *Devil's* sails hard enough to blow 'em right the way back to shore. Weren't no such things as giants.

"What's ev'ryone gawkin' at?"

"Be quiet, you stupid oaf." Horace didn't look 'round, but he sensed Dunal step up close beside him.

"You knows I don't like when you calls me that, Hory. I let you have one 'cause it seemed like you thought it were somethin' impo'tant. Don't call me that no more."

"Fuckin' shut it, simpleton."

In the second between Dunal's block-o'-wood hand slappin' his back and the shock o' hittin' the sea, Horace had time to think the o'ersized child mightn't have meant to put him in the drink. The instant he entered the water, thoughts and ev'rythin' else but panic left him like rats fleein' a punctured bilge.

The ol' sailor knew the sea'd be frigid despite what a day like this tried to make a man believe, but it surprised him into gulpin' a salty mouthful o' water, anyways. When his head broke the surface, he coughed and sputtered the ocean outta his lungs, then glanced up at fifty pairs o' eyes starin' at him from the deck. He waved his arms o'er his head but already knew this'd be his end. No man were gonna risk fishin' anyone outta the water when the shore weren't near. May as well've signed his name on the family gravestone the instant his feet slipped from under him, scribin' Horace Seaman below his long-dead father, Nedren Seaman, and o'er the spot reserved for his son, Rilum Seaman.

Bein' a good man, Horace should've accepted his fate calmly and with honor. A good man would've tread water quietly, waitin' to either drown or for some beast from underneath to come up and take him, but seein' them eyes starin' at him, doin' nothin' when they coulda thrown a rope in and pulled their mate out, added anger to the panic already makin' ol' Horace want to swim for his life.

He thrashed and flapped his arms, splashed water at the ship's side and shouted, implorin' his fellers—some he'd practically grown up with on one ship or another—to save his sorry sailor ass. They answered by tellin' him to shut his gob, to just fuckin' drown and leave them outta it. Someone threw a wooden block his way and it splashed in the ocean less'n an arm's length from him, tossin' water in his face.

"You can throw scraps but you can't toss me a rope?" Horace yelled.

A shoe with a hole where the toe shoulda been hit the sea and floated near his shoulder. A second later, a hard object hit his head, doublin' his vision, and warmth flowed down his forehead. He reached outta the water and touched his head, winced at the pain it brung, then examined the washed-out pink color of his own blood upon his fingers. None of them was gonna help, no matter how much he shouted and kicked. As he stared down at the blood on his hand, seein' his submerged body visible in the water beneath, a black shape slid past in the depths below. It took more'n a few heartbeats to do so, but Horace Seaman didn't know how many, 'cause it seemed his own ceased beatin' at the sight.

Horace forgot the blood and peered up at the men on the deck above. They'd seen the swimmin' shadow, too, all their gazes focusin' past their mate now, gapin' at the thing in the water, the God o' the Deep come to make the *Devil* pay.

The water trembled 'round Horace, and his body went cold; colder'n the water, colder'n the deepest day in winter's heart. The sea lapped 'round him, the waves growin' bigger and bigger until one washed right o'er his head. When he broke the surface again, he glimpsed the crew standin' in an open-mouthed line along the wale, but none of them was observin' him. Their eyes was lifted offa the sea, directed towards the sky as a shadow fell across him and, in his life's last moment, the ol' sailor wondered who the man were what he'd seen floatin' atop the sea, then he hoped they'd mention Horace Seaman in the tales told at ev'ry tavern along the coast.

II - Teryk and Danya - River Under the Castle

*T*ERYK WHIRLED AROUND AT a sound behind him, muscles tense and an excuse at the ready. He'd already planned for Trenan if the master swordsman found him—a semi-plausible story involving some bauble long lost during his tenth turn of the seasons. The man likely wouldn't believe him, but it mattered not. He'd been doing nothing bad enough for Trenan to tell his father, so it would be kept between the two of them. Not so if he discovered him in the water, or worse—on the other side of the bars.

But instead of Trenan finding his way past the shoulder-high hedges, Teryk peered into the smiling face of his sister.

"You're not going swimming without me, are you?" Danya's eyes shone as she danced between a hedge of witch's brew and a shock of creeper vines.

The prince let out his breath. "You startled me. I thought I'd been seen, but Trenan got lazy and sent the dogs after me, you made so much noise."

"Pfft. You didn't know I was here until I wanted you to know."

She strode across the bare dirt to where he stood on the bank of the river. The sound of its rushing water—a constant hum heard in most every room of Draekfarren—became no more than a burble here where it slipped through the bars into the channel beneath the castle. Birds sang more loudly in trees around them, whistling tunes to celebrate another day of warmth and peace.

"It's been a long time," Teryk said, watching the water. "When is the last time we swam?"

"Swam? Not so long ago." Danya giggled.

"Under the castle, I mean. I think I'd seen twelve turns of the seasons, and you eleven."

"It was the day of my twelfth turn, remember? We sneaked away after the banquet and, when Trenan found us, he made a fuss but didn't tell mother and father."

The prince shook his head and laughed. "Trenan said if he ever caught us again, he'd tell the king." He rubbed the back of his neck, staring at the water, wondering if it was worth the risk. "Hard to believe a half dozen and one have passed."

"Not quite so many," the princess said and took a step to stand beside him and survey the gently churning flow. "It's still one more moon before the day of your twentieth turn of the seasons comes."

"One more moon. Where does youth go?"

"Ha." Danya nudged him and he smiled at her. "If it's youth you want to experience, spend a day with father. Seeing the way he acts should make you feel young again."

Teryk looked at her feet and saw Danya already without her shoes. He wondered if she'd taken them off upon finding him here, or if she'd been barefoot for some time. With her feet hidden beneath the skirt of her long dress, footwear was a custom Danya avoided whenever possible. The option didn't exist for Teryk because everyone would notice if he strode around bootless.

He inhaled the aroma of the garden and the river, the chalky scent of the wall through which it flowed. *Only a moon until the day of my twentieth turn of seasons. So much time gone, and never a step beyond the walls of the inner city.*

"What do you think father would do if he found out?"

Danya gave him another shove, firmer this time. He leaned toward the water, absorbing it.

"First, brother, he won't find out. Second, it's swimming in a river, not laying with a peasant cleaning girl." She raised an eyebrow and gave him a knowing look; he diverted his gaze. "I think he'd do nothing. Trenan only told us stories of how angry father would be to keep two curious children from trouble."

"Hmph. I suppose that could be the truth of it."

"Come on."

Danya pushed him again and Teryk side-stepped to keep from treading off the bank and into the river.

"Hey," he cried. "You'll ruin my boots!"

He took a step away from the water lest she push him again, but his sister had moved away to pull the ivory comb out of her hair and let her dark brown tresses fall past her shoulders. She shook her head, loosening them, then turned her back toward him.

"I can't reach," she said, stretching her arms behind her and slapping comically at the buttons. "Undo my dress for me, brother."

"Women. Can't dress or undress themselves."

"You know I'd rather wear shirt and breeches, like you," she said, fumbling with the top button.

"And waistcoat, and jerkin, and—"

"Don't complain. You can get in and out of them all yourself, can't you?"

He obliged and the dress slid off her shoulders. She shimmied and shook and pulled until it lay on the ground at her feet, leaving her in underclothes that still covered as much of her as Teryk's shirt and breeches did of him.

"It's dreadfully hot under all this dress-up, too," she said stepping out of the dress. She picked it up and surveyed the garden around them, searching for somewhere to secret her clothes.

"Maybe swimming isn't such a good idea," the prince said, his hand hesitating on the buckle of his belt. "We're bigger than we were then. We may not fit through the gap."

"Nonsense," Danya said dipping her toe in the water. She pulled it out and considered her brother hopefully. "It's beautiful."

"Danya, I—"

His sister jumped into the river, the splash of her body hitting the water and the giggle that escaped her lips cutting his protest short. Her head disappeared beneath the rushing water for a second and an inexplicable surge of panic tugged in his gut; no more than two breaths later, her head reappeared, hair plastered to her head and a wide smile upon her lips.

"Come on, Teryk. Have some fun before you become an old man."

He frowned, hating it when she mocked him, though he knew she meant no harm by it. He'd told her his worry over the approach of the day of his twentieth turn of the seasons. All the time gone by and he'd accomplished nothing of any import. By the time their father reached the same age, he sat the throne and dictated policy. Two turns of the seasons later, the uprising happened, and then the battle that turned their father from another king in the line to a legend.

But what had the prince accomplished? Schooling and nothing more.

Princess Danya must have read his thoughts by the set of his expression, for she sent a spray of water from the river with her hands, splashing the legs of his breeches and his precious boots.

"Hey!" He pranced back a step, then raised his eyes and glared at her, a smile fighting for purchase upon his lips. "You'll pay for that, sister."

"You'll have to get wet to make me pay," she said and splashed him again.

Hopping on one foot, Teryk pulled off one boot, then the other, stowing them amongst a twist of creeper vine. Next, he removed his sword belt and lay it beneath the same witch's brew hedge where the princess secreted her dress. Last, he took off his waistcoat, shirt and breeches, rolling them together into a bundle and stretching on his toes to jam them into the elbow where a Bunyon tree's branch joined the trunk.

He stood on the bank in his underpants, enjoying the kiss of warm sun on his bare skin and watching his sister tread water in the middle of the deep river. Danya gestured for him to jump in.

"Hurry, before someone comes along."

"No one will come along," he said, running his fingers through his short, blond hair. "Unless they're looking for us."

He stepped up to the edge of the river and slid one foot into the water. The river rushed around his ankle, caressing his skin with its cool touch, tugging him, coaxing him to step farther in. He did, putting the other foot in and standing on the shallow side. Two steps farther and the side would fall away as the river grew quickly deeper.

"What are you waiting for?" Danya chided. "Goddess Festival?"

Teryk wanted to jump in, to throw up a splash that sloshed the river against her face and taught her a lesson for teasing him, but he didn't. Too much noise, and noise might attract attention. Instead, he walked the next two steps until his toes jutted over the edge of the drop off, then he allowed his body to slip into the water.

The current was mild here, but still enough to draw him toward the grate if he didn't swim against it. He let it have its way with him, bobbing in the cool, refreshing water as it floated him along in the direction of the bars, watching Danya dive below the surface. He stroked hard to reach the bars before her.

Teryk gripped one pitted and rusted bar an instant before Danya resurfaced beside him. She shook her head and laughed, throwing droplets from her hair into his face. He stopped her laughter by putting his hand on the top of her head and pushing it under the water, a ritual they'd repeated every time they'd come here since they first learned to swim.

"We shouldn't stay long," Teryk said when her face came above water again.

"You worry too much, my prince."

"Trenan will be seeking me soon. I have pike training just after the height of the sun." He glanced skyward at the sun climbing toward its zenith. Time remained yet, but better early than late.

"As do I."

Teryk snorted. "If you call that thing you wield a weapon."

"Don't laugh or I'll have to teach *you* a lesson."

"Never mind that now," the prince said. "Which one of us will—"

His sentence lay in the air unfinished when Danya dove under the water, gripping the bars and pulling herself toward the bottom of the river. It was another part of the ritual, in which he asked who'd go first and she took the initiative. Teryk always wanted to lead the way, but his sister invariably beat him to it.

The prince huffed a perturbed breath and waited, the surface of the bar he held rough against his hand, and he wondered how long these bars had been in place. The castle had straddled the river for as long as history itself, but had the grate been in place all that time? Did the bars rust away over time and require replacement? The only answer to his questions came in the form of his sister's head breaking the surface on the side of the bars opposite him.

"See?" she said, her smile broadening. "Still fit."

"You do," he said. Danya wasn't much bigger than she'd been the last time they swam under Draekfarren. Teryk, however, was both taller and broader, a testament to the effectiveness of the fitness regimen Trenan dragged him through each morning.

"It will be fine."

He peered between the bars at his sister, her eyes shimmering like the sun on water, her smile a beacon to light any darkness. Beholding her through the grate, she seemed like a prisoner, and he a jailer. They'd played this game in their youth, pretending the bars belonged to a cell in Dreemskerry, but the river's course didn't cut through the prison, and they'd grown too old for such games of fantasy. Teryk's stomach tightened—what if he got through the bars, but couldn't get out? Then it truly would be his jail.

"I don't—"

"Come on. What are you afraid of?"

He opened his mouth to tell her, but stopped; she'd never let him live it down if he did. She already had more than enough fodder to use against him; refusing to follow her would only add more. Instead of admitting his fears, he filled his lungs with air that tasted of sodden earth and cool water, and plunged beneath the surface.

With one bar in his hand, he pulled himself down and down and down. It proved easier than in his youth; he was older, bigger, stronger now. He remembered it being a struggle, coordinating the holding of his breath with the downward pull, and he recalled the current seeming more forceful, attempting to pull him against the bars and threatening to pin him there, drown him.

Down and down and down.

The pressure of the river's depth discomforted his ears, the rub of silt in the water grated against his eyes, but the prince soon spied the bottom and the end of the bars. To his right, the space formed where bottom and bars and side converged. He pulled himself toward it, air warming in his lungs.

Teryk dragged himself along the bottom until he reached the side. The gap appeared narrower, as though filled in with silt and dirt and rocks washed along by the river's current. Or maybe, since he was bigger, the world at large seemed smaller.

Danya got through.

The thought proved the opening hadn't shrunk, and prodded him to continue despite his misgivings. If his sister did it, he could, too.

Teryk gripped the horizontal bottom bar of the grate, pulled himself toward the opening the way he'd done so many times in their youth. The excited thrill of danger he hadn't felt for so long tingled along his limbs, noticeable even under the cool water. It fluttered in his stomach and clenched his chest around his lungs working hard to hold in his breath.

He swung around and put his feet through the gap, the way he'd always done. His ankles slid through, his knees, his thighs. He released a puff of air through his nose to keep water from entering his nostrils, bubbles racing toward the surface. His lungs strained with the pressure of his remaining breath.

The prince's hips went through the opening, seeming a tighter squeeze than he recalled. His stomach brushed the bottom of the rough metal, scraping lightly, and he considered extricating himself and heading back to the surface, thereby giving his sister the satisfaction of his failure, but he didn't. He couldn't let her have that.

The bottom of his rib cage went through and he put his arms up over his head, using his feet against the river bottom to pull himself on. The metal rubbed along his flesh, tightening on him, holding him, pushing his back down against the bottom. Rocks and dirt scraped his flesh, but he continued moving through.

When his nipples drew under the horizontal bar, his progress ceased.

Teryk dug his feet into the river bottom, pulling hard with his legs, the muscles in his calves flexing until a cramp seized him. He opened his mouth and cried out, a mass of bubbles spilling out of his lips instead of a pained yell. His lungs burned with the air remaining in them and he tried to calm himself while he waited for the pain in his leg to dissipate, but the distress in his chest overcame his desire for calm.

His feet flailed, kicking an invisible current in the depths of the river as he tried in vain to pull himself through or push himself back. The cramp in his calf gripped tighter, rendering his left leg useless, and one leg wasn't enough to free him from the trap he'd put himself in. He moved to lower his arms and grab the bars, use them to leverage himself through one way or the other, but he'd jammed himself through enough he could do no more than brush the metal with his fingertips.

The prince thrashed and another burst of air escaped his lungs, leaving room for panic to rush in and fill the space left by his fleeing breath. He wiggled side to side as much as his predicament allowed, but the grate's grip on him didn't loosen.

The distress in his chest grew into a great weight pressing on him, as though the water above weighed more than a block of stone. Without intending to, he opened his mouth and let water in past his lips, and what he expected to be his last thought entered his mind.

In a family of warriors, statesmen and kings, I die trapped at the bottom of a slow-running river.

The muscles in his legs ached, the air in his chest burned, and the prince ceased struggling. With life moments from ending, he saw little dignity in the manner of his death, so he thought to at least find a shred for himself in how he acted. He let himself fall, head resting on the silty bottom, awaiting his end.

Something touched his leg and, at first, he thought it the product of his air-starved mind, but then it came again, grabbing and insistent. Teryk raised his head a few inches to peer through the bars and saw Danya, her long hair floating out around her head like a halo. Her expression appeared taut with concern and reflected the desperation he'd already given in to.

She grabbed his ankles and swung herself around, put her feet against the bars, and pulled. The prince shifted, the horizontal bar scraping his chest, the rocky river bottom abrading his back. He gritted his teeth hard against the pain as rocks and metal dug into his flesh, grated against bone.

His shoulders wrenched through and the bar caught under his chin. A gulp of water entered his throat and he fought to keep from gagging even as he twisted his head to the side. Danya gave another stiff tug and pulled him free of his underwater deathtrap.

The prince knew he should kick his legs, stroke with his arms, but his limp and useless body refused to obey, his muscles spent and begging for air. His sister came to his rescue again, snagging him under one arm and pushing hard against the river bottom with both feet, launching them toward the surface.

Teryk tilted his head back, watching out for the water's surface above, praying they'd reach it before he was no longer able to keep his lungs from drawing a watery breath and pulling death into his chest.

A moment later, they broke through. The prince gasped and sputtered, coughed water out of his lungs and struggled to replace it with air flavored by must and mold, but tasting better than any breath he'd taken in his life since his first.

Danya held him up, ensuring his head stayed out of the water, and hammered him on the back with the heel of her hand. A minute later, he drew labored breaths and wished she'd stop hitting him.

"Stop," he gasped, grimacing at the pain from the scrapes left by the river bottom. "Stop. I. Can. Breathe."

Danya did and relaxed her grip. Teryk's chin dipped below the water and an instant of panic flashed through him, but his exhausted limbs began working again, stroking hard enough to keep his head above water.

"You scared the life out of me," Danya said, and Teryk read in her expression that she meant it.

"Scared you?" he said, then stopped to cough. "I thought that was the end of me."

"What were you thinking, playing around like that?"

"I was stuck," he exclaimed, incredulous. "I couldn't get through."

"Don't ever do that to me again." She slapped his chest, splashing water into his face. The prince jerked his head away, hacking and gasping again, though his throat drew breath.

"I have to get out of here," he wheezed between coughs.

His sister reacted to the desperation in his voice, grabbing his arm and towing him toward the side of the canal cutting beneath the castle.

The channel through which the river ran was carved of the same stone as the castle itself, set in place with the building of the stronghold. On either side, a ledge followed along beside the river; why they'd been built, Teryk didn't know—he'd never heard of them being used—but today, he thanked the builders for creating them.

He threw both arms up onto the ledge and rested on his elbows, swallowing great gulps of air. After a minute, his light-headedness passed but the pain of the scrapes on his chest and back remained.

"Help me out," he said over his shoulder to Danya treading water at his side.

She put her hand into his armpit and pushed, her fingers digging into his flesh, and the prince wondered if she might have meant it as punishment for scaring her. He leaned against the edge, pushing with his arms, feet seeking purchase on the slimy side of the rock channel. After a few seconds of ungraceful struggle, he heaved himself up to sit on the edge, legs dangling in the water. Danya looked up at him from the river.

"What now?" she asked.

Teryk shook his head. "I'm not swimming." Truthfully, he thought he might never swim again.

"How will you get out then?"

The prince filled his lungs with a shaky breath and peered into the darkness where the river ran deeper into the castle, the canal forcing it into an unnatural straight path. They'd once followed it all the way until they discovered another set of bars where the river exited the castle on the seaward side, then flowed through the inner city until it reached the shore. On that occasion, they hadn't been searching for another way to exit the channel, nor had they seen one.

"There must be another way."

"Why would there be?"

"I don't know. There just has to." Teryk touched his fingers to the scrape on his chest, sucked a quick, pained inhalation between his teeth, then inspected the blood on the tips of his fingers. What excuse could he give Trenan to explain his wounds? "The cleaners must have a way to get in and out in case something gets through the bars and gets caught."

"Like us."

"Yeah," Teryk conceded. "Like us."

Danya pushed away from the wall, gliding out into the middle of the river. Teryk saw his sister's outline beneath the water in the light shining through the bars, her arms spread at her side, head back, hair arrayed around her. She floated for a short time, then righted herself.

"We've been up and down the tunnel. There's no other way."

"We've only done it in the water." The prince struggled to his feet, wincing at the knot still gripping his calf. He got himself upright and found the ledge wide enough for one man, and no wider. "We can try along the sides."

His toes squelched in damp, slippery moss that climbed out of the water, across the ledge, and part way up the wall. In the dim light, it appeared black, though he assumed it was actually green. He hoped it was—black moss was poisonous enough to cause an itchy, stinging rash, and the scrapes already gave him enough to explain.

"You try," Danya said with a stroke of her arms taking her deeper into the tunnel. "I'm not the one stuck in here."

—⁓—

With the half-moon of the tunnel entrance reduced to a distant glow, absolute darkness surrounded Teryk and Danya as they inched their way along the channel.

Treacherous footing slowed the prince's pace, and the narrowness of the path forced his pained back against the side, arms spread out beside him as he tried to avoid slipping off and back into the water. He didn't want to be in the river again any time soon. His thighs and calves ached and Danya splashed along beside him; he called out to her occasionally to ensure she didn't get too far ahead. Given a choice, he'd have turned around and gone home, but trying the space under the grate again struck him as a poor option.

"Trenan will be looking for us soon," Danya said, her disembodied voice floating out of the river in the darkness.

"I know."

"Do you think he'll look here?"

"Eventually. It's been a long time since he pulled us out of the river."

Teryk crept along, the wet, slick moss squelching between his toes and on the soles of his feet. Three times he'd slipped but kept his feet under him each time, heart pounding hard in his chest.

The river rushed past, but the air in the tunnel stood stagnant around them. The loamy odor of moss and the rank scent of old mold sat upon it, sticking to the inside of the prince's nostrils, making his nose itch for fresh air, a breeze. But they'd find neither down here, and it soon struck him that the place's stink reminded him of a graveyard. The thought caused a shiver.

Teryk took another step, another, each one chipping away the hope they'd find an alternative way out, each one forcing a sliver of fear into his chest that he'd have to brave the water again, struggle his way under the bars.

We know it's tight. Danya will help me this time.

Though her help might get him through, it wouldn't assuage his already bruised ego. If they found an alternate exit, at least he might retain some semblance of manhood, in his own eyes, if not in his sister's.

"Find anything yet?" Danya called.

"No."

He shuffled along four more paces when the wall disappeared from under his leading hand.

"Wait."

He stopped and his sister, swimming a short distance in front of him, splashed around to return to the sound of his voice.

"What is it?"

"I'm not sure. Hold on."

Teryk slid along, arm extended. His wrist passed over into the open space, his forearm. No air wafted out of it, no breeze or sound of running water beyond that of the river. His shoulder was even with the place where the wall ended before his fingers found it continuing—an opening as wide as the length of his arm.

"I think it's a doorway," he said over his shoulder. Danya stroked her way to the side to lean on the ledge near his feet

"Is it locked?"

"Hold on. I don't know."

The prince maneuvered himself in front of the opening, facing it, one hand on either side. A moment of vertigo overtook him as he stood there, not knowing what lay before him in the dark. He jammed his hands hard against the wall's edges, using them to find his balance. When the unsteadiness passed, he drew a deliberate breath, held it a second, and let it go. Recovered, he moved his hand from the wall and reached out into the darkness, moving with slow care to avoid cramming his fingers against something unseen.

Or something dangerous.

He worked his lower jaw side to side, grinding his back teeth as the tips of his fingers inched forward, searching.

"What is it?"

Danya's voice startled him and made him jump. He huffed an exasperated breath and glared over his shoulder, meaning to admonish her, but the dark kept her from his sight. That meant she didn't see him, either—the way she'd startled him or the fear on his face.

"Not sure yet," he said between clenched teeth. He edged his hand farther into the gloom.

His fingers touched wood.

"Wait. I've got something."

Touching a recognizable surface gave Teryk courage to move with more confidence. He dragged his hand around the outside of the door, the pads of his fingertips tracing the rough grain of ancient wood and finding rusted iron strappings running across it near the top and bottom. To the right, his hand touched a metal ring.

"It's a door, all right."

"Help me up, then."

"Let me try it first," Teryk said.

He grabbed the ring and lifted it with the teeth-rattling squeak of metal rarely moved. The sound echoed along the tunnel, making him flinch until he remembered they were the only ones near enough to hear.

Unless someone lurked on the other side of the door.

Teryk waited a few seconds for any reaction to the sound, but none came. He gripped the ring firmly and pulled; it didn't move. He pushed with the same result.

In the dark, he had no way to discern whether to push or pull to open the door. If he saw the hinges, he'd know, but they were as invisible to him as his sister leaning on the ledge near his feet. He'd have to feel them.

With one hand still on the ring, Teryk reached out with the other and ran his fingers along the left edge from top to bottom. He touched nothing but wood door and stone wall.

"The hinges are inside," he called over his shoulder. "I'll have to push."

"Push then. I'm getting cold."

The prince leaned into the door, putting more weight on it as his sister's prompting made him forget the potential danger awaiting on the other side. It didn't budge, so he put his shoulder against it and pushed, a grunt escaping his throat. It didn't move.

"It's no use," he said.

"Very well," Danya said with a splash. "Do you want to climb back in the water and swim to the grate, or would you prefer to walk?"

He didn't need to see her face to know a teasing smile tilted her lips as she spoke the words. She'd teased him enough times for him to picture it in his mind—the one smile of hers he hated.

"Fine. Get up here and help."

"Give me a hand out."

He reached out, groping the air in the dark until their fingers touched. They locked hands and he pulled while she levered herself out of the water. A few seconds later, she stood on the ledge beside him, the sound of water dripping from her hair and underclothes adding to the sound of the river sliding by.

"It should be wide enough for both of us," he said, his hand on her arm to guide her into the doorway.

Danya squirmed her way in beside him and they both leaned their shoulders against the door, facing each other. Water dripped off her onto his toes.

"This is exciting, isn't it?" she said and her breath touched his face, though he still didn't see her, even standing so close.

"Sure," he said.

He'd never shared his sister's sense of adventure; it had been she who suggested swimming under the grate the first time they did it, and her idea to come back this time. If he put thought to it, every time they'd done anything—and every time they'd caught hell from Trenan—it had been her idea, her desire, her dare.

"Shall we go on three?" she suggested.

Teryk moved his jaw back and forth. "Three. I'll count. One...two...three."

They pushed together, straining and grunting, and the door moved by the thickness of a fingernail; or maybe it didn't.

"It won't open," Teryk said, his heart beating faster at the prospect of diving into the river again and swimming to the grate.

"No, no. It moved a little, I'm sure of it." Danya's voice carried the familiar, excited tone it took on when she thought adventure loomed. "Try again."

Teryk huffed a breath, aware of the exhaustion filling his limbs, the burning in his muscles from his underwater struggle and the tension of maintaining his footing on the slippery ledge. His shoulders sagged, but then he remembered Danya stood close by him and he didn't want his sister to realize his feeling of defeat. He stood straight and nodded in the dark.

"Right. You count this time so I can put all my energy into pushing."

She tittered and he ground his teeth, then she counted backward from three, to be different from him.

"Three...two...one."

They pushed and the door shifted modestly but noticeably behind their weight.

"Once more," Teryk said, and they pushed again.

The door swung inward, hinges shrieking with the high-pitched squeal of a tormented soul, and the siblings stumbled through into the room beyond.

After spending their journey along the passage in darkness, the first and most obvious thing they should have noticed was the light. It shone down from high above, illuminating the entire room with four pillars of light that danced and swayed with the billow of dust thrown up by the movement of the door. Instead, the room itself captured their attention.

The ceiling soared high overhead, higher than any room in the castle, including the throne room and the great hall, and the prince and princess had been in all of them. All save this one. Veins of white shot through the red marble walls unadorned by the paintings and tapestries on display in every other corner of Draekfarren castle. A line of gray and black flecked granite pillars marched along each wall, reaching all the way to the ceiling above, and beside each pillar stood a suit of armor.

"Where are we?" Danya whispered. The room took her small words and threw them around against the walls and up to heights, echoing them back and forth until they disappeared.

"I don't know."

The prince stepped fully into the room, tilted his head back to search the ceiling. No torches cast light from above, no lanterns, candles or tapers, so he presumed the illumination must be sunlight, directed into chamber by some system of hidden mirrors. The ceiling itself bore no decoration.

Three short stairs led down to the floor, and Teryk traversed them with care, worried a trap might be sprung by their footsteps and catch them, and he'd already been caught in one trap too many on this day. Danya skipped down the steps and past him, her head thrown back and arms held out to the sides as she turned a circle throwing more dust into the air to dance across the beams of light.

"It's spectacular," she cried.

"Sshhh. Stop it. Come back here."

As usual, she didn't listen to her older brother, and Teryk found himself chasing her, his gaze trailing off to the suits of armor lining the walls by the pillars. He slowed to a stop, catching his sister by the arm as he stared at the armor.

"Do you know who they belonged to?" she asked.

"No. They're not familiar. They don't belong to any of the kings of Northward."

He tiptoed across the concourse, Danya in tow, and approached a suit of armor fashioned of red enamel with silver highlights. Long, curved horns protruded from the helmet in a manner unlike any helm Teryk had ever seen.

"They're ceremonial," he said. "No one could wear something like this in battle."

"Except giants, maybe."

As he leaned his head back to stare up at the helm's face plate, Teryk realized the true size of the armor. Standing in the doorway, the huge room made the suits appear small, but anything would when compared to the massive columns. Teryk himself stood twenty-four handspans, and the top of this armor's helmet towered another ten higher than him. The horns added at least another six beyond that.

"Let's see what else we can find," Danya said pulling away from her brother's grip.

Awe-struck by the enormous suit of armor, he let her go. The slap of her bare feet on the granite floor echoed through the room, but the prince barely noticed. He took a step closer, leaning in for a better inspection of the quality of workmanship displayed in the armor.

The enameling was flawless, the precision of the casting and smithing beyond anything he'd seen produced in the inner city. The lines of the silver highlights were exact, with a perfect straightness separating it from the red. He leaned closer, squinting at the shimmering markings.

"They're letters," he whispered, and the room carried his words to lofty heights.

"What did you say?"

His sister's voice broke the armor's spell. He glanced at her, sensing danger as she approached the only other item in the room: a lectern carved of marble.

"Don't touch it," he said and hurried across to her.

"I'm not touching it," she said, hands clasped behind her back in the manner of a child caught sneaking sweets from the pantry. "What did you say when you were looking at the battle suit?"

"I think the silver bits are words."

He moved past her to see what the lectern held and found a rolled parchment sitting atop it, but nothing else.

"Words? What did they say?"

Teryk took a step toward the rostrum, barely noticing his sister's words. "What?"

"I asked what the words said."

The prince shook his head. "I'm not sure. It's another language."

"What other language?"

"Quiet," Teryk snapped and raised his hand. A hurt expression on her brow, Danya opened her mouth to protest, but didn't. "Do you hear that?"

A tiny sound—completely unnoticeable when either of them spoke, lost amongst their footsteps when they moved, hardly there compared to their heartbeats—but he heard it. The faintest of hums masquerading as a buzz, pretending to be a breath. He took another step toward the lectern.

The sound emanated from the roll of parchment.

"I don't hear anything."

"Sshh.'

Teryk crept closer. The noise didn't grow any louder, but it became more distinct—not a hum or a buzz or an exhalation, but a susurrant tangle of whispers, each indistinct on their own, but together combining to the softest of murmurs.

"It's saying something," he said, near enough now to reach out and touch the scroll if he wanted. He leaned his head closer still, listening, straining to perceive a recognizable word. "You can't hear that?"

The pad of Danya's bare feet on the stone floor sounded a cacophony in comparison, assaulting the prince's ears and making him want to press his hands to the side of his head, but then she stood beside him and the tumult ended. They both held their breath, the only sounds in the room the beat of their hearts and, hidden beneath, the whispers of the scroll.

Teryk counted twenty heartbeats pass before Danya shook her head and parted her lips, but he raised his finger, stopping her. Ten more beats, the scroll murmuring to him, talking to him. If only he understood it.

Why can't she hear it?

A feeling easily mistaken for satisfaction settled into the prince at knowing a thing she didn't, but it disappeared in an instant. Danya understood languages better than he, as she was better at most things. He wished she could tell him what language it spoke, what it said, what it wanted from him. He leaned closer, his sister leaning with him, his ear a handspan away from the edge of the rostrum, and then he understood.

"It wants me to take it with us."

"What?" Danya straightened and put her hand on his arm. "No, Teryk. We can't. We don't even know how to get out of here."

"I have to."

He shrugged her off and took the last step to the lectern, raised his hand toward the scroll. Before he stretched his hand out to touch it, before Danya did or said anything to stop him, the roll of parchment leaped into his hand and the whispering ended.

I was right.

Teryk held it up, staring, sensing his sister's eyes on it, too. The parchment was rough against his fingers and smelled old—two qualities one might reasonably expect of an ancient paper. A spot of blue wax pressed with an unfamiliar seal held the scroll from unrolling. When the prince rubbed his thumb across it, chunks of the brittle material flaked away.

"We have to find a way out, Teryk," Danya said.

"What's your hurry?" He didn't move his gaze from the roll in his hand.

"Trenan will be looking for us, remember? You have pike training."

Teryk redirected his gaze from the scroll to his sister, his eyes moving lazily, as though mired in the royal cook's version of oatmeal. They crossed the void between them, seeing the dust dancing in the light, the gleaming stone floor, the red with white pillars soaring toward the ceiling.

And the battle suits crossing the floor in silence behind her.

Blood rushed away from Teryk's face, turning his cheeks cold and making him suspect his eyes might pop out of their places. In an instant, his fearful and surprised expression spread to his sister, who glanced over her shoulder to find out what behind her caused her brother's distress. Before she turned fully, the prince grabbed her arm and pulled her away, heading toward the end of the room opposite where they'd entered.

An archway set in the wall suggested a door, but there was none. The slap of the siblings' bare feet echoed through the room, disguising the movement of the battle suits, mixing and milling with the sudden pounding of Teryk's own pulse in his ears. Seconds ago, the world had been silence, nothing but the whisper of ancient voices trapped here and waiting for the prince's ear. Now, footsteps and heartbeats grew and multiplied like a thunderhead breaching the horizon.

They stumbled up the three short stairs to the archway, panting and fearful. Neither of them looked back, afraid of what they might find pursuing them.

Teryk threw himself into the wall, jarring his shoulder and nearly dropping the parchment, but nothing moved except his bones. He stuck the scroll in the waist of his underpants and put both palms flat against the wall, pushed and pushed. Nothing.

"Help me," he yelled to Danya, who was searching the edge of the archway.

"There must be a hidden switch," she said.

Teryk pushed again, ignoring her.

"Please," he said, their other noises enough the room didn't take these words and toss them into the heights of the ceiling for fun. "Please open the door."

A click sounded, followed by the grinding of an ancient mechanism, and the wall pulled to one side as though he'd spoken the magic words.

"Come on!"

He grabbed Danya's arm and ushered her over the threshold ahead of him, then jumped through as the wall slid shut behind them. Before it closed all the way, he peeked between the wall and the edge, expecting to find giant-sized suits of battle armor reaching for them, a hair's-breadth from snagging them and ending their lives.

He saw a lectern, columns carved of granite, and no armored suits at all.

III - Ailyssa - Lines of Chalk

*T*HE CHALK QUIVERED IN N'th Ailyssa Ra's fingers as she raised her hand toward the wall, preparing to inscribe the ninety-eighth line. Never had she drawn more than thirty-two, except when a child grew within her, and most times never exceeded the twenty-eight chalk lines expected between bleeds.

She closed her eyes and expelled a shuddering breath, reminded herself she'd been aware this day would come, as it did for all Mothers, all women. But she'd imagined it differently, thinking she'd move from Mother to Matron and be an elder of the church, like had happened for N'th Adesi Ra no more than four moons ago.

N'th Adesi Re, she corrected herself.

Ailyssa opened her eyes and took the last step toward the wall, pressed the flat end of the chalk against the stone. With a final sigh, she drew it downward, marking the ninety-eighth rising of the sun since her last bleed.

More than three complete turns of the moon.

With her last coupling five moons gone, far too much time had passed to be carrying a child and not showing signs. Sometimes the blood might fool you and continue to flow for moons after conception but, at her age, the belly couldn't conceal its secret for long. The times she'd been with child, her heart had been aware of the little soul's presence before her body announced it to the world.

N'th Ailyssa Ra set the nub of chalk on the ledge beneath the marks, wiped its dust from her fingers on the front of her smock, and tilted her head back to observe the scores on the wall above the chalk lines. These ones had been scratched into the stone, meant to be permanent, not erased every twenty-eight sunrises—give or take—as were the spotty white smudges she drew each morn.

It took her a moment to count them, though she knew how many she'd find: fifty-four. She'd been counting them often of late. The more chalk lines she drew on the wall, the more she counted the carved marks, it seemed.

The twelfth line was wider and deeper than the others, indicating her first bleed, the day she earned the title N'th. She recalled it as though there were not more than forty other lines drawn in between it and the last. Her joy at waking to find her bed sheets spotted with the Goddess' will that morning had been nearly enough to overshadow it also being the last day she lived with the woman who brought her into this world. The next day of her birth—her thirteenth—marked the first time she carved a line in the wall herself.

She traced the mark with the tip of her finger, remembering N'th Pedra Ra who gave Ailyssa life. They'd followed the Goddess' wishes, and Mother and Daughter were separated after Ailyssa's first bleeding, and she often wondered what became of the woman who birthed her. Did she go on to become N'th Pedra Re? Or did Ailyssa's lack of Daughters, and her Daughter's lack of Daughters, lead to her expulsion?

Perhaps Pedra bore other Daughters who brought honor to the order and the Goddess.

Ailyssa moved her hand away from the deep wound in the stone and blinked back a tear. Her fingers hovered over the next row, where circles ringed three of the marks, the first crossed out by two lines. She kept her touch and her gaze away from this one, knowing tears came easily at its sight, but she rested her fingertip on the second. This one recorded the birth of her Daughter, Claris, when the Goddess had seen fit to bestow upon her the title of Ra—Mother.

Thirty-four marks had been carved in the wall between that circle and the last line, and still N'th Claris hadn't been blessed to become Ra. Ailyssa heard word of her now and again when one of the Matrons traveled and brought back news, and they'd told her that the Goddess did not yet judge her Daughter fit to give birth to a Daughter of her own.

Her hand moved to the final circled scar, one separated by thirty-two similar lines from the most current mark carved fewer than two moons ago. No other circles disturbed the rows between, and this last one represented Ailyssa's greatest pain. When she'd given birth to her first son—her first child and the first circle on the wall—it seemed natural he be taken from her, and she knew no different. She'd drawn the line through his birth circle without second thought; it wasn't until she held her second child in her arms that she understood what she missed with his absence. Before then, she'd never thought to wonder what became of him, it simply was what was: the will of the Goddess.

The last circle represented her second son, also taken away as a babe; a child she'd not seen since and never expected to see again. His birth had been the most difficult for her and, at times, she'd wondered if the struggle was the reason she'd birthed no more children in honor of the Goddess. Though it may be, she realized the circumstances of his birth were also why she mourned him so. Unlike when her first baby came into the world, her young daughter still nursed at her breast when the third came, and she knew what it was like to love a child.

The pain of his loss wounded her, leaving a scar on her heart far deeper than the one on the wall—a pathetic representation of a child whose fate she'd never learn. She'd been unable to bring herself to inscribe the mark of 'son' across it as she'd done the first, unable to act as though the birth and the child it brought never happened.

Ailyssa had memorized the writings as did every Daughter before they became N'th: *do not mourn a son, for they are worthless*. But, even after carving thirty-two lines in the stone, sleep eluded her some nights, leaving her to lay awake, wondering...wondering. She couldn't even bring herself to look upon the first circle.

Her hand dropped to her side and she counted marks again.

Ninety-eight since her last bleed.

Thirty-two since her last child.

Forty-two since her first drops upon the sheets.

That meant near forty-two times thirteen moons she'd wiped the chalk markers from the wall and began anew. She hung her head, wishing for her blood to come and allow her to erase their menacing implication one more time.

"N'th Ailyssa Ra. It is time."

She raised her head and saw N'th Adesi Re framed in the doorway, the smile on her lips laced with the same sadness and resignation Ailyssa held inside herself.

At least they sent a friend.

"It is time already?" Ailyssa said, climbing to her feet.

Adesi nodded. "Your coupling partner is readying himself. It is time for your preparations."

Ailyssa clasped her hands and bowed her head in deference to the Matron. Before she let go and raised her eyes again, she noticed chalk dust trapped beneath her nails, accusing her of failing the Goddess.

N'th Adesi Re led her from her room.

The laving ritual took no longer than any other of the countless times she'd participated in it, but to Ailyssa, it stretched on for a quarter turn of the moon or more. Three young girls who'd not yet been blessed with their blood and therefore not acquired the title N'th attended her, scouring every part of her with pumice rock and lye soap until she cringed at their touch. The Goddess wanted her cleansed for the coupling—cleansed of dirt and sweat, cleansed of impure thought, cleansed of sin. Cleansed of her very skin, Ailyssa sometimes thought, but never said so aloud for fear of prolonging the sacrament and drawing it out until she was raw.

With the cleansing complete, they brought out the Goddess' blade and removed every hair from Ailyssa's body, from her head to her toes. Some areas required more attention than they had in your youth, some less. After the blade came the lotions. Ailyssa closed her eyes and let them complete their duties, taking no joy from the touch of their hands.

When the attendants finished, she waited while they retrieved the simple white shift she'd wear for the coupling. Water dripped from her to the warm rock under her feet. She peered down, past her breasts drooping more than they had seasons gone by—from age, not from nursing babes, which they hadn't done in so long. Beyond her chest, her belly lay too flat for not having birthed half the number of children as many of the Ra. She looked past her body, which had betrayed her, at the spatter of droplets drying on the stone, disappearing the way she felt her life would soon, too.

The attendants returned and rubbed her with oils to stem the flow of blood from any scrapes made by pumice stone or sharpened steel. They draped the shift over her head, tied it at her waist with a length of white rope, rubbed her shoulders to ensure she was relaxed.

N'th Adesi Re returned and the attendants took their leave. The Matron offered her hand and Ailyssa took it and the friends held onto each other as they made their way along the long hall to the coupling room.

"They say he is the most fertile of men. He has sired dozens of Daughters, many of whom have become N'th, and three are already Ra."

Ailyssa forced a wan smile.

"At your age," the Matron continued, "if you produced a Daughter, I think the elders would look well upon your situation."

"Do you?" She struggled to keep a cynical tone from her voice.

"I do."

They paused before the door, and Adesi put her hands on Ailyssa's shoulders, looked in her eyes. Ailyssa's gaze wandered, unable to hold under the Matron's scrutiny. Instead, she focused on her friend's ample bosom that had provided milk to half-a-dozen Daughters, at her rounded goddess body made that way by honoring the order and the Goddess. Seeing it squeezed Ailyssa's heart.

What will I do if they cast me out?

N'th Adesi Re gave her friend a gentle shake, prompting her to raise her head, then spoke as though Ailyssa had uttered her thoughts aloud.

"This is your last chance," she said, eyes shining with concern Ailyssa hoped was genuine. "Take as long as you need. Do whatever you must."

The Matron stepped aside and pushed the door open. N'th Ailyssa Ra hesitated, watched her friend who offered a smile likely meant to reassure but which increased her nerves, then she crossed the threshold.

The portal clicked shut behind her and Ailyssa's gaze dropped to the floor. She'd stood here many times before and, each time, the butterfly flutter of nerves in her stomach kept her from gazing upon the man with whom she'd couple. This time, the butterflies were angry, the flutter a quake. If she'd bothered breaking fast this morn, she wasn't sure the food would have stayed put.

"Ahem."

She looked up at the sound of the man clearing his throat and saw him standing beside the coupling bed, naked and erect. Ailyssa kept her eyes on his face.

"I am Ailyssa," she said, hesitant.

The man shook his head, dark hair brushing the tops of his shoulders. "Your name does not matter."

Ailyssa found a sheen of perspiration on her palms; she wiped them on the front of her shift, then wondered if this man might find her doing so unattractive. The thought surprised her, for she knew coupling had nothing to do with attraction. How could a man and a woman possibly consider each other comely? The man sat on the edge of the bed, his erect manhood pointing at the ceiling.

"What..." Ailyssa began, but forgot the question she meant to ask, searched for something else. "What is your name?"

She chastised herself silently as soon as the words were spoken. Men kept for breeding didn't have names; slaves alone did, and then only so they'd recognize when their mistress required assistance.

"Judging by the lines on your face, I'd not have taken you for an attendant," he said. A warm rush of blood filled Ailyssa's cheeks. The man patted the coupling bed beside him. "Nor would I expect you to be nervous. Fear not, you are not my first older Ra."

Ailyssa said nothing. He tilted his head.

"You are Ra, aren't you?"

"Oh, yes," she said and took two steps toward the coupling bed. The shift she wore—the same one she'd worn so many times before—seemed very thin today, very transparent. She'd never worried about its ability to hide her body before. "I'm just not used to a man speaking so many words."

"Many say they enjoy my voice. I can speak less if you like."

She shook her head. "It's fine."

"Good. Come sit with me, then." He patted the mattress.

Ailyssa inhaled deeply through her nose, smelled the scented oils the attendants had rubbed on her skin and the aroma of the ones used to anoint him. The fragrances blended in perfect harmony, forming a concoction worthy of the Goddess, as they were meant to. The perfume calmed her, and she took the last few steps across the room to sit beside him, though not close enough that their thighs touched. He laid his hand on her leg and the calmness brought by the scents fled from her.

"You are tense," the man said. "Perhaps the attendants did not complete their job. Shall I rub you with more oils?"

"Yes."

Ailyssa didn't want more oil slopped upon her skin and dreaded the thought of more than the thin shift touching her raw flesh, but if she could delay the coupling, she intended to do so. The man leaned in, kissed her on the cheek, then rose and strode across the room to a shelf mounted on the wall. Six ornate bottles sat upon it. He perused them, lifted one and held it to the light, then put it back. He took another down, removed the stopper and inhaled its scent.

"Rose oil?"

Ailyssa didn't answer. She couldn't. Her gaze stuck on his right shoulder blade, where a wine-colored birthmark stood out against his olive skin.

"Have you—" She stopped and swallowed hard; he regarded her over his shoulder. "Have you always had that mark?"

He craned his neck, attempting to see his own back past his long hair. "On my shoulder?"

"Yes."

"As long as I can remember." He returned the bottle of rose oil to the shelf and chose another, wrinkled his nose at the odor. "I've never liked hibiscus."

Ailyssa scarcely heard what he said. Her head spun, making her dizzy and her stomach churn with nausea. She stood from the edge of the bed, knees wobbling.

"Where...where were you born?"

"Ha!" The man replaced the bottle on the shelf and faced her. He gestured toward his swollen manhood. "Do you not see this? I am a man. I was not born; I have no mother."

Ailyssa swallowed hard and put her hand on the wall to steady herself and keep from falling. The saliva in her mouth dried up, but she licked her lips despite the lack of wetness on her tongue, desperate to get out the words she needed to say.

"Yes, you do," she croaked and used her other hand to wipe away a sheen of sweat from her freshly-shaven head. "I am your mother."

IV - Horace – Washin' Ashore

A SANDY SCENT FILLED his nose and he coughed salty water outta his mouth, the result of a breath he weren't never expectin' to breathe.

Horace Seaman lay with cheek pressed against the beach, waves lappin' 'round him and washin' the sand out from underneath him. The briny stink, the sun's sticky heat, and the watery sound rushin' near his ears all suggested he may yet be livin', but he hardly believed it, so he didn't bother openin' his eyes. If he did, he feared findin' out bein' inside the God o' the Deep's belly smelled and felt precisely like a beach and he might, at any moment, get shit out into a hell beyond a man such as himself's imaginin'. He didn't relish the thought o' hell, and he didn't much appreciate the idea o' bein' shit out, neither.

Somewhere above, a gull squawked. Somewhere distant, another answered.

Ain't no birds flyin' 'round in the God's belly.

He parted his lips and blew out his air in a stream; it burbled in water sittin' by his face.

Is there?

After a moment, he thunk up how to know for true, and it involved openin' his eyes and havin' a peep. He inhaled another careful, unexpected breath past the water near his mouth, takin' yet more time to convince himself this were necess'ry , that he couldn't just lay here forever waitin' to see what'd happen. Be it worse knowin' you was gonna be shit out into hell, or waitin' for the bowel movement to surprise you? Horace ground his teeth together hard and convinced his eyelids they should part company.

At first, he saw nothin' but light and remembered a story that one hell were full o' fire, with people burnin' and burnin', awaitin' the end of time to put a stop to their misery. Here's one thing Horace knew: no matter where you found it burnin', fire didn't stink of ocean and beach, nor sparkle like the sun upon the sea. After so much time with a ship's deck beneath his feet, the stench o' the sea and the day's shine upon the ocean'd be two things Horace reckoned he recognized without no trouble.

He blinked to clear the stingin' salt water outta his peepers and made to raise his head for a better peek, not sure if the thing'd do what he asked of it. It did, providin' him a wee, uncomfortable twinge to his neck and an ache in his forehead along the way. Didn't seem nothin' like what he thought bein' dead'd be.

With his head held up, he laid eyes upon a beach stretchin' away into the distance. A line o' green and brown seaweed cut across the sand, a border keepin' the ocean from crawlin' into the tumble of rocks in turn holdin' the forest back from meetin' the sea. He rolled with a grunt and looked the other way, spyin' nothin' but the same thing, only layin' in the other direction.

"Fuck me dead," Horace Seaman said aloud, surprised to hear his own voice again, though it came out no better'n if a frog spoke the words. "I be livin'."

He moved his arms and found them workin' without much protestation, then propped himself up on his elbows. Straight ahead were more o' the same: sand, seaweed, rocks, forest. Limbs o' unfamiliar trees swayed with a gust of wind, long needles quiverin' against one another and whisperin' a tune what brung a chill to ol' Horace's warm, wet flesh. Bumps crawled along his forearms, beggin' for him to get himself outta the water.

His feet churned and splashed in the hated ocean. His toes dug into sand, slipped, dug in deeper. He lurched forward, pushin' himself farther onto the beach, toward the border of seaweed, the rocks, the trees. Somewhere beyond lay a world without no boats and tides, without no gales makin' waves what'd toss a man 'round in the manner of a child's plaything, and without no god lurkin' down below what wanted to make a meal outta you and shit you out in hell. Horace didn't know where he'd landed or what world it might be, but he intended to find out rather'n layin' 'bout awaitin' the tide to come in, bringin' the ocean ashore to finish what it started.

Horace Seaman got his knees up under him and crawled away from the sea. His hands splashed in wet sand, water swirlin' 'round his fingers, and he kept goin' until one palm rested in dry powder. He stopped and looked at the grit pressin' up between his digits, lifted his hand and gazed at the fine grains stickin' to his wet palm, and Horace Seaman laughed.

He shuffled forward more quicker until he reached the seaweed border. Its pungent odor invaded his nostrils, each strand smellin' as though it contained the whole ocean inside it, the stench threatenin' to roll his stomach upside down, though weren't nothin' in there for him to puke up. Crunchy brown ends o' dry seaweed crinkled under his hands, and wet, green strands squished and squelched beneath his knees. He dragged himself across the verge and energy filled him, like a bird finally free o' the cage he'd been locked in for nigh on to thirty-five turns o' the seasons.

Horace rested his hands on the closest rock, its surface warmed by a day spent lyin' in the sun like he'd done, and pushed himself upright. Water dripped outta his wet hair and stubble, his soggy shirt sleeves, his sopping shirt front. He shook himself hard, sent a watery spray flyin' onto the rocks, and climbed to his feet, wobblin' all the way. His knees quaked, habit makin' them adjust to a heavin' deck no longer beneath his feet, and he bent down and put a hand upon the rock again.

He stayed that way for a time, wonderin' what anyone watchin' might think 'bout a man what looked akin to a baby takin' his first steps in the world. But weren't no one spyin' on him, Horace knew. And if so...fuck 'em, anyways. He were alive and them seein' him teeterin' like he ain't never stood before weren't gonna change the fact, only proved it.

After a while, his knees ceased shakin' and Horace laughed. He laughed louder and longer'n he ever remembered laughin' before. He laughed for his feet standin' on dry land, he laughed for bein' free of the cursed ship and the cursed sea what bore it, he laughed for bein' alive and, most of all, he laughed for not bein' shit out into hell.

Horace straightened again and found his legs happy to hold him upright this time. In fact, he felt pretty good on the whole for a man what been drowned like a bilge rat and ate by an angry god. Pretty damned good, indeed.

He took a step and pain shot through his foot. Horace glanced down to see one o' his boots gone, lost somewhere between fallin' in the water and washin' up on the beach. Maybe that's ev'ry bit o' him the God o' the Deep ate—just one boot. Could be he'd swallowed him after all and spit him out, likin' only the flavor of his left boot and the rest of him turnin' his godly stomach. Horace moved his barefoot offa the rock diggin' into his sole and laughed again. No matter why he were without a boot, no matter why the god did or didn't burp him up, he were alive enough to cut his sole on a rock, and doin' so made him want to laugh and smile in spite o' the pain.

Horace moved forward again, pickin' his way amongst the smaller stones, limpin' on his hurt foot and glad to be doin' so. As he hobbled across the rocky patch leadin' toward the trees, his mind finally turned to wonderin' how long ago the simpleton sent him tumblin' o'erboard, and where he'd set ashore. Without knowin' the length o' time the sea'd been carryin' him, or what tides'd picked him up, it weren't possible to figure where he'd landed.

With the last stretch of rocks and the length of ten tall men separatin' him from the first line o' trees, Horace Seaman stopped dead in his tracks.

Did I float right the way to the Green?

After all them turns hatin' the sea, maybe it turned out the sea hated him, too, and floated him into more danger'n he ever imagined. Could be the ocean wanted him dead but didn't have the sand in its sack to do it, so sent him somewhere for a mess o' Small Gods to eat him after the big one didn't like the taste o' nothin' but his left boot.

Horace ain't never been on land anywhere near the Green before, only ever spyin' it while standin' on a ship's deck with his staff shrivelin' and his ball sack cowerin', but distance enough between him and it to keep his man-parts safe ev'ry time he had to sail the turn. He knew the stories 'bout the Small Gods as surely as he did the ones 'bout the God o' the Deep. Weren't no tellin' which to be more afraid of. With his feet closer to what might be the Green, his eyes starin' into the curtain o' danglin' tree limbs and tangled brambles, he weren't sure he wouldn't rather be back on a boat.

The sun frowned down on Horace, dryin' his clothes and heatin' his skin, but he shivered nonetheless. The *Devil'd* been a hundred leagues or more from the turn—no way a feller coulda floated so far without drownin'. Weren't possible for a man without his wits to stay alive so long.

Were it?

He squinted into the messy tangle o' thorns and needles, branches and limbs, each one resemblin' a twisted arm, a taloned hand. A windy gust shivered through the trees, whisperin' and tauntin', invitin' him into their shade to see what lay beyond.

Horace peeked back o'er his shoulder at the sea what spit him out on the beach, the wind what set the branches quiverin' throwin' waves across the water. Where were that wind when the *Devil* lay like a corpse upon the sea?

The waves rolled up the sand, reachin' for him, graspin' at the air to find him and drag him away, but ol' Horace Seaman weren't gonna have none o' that. The sea'd had its chance to end him when Dunal slapped him o'er the wale, and near on thirty-five turns o' the seasons opportunity before that. If it hadn't managed by now, weren't no way Horace'd give it another go. Weren't no sayin' if he'd drifted all the way to the Green or not but, if he did, maybe the Small Gods wouldn't enjoy his flavor no better'n the God o' the Deep. Maybe he tasted like shit to ev'ry god there were.

A deep breath reekin' more of fresh sap and decayin' foliage than hot sand and briny ocean filled Horace's chest. Weren't enough to fill his heart with courage, the way a deep breath tended to do for the heroes of the tales told at ev'ry tavern along the coast, but Horace Seaman weren't no hero—never thought, expected, nor wanted to be one. Horace Seaman were a man afraid o' what lay ahead o' him barely a cunt hair less'n what lay behind. But a cunt hair is a cunt hair, and that be a damn wide distance when a man's life be at stake.

Before proceedin', Horace reached 'round to his back pocket and found the rag what weren't there for no purpose but wipin' sweat from his brow, surprised to find it still hangin' 'round when his left boot didn't come along for the full journey. He wrung the sea water outta it as best he could and bent forward to wrap the cloth 'round his foot, tyin' it off at the ankle, finally givin' the fabric square another reason to be. When it were done, he took a step, placin' his rag-wrapped foot careful on the ground and pleased it protected him from stones. In his haste to protect his bleedin' sole, he didn't hear the quiet plop of a possum tail he kept in his pocket for the purpose o' bringin' him luck fallin' amongst the rocks.

Another breath what still didn't make him into no hero entered Horace's lungs and he set out into the trees, hopin' too much time hadn't passed, hopin' he hadn't floated too far. Meetin' one huge god were enough for any man's lifetime; he didn't want to go introducin' himself to no gaggle of little ones.

Horace picked his way into the forest, on the one hand hopin' not to've floated all the way to the Green where lived the Small Gods they told stories 'bout at some o' the taverns along the coast nearer the turn, and on the other hand hopin' to find one o' them taverns, 'cause he could sure use himself a pint o' ale.

That'd stop his hands from shakin'.

V - Teryk and Danya - Lessons

*T*HE DISTINCT SOUND OF sword clashing against plate assaulted Danya's ears, but she didn't turn away from her own opponent. As sparring partners went, Droinfeld's skills had deteriorated with age, but he possessed enough to keep the princess on her toes. Still, she wanted to see if her brother was finally getting the better of Trenan after seasons of practice.

She parried, swung, and danced away, spinning the old knight around to give herself a glimpse of Teryk and Trenan over his shoulder. Whatever had happened, she'd missed it, because the two of them were stalking each other in a tight circle, Trenan presenting his sword at just the right angle to attack or defend. The left sleeve of his shirt hung limp at his side, the end tucked into his sword belt. Even with one arm, Trenan could better any swordsman in the kingdom.

Teryk, in comparison, held his weapon at a precarious angle that required unnecessary extra energy to wield, and his shield sagged by his knees, improperly taunting his opponent and inviting attack. Danya wished for the master swordsman to grasp the opportunity and teach her brother a lesson this time.

Trenan swung his sword in a slow, looping arc that Teryk deflected with his shield. Seeing the ease with which her brother defended himself, she understood today wouldn't be the day for the prince's real-life lesson.

Danya returned her attention to Droinfeld, a man of more than sixty-five turns of the seasons. His white mustache drooped at the ends and sweat streamed from beneath his helm, causing him to blink incessantly. The princess realized that the drooping, the blinking, and the pink glow in his cheeks meant she was wearing him out, as she always did when she allowed their sparring to last long enough to give her some exercise instead of vanquishing him in short order.

To his credit, Droinfeld kept coming at her—as he should, given his job was to teach her the art of the sword. Despite the heaving gasps struggling their way into his lungs, and the pronounced effort his arm required to swing a good blow, he remained on the attack.

Sometimes, Danya wasn't sure who was teaching whom the art of the sword.

Their swords came together with a clang that shuddered up her forearm, the corked tip of Droinfeld's weapon waving a hand's-breadth from her face, but she had full control of his blade. The tip ended its path exactly where she meant it to, the shudder in her arm efficiently absorbed. The edge of her blade scraped along his as she flung it aside and lunged at him. To say the old knight danced out of the way might have been a flowery exaggeration, but he awkwardly managed to dodge her attack. They each stepped back, opening space between them, and Danya smiled.

"Well done, sir," she said and bowed her head without removing her eyes from his.

Droinfeld's mouth opened as though he might reply, but only a great huff of breath leaving his lungs passed his lips. Instead of speaking, which seemed as though it might have been beyond him right then, he nodded.

The young girl and older man rejoined the fight. His shield rebuffed a thrust from the princess; she sprang out of the way of a round-house swing that sent Droinfeld stumbling. His miscue gave Danya the opening she needed to finish him, but she caught another glimpse of Teryk and Trenan behind him and stayed her finishing blow.

Trenan was on one knee, blocking Teryk's overhead swings with his blade. It was obvious to the princess he could have extricated himself from the predicament with little effort—each time the prince raised his sword, he left himself exposed to being hamstrung, or run through the belly, but Trenan passed up the opportunity like a novice sparring for the first time.

"Ha!" the prince exclaimed, his sword coming down again and knocking the master swordsman onto his back. Danya watched him step forward and put the tip of his blade to Trenan's throat; the trainer let his sword fall to the dusty ground, surrendering.

An instant later, Danya felt a pressure against her stomach and glanced down to find the corked tip of Droinfeld's weapon pressed against her belly. She let her own sword and shield droop to her sides and looked up at the old knight smiling at her, his sagging mustache all but hiding the curl of his lips.

"You...should...," he gasped, struggling to make his pants form words. "Pay...attention...to..."

"Yes, yes," Danya said, brushing his sword aside with the hilt of her own. "Pay attention to my opponent. That's all for today, Droinfeld."

The old knight held her gaze, enjoying the moment of his triumph, and well he should—it had been many turns of the moon since last Danya let him best her. She couldn't dispute him, though; she needed to worry about the opponent in front of her, not what went on around her, but she wondered why Trenan let Teryk defeat him every time.

Droinfeld bowed low at the waist and, for an instant, Danya worried he might not be able to right himself. He did, then drew a long, slow sigh and took his leave from the practice ring. When he stepped aside, she saw Teryk offering a hand to help Trenan up out of the dirt.

"Beat him again. Did you see, sis?"

Trenan refused the prince's assistance and planted the corked tip of his sword against the ground to push himself up. Other than a smear of dust across his cheek, he didn't appear any the worse for wear after his sparring session with the prince.

"I saw," she replied, doing her most to sound happy for him, but she found it difficult. She wished Trenan would allow her and Teryk to spar just once, because she wouldn't hesitate to teach her brother the lessons he needed to learn. The thought brought a smile to her face and she used it to fool her brother into thinking his victory delighted her.

Teryk slapped Trenan on the shoulder, sending a puff of dust into the air.

"Are you all right? I didn't hurt you, did I, Trenan?"

To his credit, the master swordsman kept from revealing the truth of the matter, as he always did.

"I'm fine, your grace. You caught me with a blow I didn't see coming." He pulled the cork off the tip of his sword with his teeth, spat it to the ground, and slid the weapon into its sheath. "You grow more skillful every day."

Danya fought to keep from rolling her eyes as the prince beamed. His cheeks weren't as pink as Droinfeld's had been, and not as much sweat seeped from under his helm, but he did touch his shoulder and his muscles after stowing his sword. She saw the fight had drained him, and not because of his age, as was the case with the old knight, but due to his technique and conditioning. If he'd only learn to defend and attack correctly, his shoulder wouldn't hurt so, and he'd be less likely to lose his breath.

She couldn't tell him these things, though, because she was but his sister, and younger than him.

Teryk's smile faded, his expression becoming grave.

"Trenan, I have something to discuss with you," he said, his eyes flickering to Danya, and she saw he meant to tell their trainer about the scroll. He'd kept it to himself for three sunrises, and made her do the same, but it had gotten too much of a secret for him to hold any longer.

"I don't think that's a good idea," she said and felt Trenan's gaze upon her.

"Well, I do." The prince looked back to the trainer. "I am to bathe the dust and sweat of my victory from my skin, then take dinner and rest. Tomorrow is a full day of classes, but my night is free. Meet me in my chambers after dinner, Trenan. You, too, sister."

"Tomorrow after dinner, of course." The master swordsman clicked his heels and bowed his head.

Teryk directed his gaze to his sister again and she pressed her lips together, gave him a hard look so he'd know she thought showing Trenan an unwise idea. They'd have to explain where they got it, which meant they'd have to tell him they'd been swimming in the river under the castle. Trenan normally kept their secrets, but as much as they considered him their friend, his service belonged to their father. If he told the king, there would be hell to pay.

The prince walked three paces before stopping and peering back over his shoulder.

"Are you coming to bathe, Danya?"

The princess shook her head. "No. I'm going to stay and practice with Trenan some more."

"Ha! Good luck. You didn't even beat old Droinfeld."

The prince walked away, his back to them as the princess stuck out her tongue. Trenan chuckled and shook his head.

"The prince is right: Droinfeld beat you. Are you sure you want to spar with me, your grace?"

"You know he beat me because I let myself be distracted." She sneered at him and raised her sword, waggled it in the air between them. "Besides, at least Droinfeld is a knight. You were bested by a boy who can't tell a broadsword from a rapier."

"Now, now, princess," Trenan said drawing his weapon. "The prince beat me in a fair fight."

"Not true. You let him win. You always let him win."

"Your brother is an excellent swordsman."

"And Droinfeld is next in line to be king," she said as Trenan crossed the yard to where his cork lay on the ground. "You don't need that."

The master swordsman raised an eyebrow, his sword tip hovering above the chunk of cork, but he didn't plunge it in. He faced the princess and bowed at the waist, a wicked grin crossing his lips.

"As you command, your imperial cockiness."

Danya narrowed her eyes and smirked back at him, then fell into the on-guard stance she'd learned the first time she held a sword. She'd taken to the discipline of swordplay right away, much to the queen's chagrin. For seasons, she'd practiced in secret, bribing any knight willing to take her coin to fence with her using branches or wooden swords. Finally, she convinced the king to allow her some formal training but even then, he assigned the lowest level swordsmen to train her, over-the-hill Droinfeld being the best of them. She could count on her fingers the number of times she'd crossed blades with Trenan and still have some to spare.

The master swordsman nodded, acknowledging her form, and took up his own pose, the grin disappearing from his lips. He shuffle-stepped to his right and Danya matched his movement.

"Why, Trenan?" she said, her eyes glued to his. "Why do you let him win?"

"I am but a trainer, commanded by the king, princess. A man such as I does what I'm told."

So father tells you to let him win.

They circled, Trenan's icy blue eyes on her, his chestnut hair hanging dry to his shoulders—he hadn't even broken a sweat as he worked out with the prince. Danya put her left foot across behind her right, stepping away.

"Do not cross your feet, princess. Crossed feet cause stumbles."

She pursed her lips and swore to herself. She knew not to take the chance of tangling her feet. If they did and she fell, Teryk might be the only opponent in the entire kingdom who wouldn't find a way to finish her.

Trenan feinted left and Danya bit, then he lunged in, quick as a viper and deadlier than two. The princess wrenched her hips around and the tip of his sword grazed the surface of her shield with a squeal of metal. He backed away a step, smiling.

"How does it serve the kingdom for my brother to think himself a skilled swordsman when a child could beat him?" Danya thought that, if she distracted Trenan, she may stand a chance.

"It gives him confidence, your grace," the trainer answered, circling again.

"But what if he has to fight?"

"The king employs an army of swordsmen to ensure your brother will never have need to fight. One day, he'll rule the kingdom, and that's all he'll have to—"

Danya leaped forward before he finished speaking, her blade whipping in. He deflected her attack aside as though he knew her mind, then parried another attack and side-stepped when she swung her sword at him.

"You're revealing your moves before you make them, princess. Conceal."

His attack came out of nowhere, his blade striking with more force than any two of poor old Droinfeld's. The impact shook her arm and rattled her armor. Her fingers slipped on the sword's grip, but she held on. She blocked another blow with her shield, ducked under a third and counter-attacked, but Trenan tilted his body and the swipe whistled wide.

Danya had barely recovered when he struck again, his blows not as firm, but faster. His blade seemed to attack from all directions at once, like she fought not one man, but many. Light flickered in his sword as it danced and struck; she parried and dodged, ducked and retreated under the attack, stumbling away. Trenan pressed her until she forgot her lessons and, in desperation to avoid his assault, cross-stepped her feet.

They tangled and Danya fell to the ground in a puff of dust.

Her shield pinned beneath her, the princess grunted and tried to roll away and defend herself, but too late. Trenan stood over her, the flat of his sword pressed underneath her chin, the point a hair's-width from her throat.

Danya froze, afraid to swallow. Her airway tightened and closed, tears threatening at being so easily defeated, but she refused to let them flow.

"You are a far superior swordsman than your brother will ever be," Trenan said. He moved the sword away from her throat. "But you have much to learn yet."

The princess made herself breathe again, swallowed the lump clogging her throat.

"Teach me."

"And let old Droinfeld at your brother? He'd likely kill him by accident." Trenan slid his sword back into its scabbard and held out his hand to aid the princess to her feet. "Who but I has enough skill to make the prince think he is a master swordsman?"

Danya took the master's hand and he yanked her up with little effort. The strength in the man's sword arm astonished her, but not so much as the balance he achieved even while being short the other.

"I still don't understand why father wants him to think he is." She stowed her sword and unstrapped the shield. A fresh gouge across the buckler where she'd blocked one of Trenan's blows looked deep enough it might have removed her arm.

"It's not my business to know the mind of the king," Trenan said, retiring from the training circle. "But worry not. Never will the day come when your brother need discover the truth. Not so long as I'm alive."

Danya watched the master swordsman disappear through the door, hoping for the kingdom's sake he was right.

VI - Teryk and Danya - Discovery

*I*N THE PRINCE'S CHAMBER on the castle's third floor, the stone walls diffused the constant burble of the river flowing beneath and made the shush of running water hardly noticeable. But on this night, the water rumbled loud in his ears, as though Teryk sat on the shore beside great rapids. Only it wasn't the river's sounds he heard.

The din emanated from the scroll.

The parchment lay open on the table, the prince's sheathed dagger lying at the top edge to prevent it from curling in on itself, his hand resting on the bottom. The scroll only made the noise when he touched it.

Teryk leaned in, squinting hard at the parchment's browned and grainy surface. He imagined swirls and shapes scrolling across it, but each cursive letter he fancied he perceived revealed itself a trick of the flickering candle at his elbow and nothing more. He'd taken repast in his chamber, studying the scroll before Trenan came as he'd asked. When the queen protested his absence at the dinner table, he claimed Master Rewn had assigned him the task of memorizing the epic poem *Ghillihan*—the history of his family's ascension to the throne—and needed the extra time to do so.

A lie, but a victimless one.

As the sun set and the light faded from day to twilight to dark, Teryk pondered the scroll, watching for a change, but it remained no more than an old, blank sheet of parchment. With his hand rested on the coarse surface, he listened to its sound, willing the paper to speak the way it had in the chamber by the river, but it remained wordless. The babble of rushing water filled the prince's ears and he had to remove his touch to rest his head and ears from its monotony.

Why conceal a blank scroll in a secret chamber?

After turning the question over and over in his mind, Teryk kept returning to one answer: it wasn't blank. If so, why couldn't his eyes see the words written upon it?

He'd leaned over the paper again to ponder the same thing for the hundredth time, his hand on its edge and ears filling with the scroll's sound, when a knock at the door startled him.

"Enter." The word wasn't fully out of his mouth when Danya did.

"Trenan isn't here yet?" she asked, closing the door and stealing across the room with silent steps, her feet bare again.

"Not yet."

Teryk removed his hand from the scroll and the parchment rolled around his dagger weighting down the top; the river sound disappeared from his ears. The prince raised his gaze to his sister. Her long hair was pulled back from her face and a circlet of flowers ringed her head. She wore the same dress as when they'd gone swimming in the river four days earlier, its hem marked by a smudge of dirt the launderers couldn't get out. Surprising their mother hadn't noticed and made her change.

"Have you found anything?" She leaned over the table, peering down at the scroll.

Teryk shook his head. "Nothing. It's blank." He leaned back and crossed his arms, a sliver of frustration tingling in his belly. "Touch it and tell me what happens."

"Touch it?"

"Yeah. Touch it."

Danya shrugged and reached for the scroll, Teryk's gut churning as she did. He chewed his bottom lip. The scroll hadn't spoken to the princess in the chamber as it had to him. Would it now?

The tip of her pointer finger brushed its surface and the prince held his breath. Danya stroked her fingertip along the scroll's length.

"Not very good quality paper," she said. "Too rough."

He prompted her to continue the examination when she looked at him. She put one hand palm down by her brother's dagger and used the other to spread the parchment out on top of the table. With both her hands on the page to hold it, her eyes flickered back and forth across its surface.

"There's nothing on it."

"Anything else?"

He sensed her gaze on him again, knew she'd have one eyebrow raised, wondering if he'd gone daft, but she didn't say a word. Instead, she leaned forward until the tip of her nose came within a finger's-width of touching the scroll. She sniffed, her nostrils flaring.

"Smells of old paper," Danya said, straightening again.

"Do you hear anything?" Teryk chewed his bottom lip again, made himself stop.

"Hear anything? No. Just you breathing on me."

She took her hands off the parchment and it rolled up again. Teryk watched it, struggling to keep from reaching out and stopping it. Danya reached under the table and pulled out the stool stowed beneath, sat beside her brother.

"Do you think it's a good idea to tell Trenan?"

"Why wouldn't it be?"

"Because he might tell father. Then we'd have to explain where we got it. And how we got there."

Teryk frowned; he hadn't thought of that. With the scroll's river sound clogging his ears and its mystery muddling his head, he hadn't paused to consider Trenan might choose to do anything other than help them solve the riddle the parchment presented.

"It'll be all right. He won't tell." The river sounds, dim and distant, reached Teryk's ears again—the rush of the real river flowing beneath the palace.

A knock at the door startled them both. The siblings both stared at its plain wood surface, neither of them moving. A second later, Danya laughed and a smile crept across the prince's face, her merriment making his tension dissipate. He inhaled deeply between his parted lips and blew the air out noisily.

"Enter, Trenan."

The door swung open and the master swordsman entered, the plate he wore during their practice sessions replaced by a leather chest piece died green to match the king's colors and a black shirt over top, the sleeve of his missing arm pinned up at the shoulder. His ever-present sword hung at his waist.

"Your graces," he said, dipping his head as he shut the door. "What is of such import I should be summoned to the prince's chambers?"

"We found something," Danya said before Teryk had a chance to speak. She bounced excitedly on her stool and her brother wondered at the youthful enthusiasm she still managed. Teryk waved Trenan over to them.

"Have a look," he said, standing and offering his stool.

The one-armed knight strode across the room and took the offered seat, peered at the tabletop.

"Your dagger? If I recall, a gift from your weapons master."

"Not that," Teryk said, pointing. "The scroll."

Trenan raised an eyebrow. "This scrap of old paper?" He gestured toward the parchment, waving his fingers toward it without touching it. "What of it?"

"Just have a look," the prince insisted.

Teryk watched his sister fidgeting on her stool, eyes wide and lips pressed tight together. She may not have heard the sounds he heard, but he saw in her expression that she sensed what he sensed.

Trenan reached out, touched the scroll with his thumb and first two fingers, then jerked them away as if he'd brushed the skin of a sea eel. He scowled and rubbed his fingertips against the pad of his thumb, then turned his frown toward the princess and prince. They both observed him expectantly until he wiped his palm on his thigh and extended his hand toward the parchment a second time.

He hesitated before touching the sheet. Teryk licked his lips, waiting for the master swordsman to unroll it, wanting to find out if Trenan perceived the sound, too, or if he'd see something neither of the siblings had. The knight's fingers hovered for what seemed to the prince like a long moment before they contacted the parchment.

The knight sucked a stiff breath through his teeth, as though the paper's surface burned his flesh, but he didn't move away. Instead, he pedaled his fingers, unrolling the scroll across the top of the table. The prince glanced across the table at his sister and found her staring back at him with no trace of a smile on her lips or excitement in her mien. She appeared as nervous as he felt. A shared moment passed between them, then they directed their gazes back toward the master swordsman.

With the scroll open, Trenan stared at its blank surface, eyes wide and lips parted. Time stretched on, oozing past like syrup on a winter day. Twice, the prince opened his mouth to speak, unsure what he might say, and both times he closed it, leaving words and questions unspoken.

A drop of sweat appeared at Trenan's temple, rolled down the side of his face. Teryk watched it leave a wet trail along his cheek and down to his jaw line. The knight made no move to wipe it away. The prince looked to his sister again and saw her nervousness had become concern. She lifted a questioning eyebrow at her brother, and he nodded once.

Danya raised her hand, brushed her fingers against the knight's shoulder. "Trenan—?"

The master swordsman gasped a harsh breath and jumped back from the table, spilling the stool onto its side with a clatter. His feet tangled and he stumbled, reached out and grasped Teryk's arm painfully to keep from falling. When he steadied himself, he looked from the princess to the prince, eyes wide and shining with a look Teryk had never seen a hint of in them before: fear.

"What is the meaning of this?" He gazed at the scroll again, moved away a step as though it wasn't paper but a snake that might strike out and bite. "Where did you get this?"

Teryk swallowed hard, wishing he'd listened to his sister, as was often the case. He didn't let his gaze stray to her for fear she'd be wearing the smug expression she favored when it played out she was right and he wrong.

"We...we found it," he said.

Trenan turned his hard gaze on the prince. "Found it where?"

Teryk couldn't remember ever having seen the master swordsman angry in this manner before. His mouth opened and closed to answer, but no words came forth. Trenan's glare burned into him, frightening the words out of his throat.

"In a secret chamber," Danya said. She'd risen from her stool and stood beside Trenan, hand on his shoulder where an arm had once been. He shifted his scowling countenance to her.

"What chamber?"

"Beneath the palace." The princess averted her gaze to the smudge of dirt on the hem of her dress. "While we were swimming in the river."

Teryk saw the muscles in Trenan's jaw bulge and flex as he ground his teeth; without meaning to, the prince mimicked the master swordsman. He stopped when he realized he was doing it, his teeth hurting.

"It's just an old piece of paper," the prince said. He reached out to pick it up off the table, but Trenan caught him by the wrist.

"Do not lay your hand upon it," he said, voice hissing through his teeth. "It's been touched by magic."

The master swordsman glared at Teryk, then at Danya, who stared at the rolled parchment, her head shaking side to side minutely. Trenan backed away a step from the table, his grip still on the prince's wrist.

"You two are coming with me."

The prince's heart felt as though it slipped out of his chest and into his stomach.

VII - Small God - Thorn and Stormbird

*T*HE BRANCH BOUNCED GENTLY under the stormbird's weight, but the bird itself sat still as stone. Though it couldn't see him, Thorn understood the feathered animal sensed his presence; birds knew things, and there was nothing to be done about it.

He shifted his loose grip on the spear. He wouldn't use the weapon, intended no harm to this bird or any other living thing. The necessary traps were set and the bird would soon be his; he simply liked the feel of the smooth shaft in his hand, it comforted him. He'd never thrown a spear, except in practice, but he preferred having it with him, nonetheless.

Thorn took another step, moving from the leafy cover of a merry bush to stand in front of the wide trunk of a cedar. His skin shifted smoothly from green to striated brown, the color flowing across his flesh the way a liquid might flow across a flat surface, the change keeping him invisible in his surroundings. The bird's head tilted and Thorn held his ground.

The stormbird's eye fell on him and, though he appeared to the bird as no more than a tree trunk, he tensed, readying to spring if need be. A breeze ruffled the bird's feathers and touched Thorn's cheek, wafting the scent of magic along with it. He inhaled quietly, examining this odor in case another of his tribe might be near, but concluded that which he scented to be merely the magic which kept the bird from flying high enough to clear the veil.

With a cluck, the black, red and yellow bird returned to feeding on tender buds, and Thorn took another step. The loam beneath his bare foot sprang up to meet his sole, cushioning it, quieting it. Three lengths of his spear separated him from the stormbird, and he sensed the power contained within its feathers, its beak, its talons. Energy danced through the air.

Two more silent steps and Thorn had himself in position. He crouched, eyes narrowing and a satisfied smile creeping across his lips; the muscles in his slender legs tensed, coiled beneath him in preparation to pounce. The bird hopped forward; Thorn sprang.

"Awawawah!" he yelled, waving his arms and dragging his feet through the creepers and moss, stirring fallen leaves and sticks.

The bird squawked at the noise and flapped its wings, the gust of wind buffeting Thorn's face as it rose into the air, out of his reach. It looked back, as though to taunt the creature who startled it from its lunch, and then flew into the net.

"Ha!" Thorn exclaimed leaping over the log on which the bird had perched before attempting to flee. "Thorn got you."

The open end of the trap cinched closed, the stormbird struggling and grousing within, and the gusts of wind stirred by its flapping wings diminished as the net limited its movements. The bird's gaze flickered across the forest floor, searching out its captor, and Thorn allowed his flesh to fade from the greens and browns of the forest around him to its normal shade of gray.

He reached over his shoulder and stowed the spear in the sling on his back, then leapt for the tree, his fingers and toes grasping the rough bark as he hauled himself up to perch on the first branch. Dangling from the branch above his head, the stormbird writhed inside the net, twisting itself to regard him.

"Thorn didn't hurt you, did he, my friend?"

"Grawwkk!"

"Didn't think so."

Thorn jumped up and caught the higher branch, swung himself around to sit on it and peer down at his captive.

"Thorn won't hurt you, pretty bird. Thorn will free you."

He grasped the woven vine rope securing the trap to the branch and pulled. The bird weighed more than he guessed it would, so he waved his hand, calling on the fibers to aid him. The net's weight eased in his grip and he pulled the bird up onto the branch beside him; it swiped at him with a taloned foot, missing his ribs by less than the length of its beak.

"Oh, you are a playful one." He sprang up to perch on his toes, not a leaf shaking with the movement, and crouched so his eyes found the same level as the bird's.

"Here's what's going to happen," Thorn said, unwrapping the thin leather strap from around his wrist as he spoke. "Thorn will free you from the binding and in return, you will carry Thorn."

"Grawwkk!"

He leaned close, lowered his voice. "Thorn is going to fly with you."

The bird blinked once and stared at him. Thorn grinned, white teeth flashing behind his gray lips. The first attempt he'd made to capture the bird, he hadn't so much as put a finger on it. The third time, it escaped the instant he loosened the net—a mistake he'd taken steps to correct. This time, he'd fashioned the snare to open on both ends, allowing him to expose the bird's feet and tether himself in place before it took wing.

"Okay," he said, shifting on the limb. It didn't bounce under his weight. "First, the binding."

Eyes closed, he held his hand over the stormbird's head, a finger's-breadth out of reach if it stretched its neck and snapped its beak—something he'd learned the second time he caught the bird. It ruffled its feathers and a breeze played across Thorn's face, cooling him. He loosed his breath through his broad nose, pictured the sky and clouds sliding by, the rush of wind in his ears, the heat of sun on his back.

The stormbird chirped. When Thorn opened his eyes again, the bird had calmed.

"That will make it so," he said and reached for the cord securing the bottom of the net closed.

With a flick of his wrist, he pulled the string free and the trap fell open. The bird craned its head, eyeing its captor's activities. It shuffled, attempting to free a foot through the opening, but its talons tangled in the strands of the net.

"Here. Let Thorn help."

Thorn put the rope he held under one foot and reached out with both hands to maneuver the stormbird's foot out of the trap. As he did, he slid the cord he'd unwound from his wrist around the bird's leg. It let out a questioning cheap.

"This is how you'll carry Thorn."

He cinched a knot, carefully tying it tight enough not to slip, but not so tight to hurt, then settled back to inspect his work.

"No bites," he said to himself, ticking things off in his fingers. "Bird still here. Spell cast. Thorn in place. Ready to go."

With his free hand, Thorn guided the net around the bird's body, careful of its powerful wings and curved beak, and lifted the woven ropes over its head. They sat together in the tree for a moment, staring at one another. Thorn gripped the short length of cord running between his wrist and the stormbird's leg, tensing the muscles in his arm and readying himself. The bird continued glaring at him and, for a length of three beats of his heart, Thorn thought maybe it didn't understand what he required it to do. He opened his mouth to explain again, but the bird interrupted him by leaping into the air.

It flapped its wings, sending a burst of mist-laced wind fanning across Thorn's face. He had an instant to enjoy the dampness on his cheeks, cooling him on such a warm day, then the tether tightened. The bird pulled him off the branch with a jerk that wrenched his shoulder, but Thorn smiled despite the discomfort.

He was flying!

The bird's wings rose and fell sending wind and spray out behind with a faint rumble of thunder that rang in Thorn's ears. A thick branch slapped his leg, twisting him on the end of the cord, transforming the forest into a whirling carousel spinning around him. He laughed, the sound burbling out of his throat to be lost in the stormbird's squawking.

Thorn titled his face to the sky, peering up through the lattice work of leaves and branches, the sun shining through in patches. He awaited the forest falling away around him as the bird's mighty wings bore them up and up. He laughed again until he realized the canopy overhead grew no closer.

Thorn turned his attention to the bird, saw it laboring under his weight. Broad leaves slapped at his face, twisted branches grasped at his legs, tore at his flesh. The bird squawked again, a sound full of hard work and distress.

Thorn is too heavy.

He struggled to stop spinning at the end of the tether, to get his bearing, and accomplished it by reaching up with his free hand to grasp the stormbird's foot. They were higher off the ground than the bird had likely ever flown, but not so high as Thorn had climbed in the trees. Not high enough.

"Grawwkk!"

Thorn reached over his shoulder, plucked his spear from its sling. The shaft slid through his fingers, smooth wood whispering across his skin, until he gripped it right below the head. With a deft flick of his wrist, he severed the taut cord tethering his wrist to the bird's foot.

The bird rose higher as Thorn fell. He tucked his head in, somersaulted between two thick branches, and landed lightly on his feet, running before he ever touched the ground.

High above, the stormbird stroked powerful wings, pulling itself through the air, a roll of thunder spreading in its wake. Thorn danced through the forest, leaping roots and ducking branches, his feet unerring in finding the perfect spot to land when he jumped, then leaving again the instant after they'd touched. He watched the bird, rising higher and higher, breaking through the branch-and-leaf latticework forest ceiling.

Thorn leapt a ditch and his bare feet landed on soft grass. Ahead, he glimpsed a shimmering mass of green looming, rising out of the ground and reaching for the sky.

He slowed his approach, the veil's energy prickling the hair on the back of his neck, sending a flutter along his skin. The length of his spear away, he stopped and leaned back, peering skyward along glittering wall. He held his hand over his brow, blocking the sun from his eyes and beheld the stormbird high above, soaring higher than it had ever flown, higher than any bird behind the veil had flown since they were banished.

Thorn's heart swelled. How it must feel to be that bird, winging above the earth, sharing the view reserved for the clouds, gazing down on creatures, trees, rocks and rivers. Thorn ached for his eyes to see what the bird saw.

And then the stormbird crossed the veil.

Thorn's eyes went wide and his spear fell from his grasp, rattling against a stray rock as it hit the ground. He rotated slowly, watching the bird drift across the open air, a plume of cloud spreading behind it, rain falling, coloring the landscape gray like Thorn's skin.

He took a step closer to the veil, close enough his nose nearly brushed its surface. The pulse of its power excited his flesh, but he ignored it, distracted by another excitement as other thoughts came to his mind.

Nothing has ever crossed the veil.

The grass around him bent under the weight of his emotions, caressed his legs and feet the way a mother might comfort her child. He watched the stormbird until it became nothing but a dot in the sky at the head of the trail of storm clouds left in its wake. Thorn raised his hand, touched his palm against the veil.

Green lightning flickered across its surface, giving it the appearance of verdant ice. Energy flowed through Thorn's fingers, up his arm. He inhaled a breath flavored with magic and grass and rain, then spun around and trod back toward the forest. Behind him, the lightning cracks in the icy veil faded, returning it to a dim green haze as another thought ran through Thorn's mind.

Thorn needs a bigger bird.

VIII - Teryk and Danya - Punishment

TEN TALL STEPS LED to the throne sitting atop the high dais.

Danya held pleasant memories of being a small child and gaping up at their father's seat of power, marveling at how high above the floor it seemed to her youthful eyes, how difficult the climb on the occasions the attendants left her alone long enough to try it.

Later, she realized the stairs had been designed to be forbidding, both to remind the regent of the responsibilities of his station and to emphasize the king's importance to his people. The dais was built to hold the king highest above everyone. As she stood beside her brother in front of these steps, awaiting their parents' arrival, they intimidated her in a way they never had before, instilling fear as they were meant to do.

Teryk shifted one foot to the other and she wondered what thoughts went through his mind. The princess wanted to fault him for this, to chastise him for not listening to her, first when she told him not to take the scroll from the chamber, then when she doubted the wisdom of showing Trenan. But she'd been at his side and had no one to blame but herself. The times in their lives she'd talked her brother into and out of things were nigh uncountable; if she'd wanted this to be another of those instead of a new adventure, she'd have made it so.

Danya glanced sideways at the prince, saw his lower lip sucked into his mouth, chewing away with his nervous habit. Beyond him, Trenan stood on the far side, to her brother's right, as if he expected he might have to use his one hand to grab the prince should he attempt to flee. But Teryk wouldn't flee, nor would she. They'd been punished by their father before, and more occasions lay in the future. One lesson they'd both learned: accept what you deserve, for better or worse.

A door creaked open behind them and Danya faced the dais, resisting the urge to look back. Seconds later, footsteps echoed up to the ceiling high above, reverberating in the room meant to hold hundreds but now only occupied by the princess, the prince, Trenan, and the new arrivals—the king, the queen, and their attendants. No reason for a scribe, or magistrate, or the multitude of others who attended the kingdom's business—this was a family affair, not a matter of the realm.

The way the footfalls bounced against the high walls, echoing and multiplying, made it seem as though a thousand people entered but, a moment later, the king passed them without a sideways glance. Marn, his squire, followed the requisite three steps behind and one to his right; the queen and her two attendants came after. She surveyed Danya on the way by, a wan smile on her lips as she shook her head at her daughter. The princess' gaze fell away to the soiled hem of her dress.

Their father climbed the tall stairs, leaving his squire at the bottom, then the queen followed, one attendant leading her by the hand, the other picking up the back of her long skirt. The high steps provided more of a challenge for their much smaller mother, but twenty-one turns of the seasons' worth of practice since she married the king gave her the ability to disguise the effort.

The two attendants left the queen standing beside the throne, hand resting in the accustomed place on her husband's shoulder, and descended the steps in a hurried rustle of skirts. The queen's gaze flickered back and forth between her children, her expression unreadable.

Silence fell in the hall as the echoing footsteps of the attendants dissipated. Danya inhaled shallowly through her nose, trying not to disturb the stillness; she heard Teryk swallow hard. Their father leaned forward, one elbow on his knee, and stroked his short-trimmed salt and pepper beard. Though not much younger than the old knight, Droinfeld, the king was more vital and most said truly didn't show his age. He always gave credit to having a beautiful wife more than twenty turns his junior.

A shadow crossed his brow and he gestured to someone standing behind his children. A man Danya hadn't realized had entered with her parents walked out from behind them, the click of his heeled boots fluttering into the hall's ceiling like noisy birds on the wing. He halted and pivoted so both the king and queen above on the dais as well as she and the prince saw what he held cradled in his gauntleted hands.

The scroll.

No one spoke. Beside her, Teryk licked his lips; Danya resisted the urge to grasp his hand, to comfort her brother under their father's penetrating gaze while drawing solace for herself.

The king gestured again and the squire rushed away from the base of the dais, Trenan following him. Their footsteps stopped, followed by the squeal of metal dragged across the polished stone floor. Danya pressed her lips together, struggling to keep curiosity from getting the better of her and, a moment later, the master swordsman and the young squire returned to view dragging a gleaming brass brazier between them. They set it halfway between where Danya and Teryk stood and the bottom of the steps, then the squire hurried off again, reappearing with a guttering torch in hand. He lit the brazier.

A wave of the king's fingers brought the man holding the scroll ahead two paces to stand at the edge of the fire. He extended his arms.

"Father!"

Danya winced at the sound of her brother's voice, and their father raised his hand, stopping him from speaking further. His brows tilted in.

"Magic," he said, then paused to allow the word to echo through the great hall. "Magic is forbidden and you brought it into my castle."

"No, father. It—"

"Silence."

The barked violence of the word made Danya flinch. Teryk's breath squeaked at the back of his throat.

"Trenan has told me all I need to know," he said, his voice booming through the hall. "You have disappointed me, Teryk. Again. And you, young lady..."

He glowered at the princess, but said no more, choosing to simply shake his head as a display of his disgruntlement.

Teryk opened his mouth again, but thought better of speaking. Disillusionment and despair emanated from him, touching Danya as though he'd reached out with his hand. As far back as she remembered, she'd been sensitive to his emotions, empathic to the point of experiencing them herself at times.

His face set as though carved in stone, the king gestured and the knight dropped the parchment into the leaping flames.

The old, dry paper ignited at once, blackening and curling at the edges as the fire devoured it like a dog left too long without food. Danya felt her brother quiver beside her, the muscles in his arms and legs tensed as though he held himself back from rushing to the brazier and rescuing the scroll from the flames. She hoped he didn't—they were in enough trouble already.

Ancient parchment crackled and popped for a time before the regent leaned back and spoke.

"You are both forbidden from entering the river," he said, voice booming through the room with practiced ease. "And you will not leave the palace for any reason, except with my permission and an escort, until I decide otherwise."

Teryk stepped forward; Danya reached out, touched his arm to make him step back, but he shrugged her off.

"Father," he said, voice cracking. He cleared his throat. "Father. Don't punish Danya. She didn't want to swim in the river and told me not to take the scroll. I accept your punishment, but she doesn't deserve it."

The king frowned. "You accept my punishment, do you? Something in my words suggested you had another choice?"

Teryk shook his head but said nothing else. A wise choice, given their father's apparent mood, Danya thought. He directed his gaze upon her and the princess wished to find a way to shrink back to the little girl who'd found climbing the stairs a near insurmountable task.

"And is what he speaks true, Danya? Are you merely a puppet controlled by your brother, without a will of your own?"

His words dug into her as if he'd jabbed her with the end of a staff. She set her feet and bit down hard, her lips compressing to a thin white line across her face. Why did her brother have to say such things? Did he not realize how it made her look?

"No, your majesty."

The king leaned back and nodded once.

"Then we are done."

"Father, I—"

Danya cringed at the sound of her brother speaking yet again, but the king silenced him by raising a hand. He glared down at his son from high, his gaze daring the young man to say another word, but Teryk chose wisely and diverted his eyes.

Their father stood abruptly and descended the stairs. When he reached the bottom, the two attendants hurried up to aid the queen, and the king's squire scurried after him, three steps behind and one to the right. He passed them on Teryk's side this time, pausing at the prince's shoulder and speaking in quiet tones meant only for him but that Danya heard, nonetheless.

"I don't know how you expect to be king one day acting this way."

He carried on, his squire following. Danya directed her eyes toward her brother, saw the twitch in the clenched muscles of his jaw and the reflection of the flames burning the scroll shining in his eyes. He sucked his bottom lip into his mouth and chewed. Their father knew what to say to hurt Teryk as surely as if he skewered him with a blade.

Before leaving the room, the queen stopped in front of them. She gazed at each of them in turn, touched the prince's cheek, held the princess' hand. Danya thought she should apologize, but when her brother didn't, she didn't, either. The queen didn't speak until she stood before the master swordsman.

"Thank you, Trenan," she said, her hand on his arm. Their gazes met and held for a moment, as though they exchanged something that needed no words, then she allowed her attendants to lead her out of the room in a swirl of skirts. The man who'd carried the scroll followed them out, leaving brother and sister alone with the master swordsman.

"It had to be done," he said—the closest to an apology he'd come. "Do you understand how dangerous that thing might have been?"

Teryk glared at their weapons trainer, his cheek deepening to red, his eyes blazing. Danya laid her hand on his arm, attempting to calm him, but he pulled away and stepped toward Trenan, leaving only a pace between them.

"You didn't have to tell him," Teryk said, louder than he needed to, his voice strained as though he struggled to hold back tears. "We could have dealt with it ourselves."

"No, my prince. It—"

Teryk spun away and stomped toward the door before Trenan finished his sentence, the remaining words left unsaid. The prince's exaggerated footfalls bounced and echoed, and the door creaked as he left, leaving it open behind him. Danya and the master swordsman stared after him until he disappeared from their view, but when she looked at Trenan, she saw regret in his expression.

"I did what I thought best, princess," he said.

"I know."

Smoke swirled and danced toward the ceiling from the parchment smoldering in the brazier. Danya stared at it for a moment, imagining she saw shapes and colors flickering amongst the flames, then she allowed Trenan to lead her to her chambers.

IX Horace - Livin'

*H*ORACE STOOD AT THE pasture's edge, grindin' the heels o' his hands into his eyes to be sure he weren't seein' things. When he took them away, the lights remained right where he'd seen them.

He staggered outta the trees and into the field, fear's chilly grip finally lettin' up on him for the first time since...when? Since before he realized the *Devil*'d lost the shore, prob'ly. Been scared when he came 'round lyin' on the beach, and he'd been scared with ev'ry step findin' his way through the forest. So scared, he barely even pulled his dick out for takin' a piss, fearin' he'd lose his one and only precious possession the way he'd lost his lucky possum tail. The fact he hadn't relieved himself in longer'n he could say became insistent with his third step across the pasture, his o'er-full bladder screamin' to be emptied. He stopped and obliged against the tallest thorn bush he'd ever laid eyes upon, careful all the while not to piss on his rag-covered foot or to prick himself. Horace giggled a little at that.

With relief given, Horace set out again, limpin' because a rag weren't as good as a boot. It might've saved him from a few cuts and scratches along the way, and for that he were appreciative, but his foot hurt as though he'd walked through a forest short a piece o' quality footwear, and rightly so.

The sticky-side-up o' the whole situation were that he be still alive. If this kept up, some possum might come along and take him for a good luck charm. He giggled at that idea, too—somethin' he mightn't've found funny another time. But pissin' weren't the only thing he hadn't done while hobblin' through the forest—sleepin' and eatin' was others. A man couldn't sleep thinkin' he might be in the

Green, and he'd tried eatin', but who could tell one fuckin' berry from another?

But the lantern glow ahead told him he weren't in the Green. Wherever it were he drifted to, it weren't home to the Small Gods, and it definitely weren't the home to no God o' the Deep so, all-in-all, Horace Seaman were beginnin' to feel pretty good 'bout his chances for survivin' a few more days, at least. All he needed for success in his endeavor were a plate o' food, a pint or two o' ale, and a bed for layin' on, and the bed weren't that important—any flat, safe spot free of rocks and threats'd do.

As he crossed the pasture, long grass wavin' 'round his knees, it occurred to Horace he might need a story to tell why he weren't from 'round here and found himself wanderin' at night shy a boot. He wracked his poor, tired brain but came up with nothin', o'erpowered as his thoughts was by hunger and thirst. It weren't until he got close enough to make out the buildin's shape in the dark when he realized the reason he thought of naught but his growlin' belly were from the aroma o' cookin' meat waftin' outta the place.

Saliva rushed into Horace's mouth, threatened to spill out the sides. He sucked it back and swallowed hard, licked his lips.

A tavern. I stumbled upon a tavern.

His stomach gurgled, the cramps he'd done his best to ignore forcin' themselves to be noticed. What luck it were the first buildin' he come across—the one what proved he weren't lost in the Green and stumblin' 'bout waitin' to die—were a place what could provide him what he needed most.

Lamp light spilled out through the windows and squeezed under the crack beneath the door. Someone'd built the buildin' fully outta logs, with a mossy roof on top and a porch out front what seemed as though it might be sat upon durin' a summer day, but it were empty this night. Horace limped up to it and stopped outside, graspin' onto the rail 'round the stoop like he didn't have no more energy to go no farther.

Before takin' another step, he patted his chest, then the front pockets and back pockets in his breeches. The rag for no other purpose than wipin' sweat from his head, which now had another purpose keepin' his foot from gettin' cut, were the only possession he had left after idiot Dunal slapped him o'erboard into the sea.

"I ain't got no coin," he said aloud, then clamped his hand o'er his mouth, worried someone inside might hear.

For a second, he considered turnin' 'round and either searchin' out somewhere else to find food or headin' back into the forest to forage and avoid embarrassin' himself. But there wouldn't be more'n one tavern in whatever town this were, and he'd tried scroungin' food amongst the forest's twigs and berries, roots and leaves. He'd ate the wrong thing and ended up leanin' o'er a fallen log, heavin' bile outta his nose, so he didn't fancy the prospect o' givin' it another try. With a shakin' head and a non-hero producin' breath, Horace pushed the door open and slouched his hungry self into the tavern.

Oil lamps hung from posts 'round the room, illuminatin' the interior with a ghostly light and throwin' greasy smoke up toward the ceilin'. It collected there amongst the rafters, formin' a hazy pool before snakin' its way through a vent at the middle. A smatterin' o' folk sat spread 'round the tavern at wooden tables no one'd bothered to spread cloths upon, some of the patron's drinkin' and laughin', some starin' at their drinks like they figured doin' so might refill 'em. A few people peeked up at Horace steppin' across the threshold and closin' the door behind him, but they went back to whatever they was at quick enough.

Horace ambled toward the bar at the rectangular room's far end, his one boot's dull thud on the floor boards followed by the muted sound of his rag-wrapped foot draggin' in the thresh remindin' him he hadn't thought up a story. He glanced down at the dirt-black cloth, then at the folk 'round him, but none seemed to notice, so he continued on his way, hopin' a tale weren't needed.

The man loomin' behind the bar stood a head taller'n Horace, close to as tall as the simpleton Dunal what near cost him his life. His hair'd crept way back from his forehead, farther'n Horace's own, somethin' the barkeep compensated for with a thick, distractin' beard what gave him the appearance of a bear someone thought'd be funny to shave up top. He were the imposin' sort, and Horace wondered if he'd find a way to wrangle a free meal and mug fulla ale from a man with that sort o' appearance.

"Oy! A stranger," the man called out upon noticin' Horace's bedraggled self. A smile broke out across the barkeep's face what made him appear a damn bit less alarmin'. "Second one today. What be your desire, my good man?"

Horace approached the bar, peerin' out from under saggin' brows and hands clasped before his chest, hopin' doin' so gave him a resemblance to a man deservin' a little charity.

"I ain't eaten in longer than I know, sir," he said, mindin' his tone matched his expression. "And I ain't got no coin, but I—"

The barkeep's smile disappeared back beneath his beard, returnin' to him the aspect of one who Horace considered he might wanna be rightfully afraid of. It were enough to stop the hungry man mid-beseech.

The big man shook his head. "Times're tough fer everyone, friend. If you ain't got no coin, I ain't got no ale nor food."

Horace's heart shrank up on him, as though it were afraid his growlin' belly might sneak up and take a bite outta its toes. He opened his mouth to carry on with his pitch, fully intendin' to offer whatever services the barkeep might need tendin', but not quite willin' to take a beatin' if it come to it. The big man only needed to tilt his head and raise a brow to convince ol' Horace Seaman the conversation on this particular subject were o'er.

The sailor's chin drooped toward his chest, an action his shoulders decided to mimic. Back to the forest it were then, to take his chances with mushrooms and berries what might be more intent on killin' him'n they was on feedin' him. At least he found out he needn't fear the Small Gods no more. It still might be possible he were near the Green, but given he stood inside a tavern with livin' folk inside, he were sure he weren't in the Green.

Horace raised his eyes once more, hopin' to find the barkeep's expression changed, but it weren't. The big man busied himself wipin' the bar with a demeanor not encouragin' Horace to ask again and a cloth what woulda made a fine replacement for a boot. The ol' sailor heaved a sigh and prepared himself for the slog back across the pasture to the forest when he felt a presence beside him. He gazed upon a feller he'd spied sittin' alone at a table in the corner when he walked through the door.

The man leaned against the bar, smilin' wide at Horace. His smooth face were free o' whiskers, with a spot o' dried blood on his chin where he'd nicked himself shavin' and nobody'd bothered tellin' him. His clothes didn't make him appear rich, but they didn't make him seem poor, neither. Somethin' in the way he gazed upon Horace made the ol' sailor feel as though he needed to have himself a bath.

"You're a hard man, Krin," the man said, speakin' to the barkeep but holdin' his gaze on Horace. "Can't you see this poor fellow is desperately hungry? Probably he needs a pint of ale, too, don't you?"

Horace nodded exuberantly, barely containin' the spittle the promise o' food and ale brewed up behind his dry lips.

"Well, he ain't gettin' none without no coin."

"Is that any way to treat a stranger? How often do we see strangers in these parts?"

"Not often, Birk," Krin mumbled. "Except this turn of the moon."

Horace wondered for a second at the barkeep's comment, but put it right from his head in hopin' this man named Birk meant to help him acquire that what his body ached for. Just then, his stomach growled loud enough to leave no doubt in any man's mind what that were.

Birk laughed. "See, Krin? This man is in need of the kind of help only a barkeep can give."

"Are you payin'?"

Silence floated upon the air like an unmanned rowboat bobbin' on the sea, and Horace held his breath, hopin' for the man called Birk to say aye. His gut grumbled again while the wait stretched on. Krin wiped the bar top with little enthusiasm; Birk eyed Horace as though appraisin' him, decidin' if he be worth a few coins.

Finally, a response came, but without usin' no words. Birk kept his eyes on Horace while puttin' two fingers in his brown waistcoat's front pocket to pluck out a coin. He tossed the copper onto the bar where it rattled 'round on its edge until Krin scooped it up before it had a chance to fall o'er.

"Get him a bowl of stew and a pint of your best ale," Birk said with a flourishin' hand gesture. "And keep the change, kind sir."

"I only got one kind o' ale," Krin remarked as he grabbed a cup from the counter behind the bar. "And there won't be no change."

Horace's gut rumbled again, impatient now it expected to get filled.

"Thank you, sir," he said layin' his hand on Birk's arm. "I cannot thank you enough."

Birk glanced at Horace's hand, the gaze makin' the ol' sailor wish he hadn't touched him, then looked back up at him before steppin' away from the bar.

"No burden, sir," Birk said, smilin'. "Join me at my table when the good barkeep has provided you a bowl."

"Yessir," Horace said feelin' he possessed no other choice.

Birk crossed the room to the table in the corner where he'd been set when Horace walked in, sat himself down and raised his own cup of ale. Horace leaned his elbows on the bar as he awaited his brew and his stew. His stomach grumbled and growled, distractin' him enough he didn't notice the barkeep sneak up until he thumped a tankard on the bar beside him. The amber nectar inside the plain cup shimmered in the lamplight and the barkeep stood in front o' him.

"Are you sure you can afford this?" Krin asked.

Horace wrinkled his face up, not knowin' what he meant. Hadn't the other feller paid? He saw him pull the copper from his waistcoat and he saw Krin snatch it off the bar. Did he mean to get paid again? Horace opened his mouth, but the barkeep shook his head and turned his back on him.

The second Horace laid his hand on the tankard of ale, his mouth got to salivatin' and he forgot 'bout the barkeep's odd comment. He laced his fingers together 'round the rough clay tankard and picked it up in both hands, all the better to keep it from shakin' and sloppin' precious ale on Krin's well-polished bar.

The ale floodin' his tongue satiated him as good as the last time his prick slipped into a cunny, though to be honest, he couldn't have said exactly how much time'd passed since that happened. Some o' the men on the ship liked to play pretend—they pretended another feller's asshole were a woman's love openin'—but ol' Horace Seaman didn't go in for that, no matter how old a seafarin' tradition it might be. Stinky old things, a man's rear porthole.

The ale slid down his throat like honey, coatin' it with goodness and returnin' a batch o' his senses to him. He gulped three mouthfuls before stoppin' to get some air, settin' the tankard back on the bar and lickin' the frothy mustache outta the stubbly one on his upper lip.

When the tasty foam were gone, Krin showed up again, holdin' in his hand a plate with a hollowed-out loaf o' bread filled fulla stew set atop it.

Fragrant steam curled up from the bread bowl, its aroma findin' Horace's nose as easy as a huntin' dog rootin' out prey. He sniffed deep, finally drawin' air what provided sustenance for his tired bones and made him feel a bit like a hero, though he knew full well he weren't one.

"Smells delicious," he said reachin' for the plate when Krin set it down upon the pristine bar.

"Hold your ponies," the barkeep said. He turned 'round and retrieved a wooden spoon from the counter behind him, clicked it down on the plate beside the loaf bowl. "It's my mam's recipe. You'll like it."

Horace's stomach wanted him to snatch the spoon up offa the plate and get to scoopin' stew into his mouth right away, but he forced himself to be polite. He didn't know where he were nor how long he'd be here, so best not to make a man such as Krin angry. *Especially* a man the barkeep's size.

"Thank you," he said, bowin' his head.

Krin leaned an elbow on the bar and waved a finger in the direction o' Birk's table.

"Don't thank me. It's him who'll want to be thanked, I expect. Birk doesn't do nothing for free."

The barkeep's words made Horace Seaman recall again the men on the ship who liked to pretend. Be that what Krin meant? The ol' sailor's porthole puckered at the idea. He'd had men try to make him before, but they wasn't able to and usually left with black eyes instead o' stinky cocks. Weren't no way Horace's shits'd squeeze out no faster than they ever had before.

"Thank you anyways," he said pickin' up the tankard in one hand and the plate o' stew in the other.

Horace made his way across the tavern toward Birk's table, his own movement blowin' the steam from the stew into his face, its aroma stirrin' his gut into a frenzy. He were already of the mind this'd be the best stew he ever ate, no matter whose recipe it be made from.

Birk sat leanin' back in one chair, a booted foot up on another, a smile on his face as if he were the ship's cat what found a bilge full o' rats. Seein' that grin made Horace's hind side contract again, but he were too hungry to fret on it just then. He'd eat now and worry 'bout protectin' his shitter if and when the need presented itself.

Upon his approach, Birk slid a chair out and gestured for him to sit. Horace obliged, grabbin' the spoon and tuckin' into the stew before his ass had a chance to settle onto the hard wooden seat.

Turned out Horace'd presumed right: the stew's flavor were even better'n the queen's pussy. Not that he'd ever had the pleasure of bein' in the same buidlin' as Her Imperial Highness, never mind touchin' his tongue to her nether regions, though a rumor'd reached his ears that an acquaintance o' his had.

He filled his mouth full o' savory stew, followin' up with a swig o' ale before the meat and veggies made it down his throat. His benefactor watched without speakin', knowin' he weren't gonna answer until he got his fill, Horace s'posed. If that's what he thought, he'd've been right, 'cause the ol' sailor wouldn't've stopped shovelin' stew into his gob if the fuckin' tavern burned to the ground 'round him.

When he scooped the last bit o' stew outta the bread bowl, Horace proceeded tearin' the bowl itself to pieces and gobblin' them up, too, swabbin' the plate with the chunks case he missed a little somethin' and doin' a better job'n Dunal'd ever done on the *Devil's* decks. He knew 'bout some gravy on his lips and the corner o' his mouth, but ignored it until he were done with the bread, then made sure he licked ev'ry last drop. Birk watched him the whole time, a grin spread wide across his mug, and Horace wondered if he were picturin' his puckerin' hole.

His meal complete, Horace took another swig from the tankard, peered into the bottom to see one more mouthful remained, then thumped the mug on the table and leaned back in his chair. He breathed deep through his noise and let go a noisy belch that tasted good as the stew. Birk laughed.

"It was good?"

"Best stew I ever ate," Horace said, wipin' his mouth on his sleeve like that'd prove it. The cloth still reeked o' the sea, so he moved it away from his nose quick, before it made him lose a tasty dinner. "Thanks."

"Oh, you are welcome," Birk said, leanin' forward with his elbows on the table. "It's clear that when a man has needs, they must be met. Am I right?"

Horace squinted one eye at the man. "I'm appreciative, to be sure, but if you be aimin' to fuck me in my hind porthole, or any other hole, for that matter, you be aimin' at the wrong target."

Birk jerked back from the table, a shocked expression knockin' the smile offa his lips. He stared at Horace a moment, head shakin' side to side ever so slightly; the ol' sailor crossed his arms in front of his chest, usin' the gesture to indicate he truly meant his words.

"You've misinterpreted my good nature, sir."

Horace unsquinted his eye and raised a brow, unsure if he detected offense in the man's tone. Didn't matter, he'd ate already. Weren't no takin' that back no matter how hard he tried.

"But you want somethin'."

Birk shrugged and leaned on the table again. "Conversation, is all."

"You wanna converse. With me?"

"You don't notice many of the locals clamoring to join me at my table, do you? Sometimes, a man wants company."

Horace squinted the other eye. "So, you don't wanna fuck me in my shitter?"

"I have no interest in your shitter. Or anyone else's." Birk shifted in his chair, seemin' more'n a bit uncomfortable with the subject, and that convinced the ol' sailor his porthole was safe, at least from this feller. If the barkeep took a likin' to him, keepin' his bumhole safe might be trouble, but Krin didn't appear the type.

"If you get me another ale, I'll talk right up to the wee hours, it you like."

"Good enough." Birk waved his hand o'er his head to get Krin's attention. "Barkeep! Another tankard of your best ale for my friend."

"I keep tellin' you: I only got one kind of ale."

"Then that will have to do."

Birk's smile crept back across his face again, remindin' Horace of a cat creepin' up on a bird. Didn't seem he had no reason to worry, though. After fallin' in the ocean with the God o' the Deep, then sneakin' through the forest worryin' 'bout bein' in the Green, it weren't no wonder he was feelin' a bit paranoid.

"You have me at a disadvantage," Birk said steeplin' his fingers. "I don't even know your name."

"Horace."

"Horace what?"

He opened his mouth and very nearly said 'Seaman', but stopped himself. He were done with the sea and anythin' related to it; if he went 'round tellin' people his name was Seaman, he'd be back on a ship quicker'n he'd get to half-mast in a whorehouse.

"Horace what?" Birk said again, his smile falterin'.

Krin interrupted with a new tankard fulla ale, givin' Horace a second to think. He drained the near-empty cup and gave it to the barkeep with a thankful nod and the big man raised a brow at him. Horace ignored him in favor o' takin' a swig outta the fresh ale. When he set it on the table, Birk was lookin' at him and no longer smilin'. Horace wiped his sleeve across his ale-moist lips.

"Horace," he said and paused to belch the flavor o' dark ale back into his mouth, thinkin' desperately 'bout what else he might do aside from bein' a sailor. "Horace Tailor."

He cringed at his own words, his lack o' plannin'. Durin' his walk in the woods, didn't it occur to him he might run into someone and they might ask his name? Couldn't he have put some time into it to avoid just pickin' somethin' what rhymed with sailor? Truthfully, he'd worried too much on the Small Gods discoverin' him to put much time into anythin' but survivin'. And now he'd gone and named himself tailor when he'd never sewn a button in his life.

"Tailor?" Birk leaned back in his chair, tiltin' it up on the two hind legs. "What kind of name is that?"

Horace titled his head and attempted keepin' the surprised expression from offa his mug. Might he get away with his fuck up?

"What do ya mean? What's your other name?"

"Simirslad. Birk Simirslad. My father was Simir."

Horace shrugged. "Guess I'm not from 'round here."

"No, I guess not." Birk returned his chair legs to the floor and took a drink from his tankard. He made it look so good, the ol' sailor did the same. "I didn't think you were when I saw you walk in. We don't usually get many visitors here."

"But you ain't got no friends here." He scanned the tavern—a couple patrons'd left while he were eatin'. The others was careful to appear as though they was mindin' their own business. "Ain't you from here?"

"I am." He twirled the tankard back and forth in his hands, ganderin' at his own fingers. "I left when I was young, went to the city to get some school. I came back after but...I'm a bit of an outsider now."

"How long you been back?"

Birk raised his eyes toward the ceilin' like he might see how long inscribed on one o' the beams above his head. Horace looked up, too, but didn't find nothin' but cobwebs.

"About fifteen summers, I suppose."

"Hmph. I ain't never been anywhere fifteen turns."

"You are a nomad, are you?"

Horace's brows inched closer together. "A what?"

"A nomad. A wanderer. One who doesn't stay in one place for long."

"Guess you might say that." The sailor's eyes darted 'round the room again, feelin' uncomfortable with the conversation but not knowin' exactly why. He suspected he might be more comfortable if they went back to talkin' 'bout Birk fuckin' him in the shitter.

The man leaned closer, glanced 'round the tavern himself, then gestured for Horace to lean in, too. The sailor hesitated, so Birk made a come here signal again, more insistent the second time 'round. Horace gave in and leaned forward.

"If you had asked me to guess," Birk said, keepin' his voice quiet so it were just between them two. "I'd have said you were a sailor."

Horace tried hard to keep from reactin'. "No one asked you to guess."

"No, I suppose no one did. But if that would have been my guess, others might guess the same."

"What'd make you think that anyways?"

"The way you're dressed," Birk said directin' his gaze at Horace's shirt. "And you smell of the sea."

Horace dipped his head toward his chest and inhaled deeply. Birk were right: he smelled o' salty brine, like stinky ol' seaweed left too long in the sun stuffed all his pockets full.

"Well I ain't."

"Too bad, I've use for a man who knows about the sea. Here, we have only tavern tales of a god living in the depths and the men it eats when they wander too far. Who trusts stories?"

Horace grunted and eyed the man who'd bought him dinner. He didn't like how this were goin', not at all, and he'd a mind to excuse himself before it went much further.

"Do you believe those tales?" Birk asked.

"I'm thinkin' I ain't heard none." Horace pressed his lips tight, teeterin' on the edge between gettin' up and leavin' or askin' why he needed a man o' the sea. If he inquired, he suspected he'd end up on someone's boat again, and that were the last thing he wanted happenin'.

Birk leaned in closer, close enough Horace expected the man might kiss him on the lips. Then he'd have a reason to punch him and leave without seemin' rude.

"Don't you want to know why I need a man familiar with the sea?" Birk smelled of the ale they'd been drinkin'.

"No, sir."

Birk ignored him. "It's because I need someone to explain to me how it is that, a quarter turn ago, the ocean washed a man up on the beach not far from our village."

Horace's breathin' stopped short, caught on the edge of the memory of a man in a white shirt and red pants floatin' in the sea.

X - Teryk - Recovery

*T*HE *SOFT DIN* OF the night wafted in through the open window, the chirrup of crickets and calls of night birds assaulting Teryk's ears. He rolled over again, putting his back toward the noise, and threw his arm on top of his head to shut the racket out, but to no avail. Neither the singing insects nor hunting birds kept him awake, it was his father's words and the vision of colored flames dancing before his eyes.

The scroll hadn't burned the way one might have expected a dry and ancient scrap of parchment to burn. It ignited quickly, right enough, but the prince had never seen fire burn blue and pink and green, the colors dancing, reflected in the brazier's polished brass. Not a soul in the great hall mentioned it. How could that be?

'It has been touched by magic,' Trenan had said.

Teryk sat up abruptly, the thin blanket covering his naked flesh falling away and leaving him exposed, but he didn't notice the touch of the night air on his skin. His mind recalled the way the scroll whispered to him in the secret chamber, the sound it made when he touched it, the way Trenan jumped back from it, scared in a manner the prince had never seen the master swordsman scared before. And the colors.

The prince threw his legs over the edge of the mattress bed and stood, then retrieved his shirt and breeches from where he'd left them hanging over the back of a chair. He dressed hastily, distracted, as he wondered if his father might have chosen to post a guard outside his chambers to ensure he complied with his wishes.

He paused beside the table on which he'd not so long ago spread the scroll that now usurped his thoughts. A goblet of mulled wine his squire had brought to help him sleep still sat untouched, and he gazed upon it as his mind sought a story to tell a guard, an excuse for leaving his room. The surface of the dark wine reflected the dim moonlight shining through the window, the shimmer making him notice the dryness of his throat. He grasped the goblet and took a drink. The wine was no longer warm, but its sweet and spicy flavor gave the relief for which he yearned.

If I tell him my honey pot is full, he'll simply empty it.

He set the goblet back on the table, wiped his mouth with the back of his hand, and scanned the room, searching for an idea to prompt him. His eyes fell upon his sword belt slung on the post of his bed.

I'll tell him I left my sword at the practice arena.

He recognized it as a poor pretext, that it might not be enough for the guard to let him go, or that the fellow may insist on accompanying him, but he'd have to try to make it work.

Teryk sat on the chair to pull on his boots, but stopped, recalling footsteps echoing through the great hall when his father burned the scroll. He realized the click of boot heels would be too loud in the silence of the night and decided to go barefoot.

With a fortifying breath filling his lungs, he crossed the room, hoping with each step that the king trusted him enough not to waste a man on the task of guarding him. He paused with his fingers touching the door handle, and listened for noise on the other side but heard nothing other than the lonely crickets and hungry birds calling through the window.

This is silly. The scroll will be nothing but ash.

He'd seen the squire light it, watched it curl and blacken as flames consumed it. Yet a compulsion drove him on, a curiosity he could neither quell nor explain. The whispers, the colors...

The prince tightened his grip on the handle, pulled the door open.

An empty stool sat to the right of the door, tight to the wall. Someone had been assigned to keep watch over the prince, but had shirked his duty. Maybe the guard left his post, desperate to make water or void his bowels, or perhaps an illicit affair prompted him to sneak away, not expecting the prince to do any more than sleep. The reason didn't matter to the prince, only the result—his room left unguarded.

He coaxed the door closed behind him and peeked along the hall toward his sister's chambers and froze. An armored man holding a torch stood outside the princess' door, his back to the prince. Teryk swallowed hard and crept the opposite direction, glad he'd forsaken his boots as the fleshy pads of his feet whispered on the cold stone floor. When he'd reached the corner and eased himself around and out of the guard's line of sight, he leaned against the wall and released his held breath.

He only hesitated a moment to relax the tightness in his legs before continuing—the other guard might return at any time, and Teryk didn't want to run into him in the darkened hall.

The prince stole down the stairs and along another hall laid with thick red carpet. The rug upon the floor deadened the sound his bare feet would have made slapping on a stone floor, allowing him to move more quickly, rushing from shadow to shadow and avoiding the light wherever he could. When he reached the staircase to the bottom level, he paused again and listened.

The palace seemed to hold its breath along with him.

Without seeing the moon, he didn't know what time of night it was, but the entire place never truly slept at once. Guards always patrolled the hallways, bakers rose early to bake, servants cleaned through the night, but he'd seen no one so far. Time crept past, stealing by like a thief in the night, and his lungs burned with the pressure of his captive air. He released a small amount through his nose, then paused again.

A sound.

It came from the hallway he'd just traversed. A furtive step? The rustle of cloth? He knew not, but it didn't come again as he continued waiting until air ached in his lungs and he could wait no more. Up on his toes to prevent his soles creating noise on the bare stone stairs, he descended the steps as fast as he dared. Ten paces later, he finally released his breath and drew another into his thankful lungs.

By the time Teryk reached the bottom of the staircase, the muscles in his calves were knotted from tip-toeing. He paused at the foot of the stairs, relieved to stand on flattened feet again, and directed his listening back up the stairway behind him.

Another sound.

This time, the prince didn't wait to find out if he'd imagined the quiet footfall or listen for another to follow it. He sprinted along the carpeted hall, his feet beating a quiet rhythm on the plush rug woven by enslaved hands centuries before his birth. As he reached the door to the great hall, he skidded to a halt, the threads of the carpet burning the soles of his feet, and peeked back over his shoulder.

He saw nothing.

Teeth gritted, he listened for signs of a pursuer still following him. Another sound—a creak of leather.

Teryk pushed his shoulder against the door, heedless of the creak he knew it would make. He'd be discovered, he realized, but he needed to get to the scroll before his pursuer caught him, he needed to see it.

The door groaned again when he pushed it shut, the noise carried up into the rafters, building into a wave that crested against the ceiling, rebounded back, then dissolved like the ocean rolling onto the shore. Teryk stood with his back against the thick wooden door, expecting a pressure against it as his pursuer followed him into the room, but none came.

A sliver of moonlight shining through a high window fell across the long, polished floor. The brazier's edge caught the glow, amplified it to a beacon calling to the prince, guiding him to his goal. But the moonlight reflected in the brass was no normal moonlight; it sparkled blue and pink and green.

Teryk pushed away from the door, his shadow forgotten, the guard outside his door forgotten, his father's wishes forgotten. The reflected moonlight consumed him as he paced down the long room, oblivious to the chilly stone pressing against the soles of his feet, the soft echo of his footfalls swirling up into the heights.

By all rights, the ancient parchment should be ash, indistinguishable from any other. There shouldn't be fragments or pieces, scraps or flakes—nothing but dust. Somehow, though, the prince knew this wouldn't be the case.

The colors told him he'd find it so.

He stepped into the band of moonlight and stopped three paces from the brazier, its edge glowing as though alight with flame. The prince tilted his head, peered up at the high window, but no moon shone through. He stared, wondering where the light came from, then returned his attention to the brazier, the colored light, the scroll.

The last three steps passed beneath his feet and Teryk stood beside the brazier, close enough to touch it. He leaned forward, peering in, its interior illuminated by the light with no right to shine, and he saw it.

The parchment. Rolled, blackened, but whole.

Seeing it thus should have stopped him. Intelligent and educated, the prince had been raised to believe in the one old God and scoff at the mention of magic. He knew nothing should have survived the flame he'd watched burning in this very brazier earlier in the evening, nothing should have been more than ash, yet here lay the scroll, charred and brittle looking, but in one piece.

Common sense told him to be afraid, to run back to his bed to cower beneath his thin blanket, but he didn't listen. Instead, he reached into the brazier with a shaking hand and touched his fingertips against the scroll.

Its rough surface didn't immediately flake under his touch, so the prince grasped it between thumb and finger, worried it might fall if he squeezed too hard, but it didn't. Despite its appearance, the scroll's surface felt the same as when he first touched it.

But it made no sound.

Teryk lifted it out of the vessel, careful not to knock it against the side for fear his fingers misjudged its condition. When his hand cleared the sides, the light shining through the high window dimmed and the color reflected in the brazier's edge faded, throwing the room into darkness.

The door behind him creaked.

Teryk whirled, the scroll held protectively against his chest. He expected to find the light of a torch spilling down the hall, reflected in the polished stone floor, but didn't. He expected to hear a guard's voice call out, or his father's, telling him to drop the scroll and return to his chambers, but didn't.

In the darkness, he observed a silhouette framed in the doorway, and a whisper floated through the great hall to his ears. A droplet of sweat ran down his temple.

"Teryk?"

His sister's voice.

Nervousness drained from him and the unintended tautness gripping his muscles eased. He paced across the polished floor, the scroll grasped in his hand and the unexplainable lure of the brazier gone.

"What are you doing here?" he asked in a hushed tone.

"I'm not sure. I had a dream."

He stopped in front of her, close enough to see the light of a wall-mounted torch shining down the passage reflected in her eyes. She wore an expression of worry on her face that made him want to touch her cheek to soothe her, but his fingers refused to release the scroll.

"A dream? What did you dream of?"

"I dreamed you came to take back the scroll." Her eyes darted to the roll in his hands, then back. "But it must be burned to ash. Isn't it?"

The prince inhaled deeply through his nose, hesitating, not sure if he should tell the princess the truth or keep it for himself. He'd told Trenan and nearly lost the parchment because of it.

This is Danya. This is my sister.

"We can't talk here," he said, pushing past her into the broad hallway beyond. "Someone will discover us."

"Teryk—?"

"Let's go back to my chamber." He crept along the hall toward the staircase without waiting for an answer, but knew she followed when he heard the door to the great hall creak shut.

Their feet whispered over carpet, padded up stairs, and they encountered no one. Teryk breathed a relieved lung full of air upon reaching the third level landing undiscovered, the floor on which they both kept their chambers. He stopped at the top, his back pressed against the wall, the scroll held against his chest, and held his arm out to stop Danya before she rounded the corner. A finger held to his lips, he gestured for her to wait while he peeked down the passage.

The guard assigned to his room had returned and the sight of him made the prince's heart sink. The man sat upon the stool set outside his door, arms crossed in front of him, head sagging until his chin rested on his chest. Beyond him, the hall lay empty. Teryk retreated.

"I think he's asleep. And your guard is gone."

He held one finger to his lips again and signaled for Danya to follow, then took a furtive step around the corner.

They crept down the hall, the princess' hand on her brother's waist. As they approached the man on the stool, a snore rattled in his nose.

The royal siblings hesitated, waiting to be sure he hadn't woken himself, then the guard's breathing returned to the deep, even breaths of sleep. Teryk glanced over his shoulder at Danya, offered a wan smile, and set out again.

They crossed the last few paces to the door, close enough to the guard to see the hairs of his mustache quiver with each exhalation. Danya raised a finger and pointed out a line of drool spilling out of the corner of the man's mouth and along his chin; she brought her hand to her lips to stifle a giggle. Teryk shot her a warning look and reached for the door handle.

The door opened, smooth and silent on hinges lubricated regularly by the prince himself since his youth—this wasn't his first clandestine trip out of his chamber. When they'd entered, he closed the door and the tension in his shoulders loosened as he eased the bolt into place.

Danya opened her mouth to speak, but he barged past her to the table. He pushed the half-full goblet of mulled wine nearer to the edge and placed the rolled and blackened parchment in the middle. The princess came to stand beside him, eyes wide, staring at the scroll.

"It survived?"

Teryk nodded.

"But how?"

"I don't know, but I doubt it's any more legible now than before."

She scowled and reached for it, but Teryk pushed her hand away.

"You should open it," she said.

He shook his head. "It might fall apart."

"If you don't try, you'll never know if anything changed."

Teryk dragged his gaze from the scroll to his sister, one eyebrow raised at her. "Why would anything have changed?"

Danya shrugged. "How did it survive the flames?"

The prince's gaze fell back to the scroll. She had a point. The parchment was scorched black, its edges curled in on themselves, though it had no right to be in one piece. If he'd wanted to retrieve the scroll, he should have needed a pouch to scoop it into.

"All right," he said. "Let's have a look."

He reached out but hesitated before touching it, fingers shaking, suddenly thinking the entire foray futile. He'd detected no sounds from the scroll on the return trip from the great hall, and its surface was burned beyond legibility, even if words had once been written on it. What could unrolling it reveal?

The prince flexed his fingers, curled them into fists, then opened them again, wiggling them above the scroll. His sister poked him in the ribs.

"Come on, then. It's a burnt piece of paper, not your attempt at a virgin."

He looked sideways at her, a retort regarding the number of virgins he'd deflowered teetering on his lips, but then noticed her smile and realized she already knew. He kept quiet, shook his head, and returned his attention to the scroll.

Nothing out of the ordinary tingled through his nerves when he lowered his hand to brush his fingertips along the scroll's surface. It felt firm and rough, as before—old paper, poorly made, Danya had rightly said—but no sounds whispered in his ears, no colors danced before his eyes, as though whatever powered the roll before had died in the flames.

He inhaled a breath that smelled nothing at all like charred parchment, grasped the scroll's edge between his fingers, and unrolled it across the table.

Danya leaned in, peeking over his shoulder, but it was blank and as black as a night at the beginning of the moon's turn. An excitement he hadn't felt building in his chest leaked out of the prince and his head sagged forward.

"Touch it," his sister said.

"What?"

"Touch it. See if it feels different."

"I'm touching it. There's nothing. It's a burnt piece of paper."

Danya huffed air out through her nose, exasperated. "Touch the inside. If you won't, I will."

She reached her hand past him and Teryk jerked his shoulder, blocking her from reaching the scroll. His hip hit the table hard, jarring it and tipping the wine goblet. He watched it tilt toward the parchment as though time slowed, leaving him powerless to stop it.

The goblet leaned farther and farther. A drop of wine slopped out, splashed on the paper, then another. The chalice toppled, spilling its contents over the scroll's surface; Teryk released his hold on the edges, jumping back from the mess.

"Look what you've done," he snapped, standing a step away from the table, hands held up in the air.

He faced his sister, intent on skewering her with an angry look to show his annoyance, but she paid him no attention. She continued staring at the scroll, now ruined by a sweet and spicy mulled wine, as if being burnt in a brazier wasn't enough.

"Danya!"

The princess raised her hand and extended a finger, pointing at the soggy scroll. Teryk's anger melted away when he saw white mist gathering around the roll of parchment.

"What in the old God's name?" he exclaimed.

"Teryk." Danya's voice was no more than a whisper. "Open it."

His head whipped around and he stared at her hard. Did she mean it? Trenan's words sprang back to his mind again.

'It has been touched by magic.'

The thought both scared and excited him, made him nauseated and filled with exuberance at once. He shook his head, but Danya still wasn't looking at him. Her eyes remained on the scroll and, when he returned his gaze to it, he saw the mist had dispersed as quickly as it had come.

"Open it."

He reached for the parchment. When his fingers touched its edge, a choir whispered in his ear with a low, musical hum.

"Do you hear that?"

Danya didn't respond.

A deep inhalation whistled through his teeth and he grasped the edge of the parchment, spread it across the table. A few beads of crimson wine rolled away onto the table, but not nearly as much as had been spilled.

The runes scrolled across the paper's dark surface glowed with faint white light that pulsed and dimmed, pulsed and dimmed. To him, they may as well have been no more than shapes, for they were written in an ancient language he'd seen once before, in the secret chamber.

Wide-eyed, the prince stared at their forms, tracing each swoop and angle with his eyes, forgetting his own need to breathe, forgetting his sister stood beside him until the princess' fingers touched his forearm.

With an effort, he wrenched his gaze away from the lucent patterns. Danya continued staring at the wine-stained parchment stretched across the table, an expression of awe and wonder lending a glow to her countenance.

"Teryk," she said, finally tearing her eyes away from the pulsing light and finding her brother's gaze. "I can read it."

XI - Teryk and Danya - Prophecy

*T*HE BLACK PARCHMENT WENT red with the wine, then faded to pink. Shapes appeared, their edges and curves radiating dim light in the dark room. Danya stared at the lambent runes, symbols she'd never seen before but knew were the markings of an ancient language, long dead and forgotten. She watched them dance and writhe on the page like living things, then they settled into letters she inexplicably recognized, formed words she somehow knew.

The princess' eyes widened as she stared at the strange message on a charred parchment that, by all the laws of God and nature, should be nothing but a heap of dusty gray ash. But it wasn't. Instead, it spoke of omens and portends, visions and prophecy. Danya dragged her gaze away and found her brother studying her face.

"Teryk," she said. "I can read it."

His brows dipped and a line took shape on his forehead. "What?"

"I can read it."

"You can read it? How?"

She looked from him to the scroll and back, waved her hand over top of the parchment.

"What is it you see?" she asked.

The prince's eyes fell to the paper, narrowing in concentration. Danya waited. She and Teryk had learned all the same lessons from the masters, were close to equals in languages and letters, but his expression told her the lines didn't appear to him as they did to her. The tilt of his brows and set of his mouth revealed that he saw only unfamiliar forms of a long-ago language scrawled across the page. She waited for him to say so, excitement building in her chest. Finally, he sighed heavily and raised his head, shaking it in defeat.

"Nonsensical runes," he conceded. "What do you see?"

"Letters," she whispered. "Words."

"Read it to me."

The princess waved her hand. "Get ink and paper first, in case they disappear when the wine dries."

He rushed across the room, his foot striking the silver goblet that had rolled off the table and sending it clattering across the floor; he stopped at the sound of it. Danya glanced toward the door, both of them waiting for it to rattle against the bolt, for a voice to call out, asking what was going on, but neither happened. The princess released the air from her lungs and Teryk went to the desk set against the wall by the window. He returned a moment later with a blue-tinted sheet of paper, an inkpot and quill.

"Damnable goblet," he muttered.

"Hurry. The light's fading."

Teryk wiped wine off the edge of the table and set the paper down while pulling the cork from the bottle of ink. He rested the inkpot beside the paper, dipped the fine tip of the quill, and held it above the blank sheet.

"Well?"

Danya wet her lips with her tongue, surprised at the tingling sensation the action spread across them. Funny what one's imagination caused in the thrall of excitement.

"Okay. You're ready?"

"Yes. Hurry."

The princess read the first line. "When days of peace approach their end." She paused while the tip of Teryk's quill scratched the words down. He dipped into the ink again and waited for her to continue.

Danya read the next line, and the next. To her ears, it sounded as though someone else read the words, though they did so with her voice. She became a child seated on a pillow, legs crossed, hanging on each word as a master read her stories of heroic deeds and mythological lands. If she'd been that child, she would have leaned forward to be closer to the words, losing herself in them so the room and people around her disappeared, leaving her alone with the story. Sensations tingled and pulsed on her skin as though she flowed along the curve of the letters, following their bends and rushing across their straight lines like a boat swept along a river, riding its rapids. She—

"Slow down." Teryk's voice broke the spell.

Danya blinked, surprised to find she'd leaned forward almost until her nose touched the parchment. She smelled the spicy-sweetness of the mulled wine soaking it, the bitter scent of charred paper and fire beneath clogging her nostrils. Clearing her throat, she leaned back, standing straight.

"How far did you get?"

"To raise the Small Gods, a Small God must die."

The princess continued reading, slower this time, and the words didn't draw her in as before. Her voice came from her mouth, the rasp of the quill on the paper and the occasional drip of wine plummeting from the edge of the table holding her in the moment. She paused between each line, giving her brother an opportunity to keep pace and refresh the ink on the tip of his quill.

When she spoke the final word, the scribbling continued for a few seconds, then ceased. Teryk held the writing implement over the paper, waiting.

"Is that it?"

Danya nodded, her gaze remaining on the scroll. The pink surface touched by the wine darkened to red, then brick and ruby. The glow of the runes faded and the color overpowered them, sucking their light back into the parchment.

"Do you see?" she whispered.

Out of the corner of her eye, she noticed her brother's nod.

The paper went scarlet, crimson, then black. The shapes and forms disappeared, the scroll rolled up on itself, and Danya's heart lurched. She tore her gaze away, directing it to her brother and the blue-tinted sheet of paper on the table in front of him, the tip of the quill hovering above the cursive letters drawn by his hand.

"Did you get it?" she asked, breathless.

"Yes." He set the quill beside the ink, knocking the cork rolling across its top to rest against the scroll. "I got it."

"What does it say?"

Teryk raised a brow.

"You don't know what it says? You read it."

"I..." If anyone in the kingdom might understand what she experienced reading the lines on the scroll, it was her brother, but she found no words to describe it. He sensed her lack and came to the rescue.

"It's a prophecy," he said, wonder and awe plain in his voice. "A prophecy about me."

Danya stared at him for a moment before the guffaw broke from her lips, uncalled and unexpected. His face went instantly angry, and she put her hand over her mouth to keep more laughs from escaping.

"I'm sorry. I didn't...I don't know where that came from."

He scowled at her, unimpressed with both her reaction and the subsequent apology.

"It says right here." He pointed at the paper with an ink-stained finger. "The firstborn child of the rightful king."

"Which king?"

"What do you mean? There's only one king: our father."

"Now, yes. But how many kings before him? How many more to come? Maybe it's referring to one of them. A king long dead, or your son."

"No. It's not. It's father."

"But if it refers to a long-ago king, that would explain why it's written in an ancient language."

Teryk shook his head and she read his frustration in the set of his brow. He rubbed his lips together, passed his tongue between them, thinking, concentrating. His eyes scanned the paper, fell on the scroll, then rose to meet hers.

"If it had been written to be read by someone long ago, or someone yet to come, then why did we find it? Why were you able to read it?"

She shook her head, lacking an answer.

"Danya," he leaned toward her as though telling a secret. "Why did it speak to me?"

His eyes shone and she perceived in them the excitement she'd experienced when she read the scroll. It had left her now, an insidious sliver of dread insinuating itself in its stead, but she couldn't argue Teryk's words. All the happenings leading them to the scroll seemed too many for mere chance, as though an unseen hand guided them through the dark underground channel to the secret chamber in which no one had ever set foot. The voice he heard, the scroll surviving the flames, her ability to read its words. It all pointed toward one thing.

"Magic," she whispered.

"We were meant to find it. This," he picked up the paper on which he'd inscribed her translation and shook it in the air, "is my destiny."

A shiver crawled up Danya's spine at her brother's words; the sliver of apprehension expanded through her mid-section, up into her chest. She knew her brother well enough to realize he meant what he said, that this wasn't a dramatic action meant to elicit a surprised response, or a laugh like so many times before.

"What will you do?"

He shook his head and paced away from the table, crossed the room to the desk where he opened a drawer and stowed the blue-tinted paper.

"I'm not sure. I need time to think." He faced her again, hand resting on the drawer's handle. "Right now, I'm tired. It's been a long day."

All his exhaustion seemed to fill his face at once, and then it leapt across the room and settled into Danya's bones. It weighed on her as though she wore a full suit of plate and carried Trenan on her back. Her knees shook and she grasped the edge of the table to keep them from buckling.

"As am I," she said and stifled a surprise yawn with the side of her fist.

Teryk returned to her side, his hand grasping her upper arm. He guided her to the door and unbolted it.

"Careful," he whispered, opening the door a crack. He peeked through, blocking her view. "Still sleeping."

Teryk opened the door wider and Danya saw the guard slumped on the stool, the line of drool they'd snickered at on his chin now a patch of dark wetness on the front of his blue jerkin. The princess dared to poke her head out and glance along the hall; the guard outside her door had returned to strike a similar pose.

She nodded to her brother and he put his hand on her shoulder. Their eyes locked, silent words passing between them to keep this discovery to themselves, to support each other as they'd done their entire lives. Danya stepped out into the hallway; Teryk shut the door gently behind her.

Despite the sleeping shift she wore, Danya felt naked standing in the corridor. At any second either of the guards might awaken and discover her, and now it would be only her, not the two of them together. She understood he hadn't abandoned her, that necessity demanded she make the short return trek to her chamber on her own, but it poked at her heart and made the unease in her stomach spread.

She inhaled shallowly, then went down the hall, leaving the guard outside Teryk's door to drool on himself until the morn.

The pads of her bare feet made no sound as she stole to her room. The guard assigned to her snored atop his stool, his rumbling breaths disguising the noise made by the opening of her door. She stepped one foot across the threshold and paused to look back at the man. His helm sat askew on his head, pushed forward when his head tilted back against the wall, his mouth open to allow air to rattle noisily along his throat. Despite the exhaustion settling into her limbs, a thought occurred to the princess. Before she entered the room and shut herself in, she leaned down and touched the guard's shoulder.

"Guard?"

The man continued to snore, so she grasped him more firmly and shook him.

"Guard."

No response. She kicked the stool, punched his shoulder and raised her voice.

"Guard!"

A louder snore echoed along the hall but she received no more reaction and Danya gave up. The tiredness that had seeped into her bones forced itself into her eyes, making her lids heavy. They fluttered as she closed the door, her mind wanting to ponder the mystery of the sleeping guards, recognizing a connection to the evening's other events, but her weary head fought against seeing it.

She reeled across the chamber and slumped onto her bed without pulling the covers over herself. When her eyes closed, she pictured letters made of light crawling like snakes, then she dreamt of a man who came from across the sea.

XII Horace - Reunion

*B*IRK'D TETHERED HIS HORSE and wagon out back o' the tavern, away from the other horses. Seemed Birk weren't the only outcast, but his mount, too. Horace didn't pay it much mind, though, because his thinkin' were on other things. Red and white floatin' things. Small Gods and a god under the water what ate your things.

The wagon slammed through a rut in the track, jarrin' the ol' sailor's teeth together and pullin' him outta his worried musin'. He gawked 'round at nothin' but trees linin' the side of the road in the darkness. Coulda been other things in there, and Horace thought if he gave it enough effort, he just might find 'em, but he didn't wanna look hard, and he didn't wanna see. Trouble were, he didn't particularly wanna talk to the man drivin' the wagon, neither. He'd've been right fine workin' for a bed in the tavern's back room rather'n go with Birk to meet the man what crawled outta the sea.

Horace cleared his throat, the thin flavor of ale and tasty stew tingin' his phlegm and makin' him wish for another tankard, another bowl.

"You doing all right, friend?"

Birk directed his eyes toward the ol' sailor instead o' the road, so Horace stared straight ahead at the horse's ass.

"Yep."

"Not much of a talker, are you?"

"Nope."

Birk flicked the reins, slappin' the leather on the flank o' the animal pullin' the wagon, but Horace knew it were for show—he didn't prompt the horse enough to make it go any quicker. The wagon driver returned his eyes to the path ahead and it felt to the sailor as if someone lifted a weight from offa him. Still, he figured he should say somethin' to the feller...he did pay for dinner and ale, after all.

Horace only cared to talk on one thing.

"When did you say this feller crawled his way outta the sea?"

Birk paused before answerin', and ol' Horace Seaman suspected one o' them sly smiles might be slinkin' its way onto his face, but he didn't take a peek to find out. He didn't like them skulky smiles.

"Less than a quarter turn of the moon," Birk answered finally. He looked skyward and Horace followed his gaze to the half-moon hangin' up high amongst the Small Gods. "Three sunrises ago, it was."

Horace nodded as though the timeline made sense to him. He thought back to the last moon what caught his eye, the night before the simpleton pushed him into the water and ensured the *Devil o' the Deep* got ate by the God. That night, the moon'd been a sunrise beyond the quarter turn, but his mind didn't recall if it were first quarter or last. How long'd he floated in the sea?

"And three sunrises ago, when this feller washed up on the beach, he were alive?"

"And remains so."

"Talkin', is he?"

Birk flicked the reins again, meanin' it this time. "He hasn't regained consciousness yet."

Horace faced the wagon driver and raised a brow toward his forehead. Birk caught the gesture and nodded.

"He's not woken up."

The sailor let the air outta his chest and tightness left his limbs. He didn't have no explanation why this feller from the sea were makin' him all tense and such—might be any ol' fisherman fell into the ocean and got himself washed ashore—but somethin' in Horace's gut told him a clumsy fish-gatherer weren't the case. If he'd learnt anythin' in near thirty-five turns with his feet set on ship's decks, it were to give his attention to whatever his gut had to say. The other thing he'd learnt were that he hated the sea.

"Is he gonna live?"

"I think so, but he needs the doc. That's why I need your help. And to find out if you know him." Horace sensed Birk's gaze on him, his grin grinnin'.

"Can't see how's I would."

His voice held a tremor, and he hoped Birk ain't detected it. They continued their trip in silence, the dead quiet of the night bein' disrupted only by shoed hooves gratin' on rocky road and rattley wagon wheels bouncin' through ruts. Horace sat on his hands and chewed his bottom lip all the way, wonderin' if a God o' the Deep were able to make an appearance on land.

No surprise to Horace findin' Birk's house on the outside edge o' town—Millstream, the place were called, on account o' the fact there were a mill and a stream. Birk lived in a small shack what appeared built by a man who went to school to get book learnin' 'stead o' figurin' out how to use tools in his hands like a man should. The shack ain't fell o'er yet, but it resembled one awaitin' a stiff breeze to finish the job. Horace licked his finger and held it up as he climbed offa the wagon. No wind, so it might be safe for sleepin' in one more night.

"She's stronger than she looks," Birk said, noddin' toward the shack as though he'd listened in on the words in the sailor's head. "Built her with my own hands."

"Figured."

Birk titled his head, then laughed, apparently takin' no offense. Instead, he set to unbucklin' his horse from the wagon and Horace gave him a hand without makin' him ask. After the man bought him stew and ale, it were the least for him to do. He wished it were all there were for him to do.

The unhitchin' done, Birk led the horse 'round behind the shack to a barn what looked to need no more'n a breath to send it topplin' to the ground, but it appeared to be holdin' its own as good as the shack. Whatever this Birk feller were doin', it didn't look pretty, but it worked to keep the rain offa his head and the bugs outta his teeth.

"Come on, I'll show you the man from the sea," he said, closin' the barn door behind him.

Horace chewed his bottom lip some more, got a bloody flavor on his tongue and made himself stop. Eatin' himself weren't no good answer.

They crossed the short yard to the door, gravel crunchin' under Horace's one foot and pushin' uncomfortably against the sole o' the other. He'd appreciated the stew, and the two tankards fulla ale, but if he got outta this encounter with his life, he hoped this man might have a pair o' boots to spare.

Birk swung the door open and stepped into the shack's dark interior; Horace hesitated before followin' him, his mind thinkin' on the man in red and white bobbin' upon the sea. But he'd not seen the man's face, nothin' but white shirt and red pants. Maybe the man didn't have no face, but a monster's face, the God o' the Deep's face.

The ol' sailor shivered despite the warm night and forced himself to step o'er the threshold and into the shack. Only a chickenturd stands in a doorway, afraid and shiverin', and First Man Horace Seaman weren't no chickenturd. He just didn't wanna be in a certain place at a certain time, nothin' more.

Horace swung the door shut behind him and stood unmovin' in the dark. The day's heat'd brought out the shack's odors, and the lack of light prompted his nose into workin' harder'n usual. It told him the thresh on the floor were fresh, that Birk'd built at least part o' the shack outta cedar, and he'd cooked himself up a chicken for his dinner. Beneath ev'rythin', clingin' to them smells like a rash on your balls what didn't wanna go, Horace sniffed the briny stench o' sea water and fought to keep his meal from comin' back up on him, 'cause pukin'd be a terrible waste o' good stew.

"A moment and I'll have the lamp lit."

Part of Horace relished the idea o' light, so his eyes'd do a portion o' the work and his nose'd stop showin' off, but another part didn't wanna see what hid in the dark. What were ol' Horace Seaman gonna do if the lamp lit up on a man wearin' red pants and white shirt?

What were he gonna do if it were a god crawled outta the sea to collect what shoulda been his?

Birk struck a flint and a spark flashed eerie light across his face, but the wick didn't catch. He did it again, the spark flashin' on the snaky grin spread wide on his lips, and it didn't light again. Horace almost stepped forward and offered to ignite the thing for him, but remembered to hold his tongue on account of he didn't really want the lamp to light. If it didn't, might be he'd be able to sneak himself out while Birk cussed o'er it, as any man'd do if it didn't catch by the third attempt.

But it did. The spark flared a third time, and the wick caught, throwin' a fluttery light across the inside o' Birk's shack. Horace tensed, his teeth bit tight, expectin' a man clothed in red and white, seaweed draped 'round his neck and ocean water drippin' outta his hair, to lurch at him, drag him to the ground and then on a long trek back to the sea.

No man awaited him in the dark, though, and ol' Horace Seaman relaxed the tension outta his limbs, if but a little.

Inside Birk's shack were a damn bit better than the outside. He'd carved it up into at least two rooms what Horace saw, and the table and chairs set in the room's middle appeared artisan-made—must've been brought from the city, 'cause the way the shacks' outside looked proved Birk didn't make them himself. Rocks o' different colors and sizes made up the mantle, also an expert's work, and Horace wondered if rockwork were somethin' Birk might've done himself, but he doubted it.

"Welcome to my home," the man said, arms spread wider'n the grin upon his face.

Horace sucked a breath in through his nose. The sea's salty odor lingered, torturin' him, and it sure as hell didn't make him no hero. Fact, his bladder gave a shake at the smell of it and he thought it might let go and make him piss himself. He told himself it were the two tankards o' ale what caused it, nothin' more. Horace Seaman weren't no chickenturd.

"Where is he?"

"Right to business." Birk gestured toward a tattered velvet curtain hung across a doorway what leaned towards starboard. "Right through there, in the bedroom."

Horace's gaze found its way across the room to the drape what he suspected might've once been a lively shade o' green, but time and wear'd faded it closer to brown. The frayed edge brushed the floor, threads danglin' from it, and behind it lay...what? A God? Death? Hopefully nothin' more'n a man.

With a hard blink and a shake o' his head, Horace forced his feet to move him toward the doorway. Thresh crinkled under his boot, then pressed into the sole o' his rag-wrapped foot, and he wondered if whatever were on the curtain's other side might know where to find his other boot.

Birk grinned and stared as the ol' sailor made his way across the room like a cat sneakin' up on a mouse, one slow, careful step after another. Horace suspected the man might wanna prompt him into goin' quicker, the way he did when he flicked the reins against the horse's flank, but he kept himself from it, and that were for the best. Horace wouldn't't've taken kindly to him slappin' a piece o' leather on his ass, no matter how much stew and ale he bought for him.

The sailor raised his hand and stretched his callused fingers—digits used to tyin' knots and workin' hard—out toward the curtain. His fingertips touched its edge, found it softer'n he imagined, and hesitated. His bladder made its desire to have a piss known again, but Horace ignored it, concentratin' on the cloth's smoothness. There weren't nothin' soft as this on a boat.

"Nothing to be afraid of," Birk said. He'd come across the room while Horace weren't payin' him no mind and stood a pace away to the side. "He's unconscious."

The sailor faced his host.

"Asleep," Birk explained.

"I know what you mean," Horace snapped. "I ain't afraid, is all."

Birk bent his head forward, his smile unfalterin', and Horace went back to the curtain to insert his hand between the cloth and the leanin' jamb. Closer to the second room like this, the sickly sea smell were stronger. The sailor's stomach clenched and he moved the drape aside, took a step.

He peered into a small, dark room without much in it. Horace caught sight o' a trunk and a bed, and on the bed lay a man's shape...a big man, judgin' by the bulges in the covers. Big, but Horace's eyes couldn't make out his features in the dark, and a blanket covered him right the way up to his chin.

"Here," Birk said, the word startlin' Horace and makin' him have to squeeze harder to keep his bladder from havin' its way. "Allow me."

Birk grasped the edge of the velvety curtain and pulled it outta the way, then held the oil lamp up for it to cast light into the room. Horace turned his gaze away toward the chest sittin' at the foot o' the bed. He found it finely crafted in the manner o' the furniture, and inlaid with somethin' what sparkled and shimmered in the lamp's dancin' light. Horace thought it might be called mother o' pearl, but he weren't sure if that were it, or if pearls even came from mothers.

Birk held the lamp patiently and Horace felt its heat against his cheek, his ears detected the flame's hiss burnin' the oil in the wick. The sailor made his eyes move up the bed from the chest, followin' the man's curves and bumps hidin' beneath the blanket. They seemed like reg'lar curves and bumps, not akin to tentacles and such bein' hid underneath, and he thought even a man o' Birk's nature would've thought to tell him if the man were possessed of tentacles.

The pulled-right-the-way-up blanket covered half the man's face, right to his nose. His eyes was closed, but weren't no mistakin' the mess o' straw-colored hair stickin' out from under like someone were attemptin' to hide a mop.

Horace's mouth fell open.

"Do you know him?"

He stared a moment, then forced his jaw shut again, hopin' Birk didn't notice it openin'. His bladder begged for relief and he fought the urge to cross his legs to make it behave.

"What?"

"I said do you know him, Horace?" Birk repeated.

"Nope," Horace said, forcin' his voice into soundin' normal. "I ain't never seen him."

Birk let out a breath what stirred Horace's hair and coaxed goose bumps along the flesh on his lower arm. The sailor's eyes remained on the shock of tangled locks pokin' out from under the blanket.

"All right, then. We'll take the fellow to the doc at first light. Maybe he'll have better luck waking him and we can find out where he came from. Here." Birk gave the oil lamp a shake, its metal door rattlin'. "Take this and I'll prepare a place for you to sleep."

Horace raised his arm and took the handle o' the lamp in his fingers without removin' his gaze from the unconscious man. He sensed Birk move away, then heard the man shufflin' 'round furniture and thresh, clearin' a space for Horace to lay himself down. The sailor ignored him, takin' another step into the small room and lettin' the curtain swing back across the doorway behind him. He glared' hard at the bit o' head left uncovered by the wool blanket, leaned in close, doubtin' his eyes, but there weren't no reason for doubt.

"Fuck me dead," First Man Horace Seaman whispered so quietly, even he couldn't've heard the words. "Dunal."

XIII Teryk and Danya - Plans and Lies

*T*HE FAINT ODOR OF burnt wood and charred cork wafted to
   Teryk's nose. Nostrils flaring at the scent, he glowered at the
empty tabletop, a black mark the size and shape of a rolled scroll
scorched onto its surface, the blackened stopper from the inkpot atop
it. He resisted the urge to bend over and search across the floor, under
the bed, by the desk. He'd find nothing but the silver goblet he'd
fortuitously knocked off the table the night before.

Not fortuitous: destined, fated.

The door swung open and his sister entered without knocking, her
custom no matter how many times he'd admonished her for it. He'd
given up the demand a long time ago. Beyond her, Teryk glimpsed the
empty stool on the other side of the threshold, his guard likely recalled
from his duty sleeping outside the prince's room to partake in far more
strenuous activities.

Already clothed for the day, Danya closed the door and strode across
the floor to where he stood. He suspected she'd been out of bed for a
while, though the dark circles under her eyes suggested she'd found
sleep no more easily than him.

The princess strode to his side and gazed down at the table.

"Did you take it?" he asked knowing she hadn't.

"No. Why would I? The prophecy speaks of the first born, remember? Not the second." Danya glanced across the room at the desk
where he'd hidden his transcript in the drawer, tilted her head in its
direction. "Is it...?"

"Still there, and in one piece." He slouched onto the blue velvet divan, arm thrown across the back. Danya perched on the edge of it beside him.

"It seems so silly now the sun is up, doesn't it?"

Teryk noticed her peering sideways at him and only grunted in response. She shifted to face him, eyes glittering, a forced smile on her lips.

"I mean, truly...magic? There's no such thing in the real world. No one believes in magic, or Small Gods, or men from across the sea. Right?"

The prince held his sister's gaze without answering for a few seconds, then turned away to study his fingernails. If he let her speak long enough, she'd decipher the goings-on in his head. The sparkle in her eyes dimmed—the first sign her realization had begun.

"Parchment can't survive fire. Glowing letters don't appear out of nowhere. Men don't sleep like the dead on guard duty and scrolls don't spontaneously burn up in the middle of the night."

She waved a hand toward the table and the charred mark on its surface, then continued to stare as though she thought doing so might make it fade away. Teryk realized she'd almost convinced herself of what he already believed.

Danya sighed and fell against the divan, her eyes rolling back as she directed them toward the ceiling. Teryk looked at her, at the way her hair rested across her shoulders, at the sprinkle of freckles on her nose. In just another moment, she'd—

"It happened, didn't it?" she said.

He nodded. "It did."

"How can it be?"

"I don't know but, believe in magic and Small Gods and all the rest or not, it happened."

"What do we do now?"

The glimmer returned to her eyes. As was so often the case, she began to see this as just another of their little adventures, like swimming in the river. But it wasn't. His heart told him it was far more.

"*We* don't do anything," he said. "*I* am going to fulfill my destiny."

"What do you mean?"

He sat up and leaned toward her, his elbows resting on his knees, letting the pause draw on until she'd have trouble containing herself from asking again.

"I'm going to find him, Danya. I'm going to find the man from across the sea."

"Don't be stupid, Teryk. The—"

"Don't call me that," he snapped, jumping to his feet.

"I didn't mean—"

"I understand what you meant." He paced away, shaking his head. When he faced her again, she'd moved to perch on the edge of the divan again, her hands clasped in her lap and concern creasing her brow. She hadn't meant to call him stupid, but the word had come out of her mouth, nonetheless.

"All my life, I've lived in our father's shadow," he continued. "At his insistence, I spend more time learning history and matters of the state than I do swordplay and strategy. What have I learned in my studies, sister? I've learned that, generations ago, our family took the throne by force. That men swung swords and won the crown for our ancestors through cunning and strength of arm without any concept of which crops command what prices and when the merchants can sell their wares."

"It's not that way anymore, Teryk. We've seen no war in our lifetime and longer. We live in a kingdom of peace."

He strode to her purposefully, went to his knee and took her hands in his.

"Yes, Danya, but it's also true I've never been outside the walls of the inner city. When my day comes, what sort of king will I be if I've not seen Woodsel or visited the dungeons of Dreemskerry? By the God, I've never set foot on the ground of the outer city, let alone the others."

The princess nodded because she couldn't do otherwise, for she lived the same life. In all their days, they'd barely been out of each other's sight but for sleep.

"What if the words you read on the scroll tell the truth?" he said. "What if Woodsel and Dreemskerry, Bywater, Riverbank, and the rest of the land are in danger from an evil no one is aware of? What if terrible things come to pass and, having known, the future king—the one named in the prophecy—stood idly by and watched?"

He squeezed her hands and a corner of her mouth rose, not in a smile, but in a gesture of agreement. She got his point, as he knew she would, as he knew she likely had before he ever began speaking.

"We must tell father," she said and Teryk's heart jumped.

"No." He dropped her hands and stood. "We cannot. He burned the scroll without opening it, without knowing the words written upon it. A piece of paper frightened him so much, he put it to the torch. What do you think he'd do if we told him what it said?"

"Trenan, then."

He sank onto the divan beside her, rested his arm around her shoulders.

"'The firstborn child of the rightful king,' it said. Not the king. Not the one-armed swordsman." He pulled her closer, leaning in toward her. "You're the one who read it."

"Of course." She smiled and pushed him away with her palms against his chest. "But I'm not letting you go alone. If you don't want me to tell anyone, you're taking me with you."

Teryk let his shoulders sag, as though giving in to her demands because he had no other choice. But he'd known the conversation would end up here. His sister loved adventure too much to allow him one on his own, and she was too devious not to threaten exposing his plans. He was ready.

"Okay," he said with a nod. Danya clapped her hands together once and bounced in her seat, then settled herself. "We leave after my lesson, three sunrises hence."

"So soon?"

"Yes."

"The scroll didn't say when things would come to pass. What if it's not for many seasons?"

"What if it's already happening? What if the man from across the sea is here? If we accept that the scroll's magic led us to find it, then we have to assume it did so at the right time."

The princess nodded. "Of course."

"Then we have no time to lose."

Danya rose from the divan and paced the room, hands clasped behind her back as she thought. Her feet—bare as usual—alternately clapped on the uncarpeted sections of the stone floor, then made no sound when she walked on the rug.

"It will be difficult to leave the inner city. By the God, it will be near impossible to escape Draekfarren," she said.

A grin spread across his face and she raised an eyebrow.

"But you have a plan."

"I do," Teryk said. "Do you have a waterproof bladder, like we used to use on our river adventures when we were young?"

"You're planning to leave by the river."

"Yes." He jumped to his feet and crossed to her. "If we go after my lesson, around dinnertime, everyone will be occupied. The river cleaners will be done their work, and we will reach the wharves after the shoremens' day is finished."

"And the grate?"

He shrugged. "If we can get through one, we can get through any of them."

"It might work." She crossed one arm in front of her chest, propping up her other elbow to rub her chin with her fingers. The habit she'd picked up from their father, more suited for a man with a beard than a fresh-faced young lady. "What happens after we get out?"

Teryk allowed the grin to cross his lips again. This was playing out as he'd hoped.

"That, my dear sister, is when the real adventure begins."

She stopped rubbing her chin and crossed her arms, studying him with one brow raised and the corner of her mouth up-turned. He recognized the expression—the same one she got when she talked him into something.

"Okay. The river, moonrise after three sunrises."

"Pack light and we'll meet at the far wall of the northern courtyard to spend as little time in the water as possible."

She poked him in the ribs. "A little frightened of the water after our last swim, aren't you?"

"No, but it will raise suspicions if someone sees us floating through the courtyard when we're supposed to be supping."

"So we'll meet by the grate?"

"Yes. We'll attract less attention if we go separately. And it will be easier to slip our guards. Until then, go about your business like any other time."

"Of course." She moved closer and put her hand on his arm, held his gaze for a moment before speaking. "Are you sure about this? It will be dangerous."

Teryk breathed in sharply, then let the air out slowly, as though finally making up his mind. He'd been planning this since he sent her from his chambers the night before.

"We have no other choice."

Danya slipped her arms around him, pulled herself against his chest and hugged him. For most of his life, the prince's younger sister had given him strength, made him see the man inside himself he often didn't realize existed. She'd encouraged him, comforted him, aided him, and he liked to think he'd done the same for her, though she didn't need it as often.

But now, he was a man, and next in line for the throne. Teryk, son of Erral, was firstborn of the rightful king, the one named by the prophecy written on the scroll by some long dead hand. His fate was determined, his destiny preordained.

But his heart ached for having lied to his sister.

XIV - Horace - Doctorin'

*H*ORACE GLANCED BACK o'ER his shoulder as the wagon bounced through another rut hard enough to lift his ass from offa the seat. Dunal's limp form jounced along with it without re-sistin', but the sacks he and Birk'd piled 'round him kept him from bouncin' right o'er the side, somethin' Horace weren't altogether against happenin'.

"Why d'you wanna find out who he is so bad, anyways?" Horace asked graspin' the edge of the seat to keep his ass from flyin' up in the air again. The road were rough enough to set his cheeks to hurtin'.

"He came out of the sea," Birk replied, his voice holdin' an excited tone. "Do you know what that might mean?"

"He's a fisherman what fell outta his boat?"

"Well, yes. That might be the case." Birk snapped the reins hard and the horse whinnied in protest. He and Horace provided load enough for the poor nag, and Dunal were near worth another two. "But if he is, he's not from around these parts."

"Where do you s'pose he'd be from, then?"

"I'm not sure. He seems too big to be a fisherman."

"I didn't know they was a certain size."

"Nobody around here is that size. Maybe he's from the Green."

Horace guffawed, makin' it sound just right. "The Green? Ain't nothin' good from the Green, and he don't look like no Small God to me."

"More than just the Small Gods live in the Green."

The sailor shifted, uncomfortable on his seat, slidin' his ass side-to-side and grippin' the edge hard enough to make his knuckles go white.

"The Green's too far for him to be from there anyways." Horace's gaze flickered toward Birk. "Right?"

"It's not so far to be impossible, but you're right." He laughed. "He is awfully big, isn't he?"

Horace chuckled along with his host, doin' his best to keep his anxiety from showin'. Mentionin' the Green made him jittery, and knowin' it were close enough for Birk to consider Dunal might've come outta it weren't no good tonic for Horace's nerves.

Birk tapped a finger against his chin near a place where he'd nicked himself shavin'—a different one'n he'd cut before. Horace watched him, wonderin' how to get himself outta this situation he inadvertently found himself in and damnin' himself for bein' so desperate for food and ale. Weren't the first time a thirst for ale caused him trouble.

"Perhaps," Birk said, raisin' a finger in the air and facin' his travel companion. His eyes glittered and his grin what had disappeared while he thought deep returned. "Perhaps he's a man from across the sea."

Horace frowned. "Ain't no men from across the sea."

"Really?" Birk raised a brow. "You seem to know a lot about the sea...Tailor."

"Maybe I ain't no tailor, but I ain't no seaman, neither." Horace diverted his gaze, glad to see a few hovels croppin' up alongside the road—they'd be to the doc's soon. "It don't take no sailor to know there ain't nothin' across the sea. Nothin' but death."

"But how do we know? No one's ever gone."

"No ship what strayed from the coast ain't never come back. No sailor what looked o'er the shoreward wale and saw nothin' but sea ever lived to tell 'bout it."

Horace's words trailed off along with his thoughts, his mind recallin' the empty feelin' in his gut when he'd seen the land were gone. He should be happy he'd survived to draw breath. He should be dancin' and drinkin' and fuckin' ev'ry day as if it might be his last, because none o' them should've been his to live. Yet he sat beside a feller with too much nose for his likin', the two o' them haulin' the one man what might tell the truth of Horace to the doc and prob'ly get him sent back to the sea.

Dancin' and drinkin' an fuckin' all seemed better choices.

The wagon's boards rattled, the horse's tail flicked a fly what landed on its ass, and Horace wondered if the other man—the man he saw in the ocean before the God o' the Deep came and ate the *Devil*—might've been a man from across the sea.

He didn't say anythin' to Birk of it, just glowered straight ahead at the road and let their trip go on in silence.

—⁓—

They unloaded Dunal outta the wagon onto a bed with big, wooden wheels on it what might've doubled for a wheelbarrow when no hurt people needed loadin' in it. Whatever it were, Horace'd gladly thank whoever built it so he didn't have to lug the simpleton's fat ass all the way into the doc's shack.

He and Birk stood off to the side while the doc—a man with long hair at the back and near none on the top o' his head and what Birk called nothin' but doc—poked and prodded the head swabbie of His Imperial Majesty's Ship, *The Devil o' the Deep*. Course, Birk and the doc had no way o' knowin' who he poked, 'cause there ain't been enough time passed for anyone to find out the ship were lost, and Dunal weren't talkin'. Yet.

Weren't no fuckin' way Horace'd ever tell and get himself sent back out on a boat. If, when he died, they lashed his body to a rowboat and sent him driftin' out to sea to appease the God o' the Deep, as were the custom with dead sailors, it'd be too fuckin' soon for ol' Horace Seaman. Never'd be too fuckin' soon.

"Where did you find him?" the doc asked without lookin' up from peerin' into Dunal's ear as if he thought he might have a chance o' findin' somethin' in there.

"On the beach. Not far from Juddah's place."

Now the doc looked up at Birk, one eye goin' kinda squinty. "What were you doing all the way over there?"

Birk shrugged. "Walking. Thinking."

"Well, don't let Juddah find you been walking and thinking too near his place. He'll have your beans off if he does."

"I'll take it under advisement. Thank you."

His tone didn't suggest he meant it, but Horace didn't pay it much mind. The doc opened Dunal's mouth to peek inside and screwed his face up at the simpleton's reeky breath.

Some things don't never change.

Next, he pried open first one o' Dunal's eyelids, then the other. He put his ear to the big feller's chest and listened, touched his fingers to the swabbie's wrist, knocked him in the knee with a wee hammer. Dunal's foot kicked up into the air and Horace gasped, thinkin' the tiny whack'd woken him up.

What'd Horace do if Dunal woke up?

But he didn't. The doc took the hammer to Dunal's other knee and got the same reaction, but the simpleton's eyes stayed closed. He didn't cry out nor laugh nor tell the doc to stop.

After more pokin' and proddin' 'round Dunal's lower belly and too close to his tackle for Horace's comfort, the doc stepped back and put his hands on his hips, starin' at the swabbie like he expected him to sit up and start talkin', but he didn't know Dunal the way Horace did. He didn't know Dunal weren't none too good at conversin' at the best o' times.

"Odd," the doc remarked.

"What is it?" Birk asked.

Horace looked from one to the other but didn't get no hint what were goin' on. The doc walked up to Birk, took him by the arm, peekin' sideways at Horace all the while.

"Can I talk to you? Alone."

Birk nodded to the doc, then faced Horace. "I'll be right back."

They left, shuttin' the door behind them as though they figured Horace or Dunal or the both o' them might take off if they didn't. Horace thought it didn't sound a bad idea at all. He glanced down at his feet and the pair o' boots Birk'd provided. They was too small and pinched his toes, but he'd be able to run in them if it came to it.

Horace turned his attention to a row of glass jars sittin' on a shelf at eye level. A bunch held different plants and roots and stuff, all dried and crumblin'. A thick-lookin' yellow liquid with things floatin' in it filled others, things what Horace didn't wanna find out 'bout. He picked one up what contained somethin' small and purple bobbin' inside—it looked as if it might've been the cock off a dog.

"Hory? Is it really you?"

The words startled Horace so bad, the jar slipped outta his grasp, hit the ground and shattered. He stared down at the mess it made and wondered if the doc heard, but the worry o'er spillin' a dog's cock disappeared right quick. Only one man in the world called him Hory.

"Dunal?"

He pivoted real slow, fingers claspin' into fists beside his legs without him intendin' them to. The simpleton still lay on the doc's wheeled table, his head facin' toward Horace and the dopey grin the sailor'd wanted to slap off him more times'n he remembered pullin' up on his mouth's corners.

"It's me, Hory. Dunal."

"You're awake."

"I been pretendin'."

"You been pretendin'?"

"Uh hunh."

Horace shook his head as if doin' so might cause the simpleton to make sense. "Why?"

"Cuz I don't know where I am or who they is." His smile disappeared, replaced by a fearful expression. "What if they wanna put their things in my porth'le?"

"I don't think they do."

"Cain't tell by the way he were touchin' me, Hory. Look what he did."

Dunal directed his eyes downward and Horace followed his gaze to the bulge in et big man's breeches. Seein' its size made the ol' sailor sorry for goats and sheep ev'rywhere.

Horace's mind raced. How long before the doc and Birk'd get back? Enough time to sneak out the door without bein' seen?

"Get up. Let's get outta here."

"I cain't. My legs ain't workin' yet."

The ol' sailor shook his head. "I guess we'll stay a spell."

"Cain't do that, neither, Hory. What if they wanna keep us? What if they won't let us go back to the boat?"

Dunal's words tied Horace's stomach into a knot what made him have to rest his hand upon the edge of the simpleton's wheeled bed to keep his knees from givin' out under him. It felt as though he were a first-time cabin boy, back on a lurchin' deck, desperate to keep from bein' thrown o'er the side, the way he were when Dunal'd smacked him.

"I ain't goin' back to no ship," Horace grated.

Dunal's eyes went wide like his shipmate told him the ocean were really the land and the land were the ocean. His mouth opened and closed twice before words found their way out.

"But, Hory. You gotta. It's yer duty."

Horace shook his head, which felt full up with more air'n it were supposed to hold. His spittle held the flavor o' brine and he thought to spit it out, but Dunal grabbed his arm, distractin' him. The simpleton's grip were weak on his wrist, light as a fly landin' on his skin.

"Don't say that, Hory. You gotta go back."

"I ain't never."

Dunal's expression went grave and serious, least grave and serious as a simpleton's mug can. His grip tightened on Horace's arm, but still weren't enough to match a young girl's. He sat up of a fashion, gettin' as close to his ol' shipmate as his beat up body'd let him.

"You gotta, Hory. If you don't, I'll tell 'em where t'find ya."

Horace bit hard enough on his teeth, he wouldn't't've been surprised if they shattered under the pressure. Weren't no way in hell he'd be settin' foot on a boat again. He'd give them his permission to fuck him in the hind porthole ev'ry day for the rest of his life if it meant not havin' water beneath his feet. No one here knew he were a sailor, so no one here'd make him go back.

'Cept Dunal.

The ol' sailor's vision fogged up 'round the edges, like someone breathin' on a piece of shiny metal, and before he realized it, his fingers found their way to Dunal's throat. When he saw it happenin', he didn't do nothin' to stop them.

A gurgle he prob'bly meant to be a cry for help, or a plea for mercy, escaped from between the simpleton's lips. His hands pawed Horace's arms without effect as the ol' sailor leaned in, pressin' his whole weight on Dunal's windpipe, loop-de-loo thoughts chasin' each other through his mind.

I ain't goin' back and you ain't fuckin' no more goats. No more ship for me, no more sheep for you.

Dunal's cheeks went pink, then red, then darker. Horace leaned in hard, squeezin' with ev'ry bit o' his might, with ev'ry shred o' hatred he held for the sea. The simpleton's throat creaked beneath his grasp, then collapsed, and the gurglin' from Dunal's lips stopped; his little girl clawin' ceased and his hands fell onto the wheeled bed's thin straw-stuffed mattress.

Horace hung on longer, still pressin' down with ev'rythin' in him until the ache in his shoulders and the tops o' his arms insisted he let go. He did and leaned away, his hands slippin' from offa his shipmate's throat, flexin' his fingers to shake out cramps he hadn't even known was formin' in them.

He stumbled back a step, starin' at what he done. A line of saliva ran outta the corner o' Dunal's mouth, along his cheek and into his ear. His face were pink, his lips sea blue, and he possessed an unnatural dent in the middle o' his throat in the shape o' Horace's fingers. The mound o' his erection still pushed the blanket outta shape.

Two thoughts jumped to the front o' First Man Horace Seaman's mind:

I killed the skipper's wife's cousin.

And:

I gotta get outta here.

Horace spun 'round and took one step toward the door stoppin' when he saw his path blocked by Birk and the doc. They both stood in the doorway, mouths fallen open, expressions of disbelief in their eyes, and Horace wondered how long they'd been standin' watchin' him. Could he make up an excuse? Tell them Dunal'd gone and died on his own?

The way Birk fixed his gaze on the ol' sailor, the accusation burnin' in it convinced him it were too late for excuses.

"What—?" the man who'd bought him stew and ale, given him a place to sleep and a pair o' boots began, but Horace weren't stayin' 'round to see what Birk might have to say 'bout what he done.

Horace exploded forward, catchin' both men by surprise and knockin' them out of his way boltin' outta the doc's house. He ran past Birk's horse and wagon, the too-small boots he'd been given pinchin' his toes while his feet hammered across the road and into the field.

Former First Man Horace Seaman lay his eyes on the forest ahead and didn't bother lookin' back to see if the men gave him chase.

XV - Teryk - Godsbane

*T*HE SUN SWUNG LOW toward the far horizon, but sweat streamed out from under Teryk's shallow helm and soaked the shirt he wore beneath his chest plate. A blow he didn't see coming bounced off his shield and Trenan growled at him.

"Concentrate," he grunted, taking another swing that Teryk caught on his blade. "An adversary won't go easy if your head is off playing in a field while your body joins the fight alone."

The prince gave his head a shake to clear the muddle of thoughts, but how could he? He'd hidden his pack and already divined both his way out of the castle and the best route out of the inner city. Beyond the inner wall, he didn't know what to expect, but he harbored no doubt he'd be up to the challenge—Trenan had been unwittingly training him for it and the prophecy proclaimed it. Now he had only one other task remaining that he'd decided to complete before stealing out on the adventure of his life.

Their swords clashed and Teryk's grip slipped; his weapon thumped on the dry ground inside the training circle and Trenan held the point of his weapon to the prince's throat. Teryk let his head sag forward and lowered his shield. It was the first time Trenan had bested him in more moons than he remembered, but it didn't matter—neither his heart nor his head were into sparring.

Trenan raised a brow. "This is unlike you, Teryk. Where's your fight today?"

"It's the sword," he said, waving his hand at the weapon lying in the dirt. "It needs sharpening."

"It fell from your grip because it's not sharp enough?"

Teryk shrugged and shuffled his feet, avoiding the master swordsman's sarcastic glare.

"Its dullness distracted me from the fight. You know I fight better than this."

"Indeed." Trenan bent and retrieved the prince's sword from the dirt, offered it to him pommel first. "Perhaps you should have it sharpened before we continue."

"I will." Teryk squinted up at the sun. "It's hot. Can we call it for today and resume tomorrow?"

Trenan took a moment to judge the time. "If your grace wishes."

"I do."

"Then we will resume on the morrow."

Teryk removed the helm and wiped sweat from his forehead and eyes on the sleeve of his shirt, then unbuckled the chest plate and handed it to the squire waiting at the edge of the practice circle to take it from him. The lad hurried off to hang it and the prince turned back to his trainer.

"Am I a good swordsman, Trenan?"

"The only other than your father who's beaten me."

The prince wiped his face on his sleeve again and noticed the master swordsman wasn't perspiring. He wasn't sure he'd ever seen a drop of sweat on the man's brow. Was lack of sweat a reward of being a master? If so, Teryk wondered why he perspired so when he bested Trenan most times. The squire returned a few seconds later, hands held out to take the prince's sword, his presence distracting Teryk from his pondering.

"Don't worry about this."

"Highness?" the lad said.

"I'll take it to the armory myself. It's been a while since I visited. Perhaps another weapon might catch my fancy."

The squire bowed his head and took his leave. Trenan stowed his own sword in its scabbard and gestured for the prince to lead the way out of the practice ring.

"I'll come with you, Your Grace. That way I can tell you about the weapons, should you choose to select a new one."

Teryk's heart jumped into his throat. The last item he needed for his journey was in the armory. If Trenan accompanied him, his plan would be compromised. Worse—Danya might suspect his lie.

"No need, Trenan. I can take care of it. Besides, don't you have a lesson with my sister first thing on the morrow? She told me last night she thinks she's gotten good enough to best you."

"Oh, did she?"

"You should stay to hone your skills and better defend your honor." He nudged the trainer in the ribs with his elbow, unsure if his story was convincing him. "If anything catches my eye, I'll bring it to you before I adopt it as my own."

"So it shall be, My Prince." Trenan bowed at the waist. "I shall see you on the morrow, either with sharpened sword or a new weapon for my inspection."

Teryk nodded his thanks and the master swordsman spun on his heel and left the practice ring. The prince slid the broadsword, which wasn't dull at all, back into its scabbard and set out toward the armory, relieved.

He strode across the training square toward the archway, the heels of his boots sending puffs of dust swirling into the late afternoon air as he reviewed his plan. He glanced toward the sun—still enough time to visit the armory, retrieve his pack and be on his way before Danya suspected his absence. Once he made it outside the walls of the inner city, he'd be beyond anyone's reach.

Teryk sighed. Deceiving his sister brought a sour taste to his mouth, but this was his burden to bear, and he'd do anything to keep from putting her in harm's way. If she came with him and ill befell her, he'd be unable to live with himself, and the king and queen would never forgive him.

The king. He'll soon see I'm ready to rule the kingdom.

He bit down hard on his teeth, the discomfort brought on by thoughts of their father driving the guilt for lying to his sister out of his head. If only the king recognized his worth, realized his potential to be more than a statesman. This would prove him worthy of their line.

Teryk passed through the arch and paused when he heard a clatter behind him. Glancing over his shoulder, he spied the guard who'd been sleeping outside his room jogging toward him, armor rattling, scabbard bouncing against his thigh. Teryk expected the man and had prepared. He raised a hand in greeting before he arrived.

"Ho! Rile, isn't it?"

"Yes, your highness." The guard skidded to a halt in front of the prince and bowed at the waist, breathing hard after his armor-clad run in the hot sun.

"You look parched, sir. Are you all right?"

"It is a hot day, my lord."

"Well, I'm merely on my way to the armory to have my sword sharpened, then I'll be back to finish my practice with Sir Trenan. Why don't you take the opportunity to fetch yourself some water and a bit of shade?"

"Very kind of you, my prince, but the king—"

"I'm sure the king did not mean for you to think you should melt while protecting me from a room filled with weapons and armor. Does he worry a stack of bucklers might fall on me? Or perhaps he thinks I'll cut myself?"

The guard chuckled then cleared his throat. "No, my prince. I s'pose he don't."

"Then run along and refresh yourself. It's too hot for either of us to be up to shenanigans. I'll see you at dinner."

"Thank you, my prince." Rile bowed and walked away at a much slower, more energy-conserving pace than he'd arrived at.

Teryk let the corner of his mouth curl up in the start of a smile. Danya had told him how she'd been unable to wake her guard when she'd returned to her chambers, so it didn't surprise him he'd so easily convinced Rile. He thought if he'd told the soldier the king required him to feed the chickens, or offered him a roll with the queen, he'd have been talked into leaving the prince be with as little effort.

He strolled past the gardens, forcing himself to a measured pace quick enough to carry him to his destination, but not so fast he'd attract attention. A mix of excitement and fear swirled inside him, making him want to hurry his step. Instead, he observed the array of colorful flora without seeing them, he waved to a maiden sniffing the flowers without recognizing her, his boots clopped on the flagstone path without noticing the sound.

He'd concealed the pack he'd take with him and the cloak for disguising himself in a patch of nerin bush near the armory, hidden behind broad, green leaves. His thoughts slipped back to the bag and the blue-tinted paper secreted within amongst the sparse belongings he'd packed. After Danya left his chambers, he'd sat on the divan and read it over and over again, doing his best to commit it to memory, but the words kept eluding him. A few fragments held on, and he turned them over in his head, attempting to reason through their nonsense.

Man from across the sea...

Small Gods...

Seed of life...

Nothing might be found across the sea but drowning and death. The Small Gods were tales told to young children to keep them from wandering off or a threat of punishment when they chose to be mischievous. And 'seed of life?' A foreign, unfamiliar term to Teryk; he had no idea to what it referred.

But he remembered one line, and it came back to him, repeating itself in his mind as the carved stone walls of the massive armory building loomed ahead of him.

The firstborn child of the rightful king.

Nothing else inscribed on the scroll mattered as much as that one line, the one proclaiming him the man to fulfill the prophecy.

A sense of pride that had eluded him through much of his life swelled in his chest as he mounted the steps to the armory; a smile crept onto his lips. He paused with his hand on the door's polished brass ring.

How strange; I am to become the most important man the kingdom has ever known, and they don't even know they need me yet.

He let the grin slip from his lips, replacing it with the veneer of command he'd seen his father wear whenever his ass polished the seat of the throne. The huge door creaked open, the bottom of the thick wood scraping on stone, and the prince entered the armory.

He'd been inside the building before, but not since his youth, when he'd accompanied his father during a routine inspection. At the time, he didn't know what made the review necessary when, other than the odd small skirmish, the kingdom had seen peace for an age. The king had explained the surveys were partly ceremony and partly preparedness, and then instructed the classroom master to increase the length of his lessons on matters of the court. Teryk never went with the king on another inspection, but the time he had was also the one and only time he'd seen Godsbane.

The air within the armory lay tepid and thick with the odor of oiled metal and fresh leather. He yanked the door closed behind him with a squeal of wood on stone, and stood in the antechamber, waiting, his eyes wandering over his surroundings.

A shield mounted to the wall bore the king's sign: a lion standing astride a fallen dear, the sun rising behind them, a scroll across the bottom that read 'The Mighty Shall Prevail.' Two halberds affixed to the stone crossed below the shield, their ornate axe heads framing the coat-of-arms. A low table and uncomfortable-looking chair provided the only other furnishings.

Teryk shifted from one foot to the other and became aware of the sweat-soaked undershirt cooling on his skin, sticking to his chest and back. He pinched it between two fingers and pulled it away, glad to be changing clothes soon.

The sound of metal clanking against metal rolled through the open door beside the shield and halberds. The prince craned his neck, attempting to spy someone to attend his needs, but he saw no one. He cleared his throat, but it surrendered no more than a squeak he'd have been loathe to admit belonged to him.

"Hello?" he called, feeling time growing short.

A scrape of something hard against stone responded, but no voice answered him.

"Hell—?"

"Hold onto ye horses!"

The shouted words bounced along the hall and into the antechamber and Teryk hoped the owner of the tongue that spoke them would follow along close behind. He crossed his arms and set his expression.

Grumbling, indistinct words tumbled through the door, followed by the scrape of leather soles on stone floor. A moment later, a man appeared. He wore a dirty green smock, dark breeches, and worn brown boots. His white hair stuck out from his head at odd angles and his cheeks and chin appeared as though the knife he'd used to shave had been far too dull.

"Can't give a man a moment's peace," he mumbled, not quite under his breath. "Almost dinner time an—"

He stopped when he saw Teryk standing in the armory's antechamber, a cross expression on his brow. The man's grumbles ceased and he bowed deep enough at the waist, the prince wondered if he'd find the strength to straighten his spine again.

"Apologies, my prince," the man said, his words directed toward the floor. "To what does a humble armorer owe the pleasure?"

"Rise," Teryk said, and the man did, his expression suitably contrite. The prince pulled his sword out of its scabbard. "My sword needs a new edge. Have you the time to accommodate me? I know dinner time approaches."

A blush rose in the man's cheeks. "A jest, my prince. That's all."

"Of course."

"But where is your squire? It's been so long since we've seen your highness in this humble storehouse."

"Exactly why I decided to come. It seems an age since I last set foot within these walls."

"I remember. You'd seen naught but ten turns, if'n I remember right."

"I believe you do." Teryk raised a brow; the man did have a familiarity about him. "So, you have time?"

"For the prince, I'll make time."

The man took three steps to close the distance between himself and the prince, then held his hands out to receive the weapon. Teryk relinquished it, placing the hilt in the armorer's right hand, the blade in his left. The old soldier stroked the edge with his thumb, then lifted it to his eye to gaze past the guard and along the blade. He grunted quietly at the back of his throat as he lowered it and trained his gaze on the prince.

"My lord, this weapon don't—"

"Sharpen it," Teryk said, dismissing the man's words with a wave of his fingers, the way he'd seen his father do a thousand times before. "How long will it take?"

"Not too long, judging by the shape of it, my prince."

"Fine. I'll pass the time amongst your stores. Call for me when you're done."

Without another word, the armorer bowed his head and retreated along the hallway from which he'd come. Teryk padded across the antechamber to the doorway and peeked around the edge, watching him until he disappeared.

The prince knew he'd be best to wait until the grating sound of the sword grinding against whetstone reached his ears, but he'd already spent more time than he'd intended. The instant the armorer's dirty green smock disappeared from sight, Teryk stole down the hallway after him, pausing when he got to the doorway to the grinding room.

With the man's back to the door, Teryk hurried past.

Beyond, the armory was a maze of corridors and doors, storerooms and display chambers. Many seasons had passed since his visit to the armory, but the prince thought he might still find his way.

Behind him, the noise of stone grinding steel began, allowing him to rush along the passages without worry of the hurried sound of his footsteps. He passed closed doors, each marked with a painted sign depicting the type of weapon or armor stored within, and Teryk wondered if the old armorer had drawn them himself.

He took a right, then a left, passed a door labeled with a sign depicting an open-faced helm, then another showing a bow. There seemed no rhyme nor reason to the placement of the different armor and weapons; the room containing arrows was located nowhere near the bows, hand axes and pole axes were stored in separate wings.

Panic built in the prince as he raced by doors marked with daggers, leather armor, pikes, javelins. Finally, he went past one with a sign depicting a sword, skidded to a stop and backtracked to it. He threw it open, convinced he'd come to the end of his search.

Racks of swords lined the walls, organized by size: short swords, sabers, bastard swords, broadswords. It took him but a few seconds to realize this was not the correct chamber. The king didn't allow Gods-bane to be kept in a storeroom with the other swords—the ceremonial sword of the crown required a chamber of its own.

Frustrated, Teryk shook his head and slammed the door. The panic in his gut spread, tingling along his arms and into his chest. He paused in the hallway, looking left then right, unsure which way to go, his breath panting between his lips. Could he have missed it?

He took a step back the way he came, then stopped, considered the other direction over his shoulder, wiped sweat off his palms on thighs. The twists and turns of the halls quieted the grinding sound of the armorer sharpening his blade to a quiet buzz. He didn't have much time before the old man finished.

Teryk passed the room of swords, continuing along the way he'd been going. Surely, he didn't miss the crownsword's display chamber. He couldn't recall what depiction adorned the sign mounted upon the door, but he hadn't seen one he thought appropriate to label the room containing Godsbane.

He rounded another corner, another. If he were in a forest, he'd have been lost beyond hope by now, but he took heart in the knowledge the armory building had one entrance and exit, and every passage led back to it, given enough steps. But would they lead him there in time?

The sound following him from the sharpening room faded away, replaced by a new one coming from in front of him. Teryk stopped, listened. The noise was far off and harsh. He took a few more steps, passing a sign depicting a round buckler, before realizing the source of the ruckus.

It was the same sound: the armorer sharpening his sword.

Teryk had traversed the maze of the armory building and come out the other side without finding the room for which he searched. His stomach sank, casting nausea into his throat.

The prophecy hadn't mentioned the crown sword—at least not that Teryk deciphered—so leaving without it wouldn't mean the end of his undertaking, but he'd convinced himself the sword needed to hang at his side. If he was to prove himself, he should do it with the weapon that represented his lineage and the kingdom in his hand.

But the time to find it was near running out.

Teryk pressed on, the noise of stone grinding metal growing louder as he advanced. He rounded one more corner and recognized the hall leading back to the antechamber, and to the sharpening room if he continued past. His head sagged, a hated feeling of defeat weighing his limbs.

"At least I'll have a sharp sword," he said aloud, pushing on toward the archway.

Two final doors, one on either side of the hall, lay between him and the antechamber. He forced himself to raise his eye to each as he approached and found the first bore a sign drawn with fire. Teryk stopped in front of it, his forehead wrinkled. He laid his hand upon the handle and pushed, but it didn't open.

Locked.

He'd found no other room in the armory locked.

Godsbane.

He bit down hard on his teeth and blew a frustrated breath through his nostrils. If he'd come the correct way, he'd have left himself enough time to figure a way to unlock the door. But as he stood before the door, staring at the depiction of orange and red flames, the dissonant grate of the sharpening stone stopped. Teryk glanced along the hall toward the door through which he'd seen the armorer enter, expecting him to reappear, calling the prince's name.

He'd failed.

The armorer must have paused to appraise his work and decided the blade required more because, a second later, the sound resumed. Teryk faced the door again, grasped the handle once more.

But why fire?

He stared at the painted lines on the wooden square mounted to the door. Godsbane had nothing to do with fire.

Teryk peered down the hall at the last door, the one closest to the archway leading back to the antechamber. Could it be he'd gone so far only to find he'd been so close?

The prince took his hand from the door handle and jogged the few paces to his last chance, his hand resting on the empty scabbard hanging at his waist to prevent it from banging against his leg. He stopped in front of the door and stared at the sign mounted upon it, his eyes wide.

A crown.

He shook his head and chuckled to himself, then remembered time was short. A keyhole below the door handle gave him pause. The room marked with fire had been locked, but did the other doors have keyholes? In his hurry, he hadn't paid attention. Neither the sword room nor any of the others had been locked. The prince's lips pressed into a line, he rested his fingers on the cool metal of the door handle.

And pushed the door open.

Godsbane lay on a display rack near the far wall, strategically placed windows in the ceiling casting light on its blade to make it shimmer as though aglow from within. Its jeweled scabbard lay on the wide pedestal in front of it, rubies and sapphires sparkling along the leather case as the sun dipped toward dinner time.

The grinding sound of a sword being sharpened ceased.

Teryk leapt into the room, rose-scented incense floating in the air finding his nose, and crossed the chamber in five long steps. He snatched the crown blade from its perch, reached for the scabbard with his other hand but paused before taking it. Godsbane's ornate, gold-trimmed hilt would be enough to garner more attention than the prince wanted; having the gaudy, gem-incrusted sheath hanging at his waist would identify him to anyone who spied it, perhaps get him arrested.

Or robbed.

He shook his head and slid the blade into his own empty scabbard, happy to find it mostly fit, leaving only an inch of Godsbane's engraved steel sticking out at the top. Not perfect, but better than the alternative.

Teryk spun and hurried back across the room, acutely aware he made the lone noises anywhere in the building. He peeked around the jamb, peering along the hall toward the sharpening room, but didn't see the armorer. Was he still in the room? Or had he finished and returned to the antechamber to present the prince with his newly-sharpened sword?

No, he'd have called for me.

Heart hammering in his chest, the prince sprinted the last few paces to the archway, through it into the antechamber. To his relief, it remained empty. He hurried to the door and pulled hard on the brass ring, his jaw clamped tight in preparation for the groan of the hinges, the scrape of the wood on the stone floor.

Still no sound from the sharpening room.

He yanked the door open and bolted out into the hot evening leaving the portal ajar behind him.

The patter of quick footsteps in the hall made Shourn raise a brow; he paused in rubbing the cloth dowsed with oil along the length of the prince's blade.

"What's he up to?" the armorer murmured.

He dropped the square of fabric on the stool and picked up another, wiped his fingers on its soft, dry surface first, then used it to wipe the excess oil from the sword. He lifted the hilt to his eye, gazed along the fine edge and nodded, satisfied with his work. The steel hadn't been dull, so he didn't know why the prince insisted he sharpen it, but it wasn't his place to question the young man who'd be his king one day. If he'd learned anything in his life, it was to kiss the ass of any man with the ability to make his life miserable just because the mood struck him.

The soft cloth whispered along the blade one more time, Shourn talking extra care not to shave the skin off his finger, but he halted at another sound.

The outer door opening.

Shourn's forehead creased. Who else needed an old man so close to dinner time? He had a few choice words picked out if it turned out to be anyone but the king himself. Distracted and a little bit more careless than usual, he took the cloth from the blade and accidentally touched his thumb to the sword. The fresh edge cut him and he sucked a breath through his teeth, jammed his thumb into his mouth. The rusty tang of blood flooded his tongue.

"Dammit," he muttered around his sliced digit.

He tossed the cloth aside, returned his injured thumb to his mouth, and stalked down the hall to the antechamber, Prince Teryk's sword in hand.

"Dis better be 'ood," he said, words distorted by a mouth full of thumb.

The door stood open, the chamber empty.

His eyes darted around the sparse room and found only the furnishings intended to be there. He leaned back and peered one way along the hall, then the other. Empty. No one had gone past the sharpening room; he'd have noticed if they did as he'd noticed the prince sneaking by earlier. Not sure why he'd needed to sneak, but the prince could do whatever he wanted, he supposed.

Shourn shook his head and popped his thumb out if his mouth.

"Prince Teryk?"

His voice echoed along the hall, but received no response.

"Your highness?"

Nothing. Shourn shrugged and shook his head, returned to the antechamber and put the prince's sword on the low table.

"What's so important a prince needs to leave before his sword's ready?"

He went to the door and looked up at the sky, gauging the time by the sun's position. Morth should be dragging his lazy ass around the corner any time, coming to relieve him so he could get dinner in his belly. About time.

Shourn pushed the door closed, still shaking his head as he sat in the chair, admiring the prince's freshly-edged blade. He returned his thumb to his mouth, sucking on the rusty flavor of blood mingled with the bitter taste of oil.

"Fuckin' printh," he murmured. His stomach growled and he settled back in the chair, waiting for Morth.

XVI - Ailyssa - Bloodless

THE EDGE OF THE bedframe pressed against the back of N'th Ailyssa Ra's thighs, the thin mattress compressed almost to nothing beneath her weight, but she didn't notice the discomfort as she stared at the wall.

It occurred to her the stone wall and its markings had consumed much of her waking hours these past few turns of the moon. The number of chalk lines drawn upon its surface remained at ninety-eight despite the number of sunrises since she drew the last mark.

Still she didn't bleed, and no child grew in her belly.

How could there be? She'd carry no babe if her blood was done. More importantly, no woman made a babe without coupling.

Ninety-eight lines which should be one hundred and five. The wall had lost count but, after most of a lifetime spent keeping track, N'th Ailyssa Ra's mind had not.

She inhaled deeply, tasting the familiar hint of chalk dust in the air, then let her breath out with a sound of resignation. Whenever she named herself in her thoughts, she did so with all of her titles, knowing the time when she'd no longer be able to use them drew nigh.

Hands on her knees, she pushed herself up from the bed, unsure what to do next. She'd said her morning prayers to the Goddess, thanking her for the sun and the moon, the grass and birds and sky, but skipping the thanks for her womb. At the end of the supplications performed by every member of the order, she added her own words, as she had each dawn, afternoon, and sunset for one hundred and five risings of the sun. She beseeched the Goddess to return her blood, to give her another chance to honor her with a fertile Daughter.

But the Goddess had forsaken her. Her blood had not renewed its flow and the man they brought her for coupling—her last opportunity to produce a child that might save, or at least prolong, her position in the order—had been the one man with whom she'd never bring herself to procreate.

Her son.

She pursed her lips and hung her head, a righteous anger she'd never experienced brewing in her belly in place of the child she was unable to conceive. It tingled along her arms, clenched her fists, tightened her throat. She raised her head, glared at the rows of chalk lines on the wall, the wounds in the stone above them indicative of her life gone by. Every one of them—etched and chalk-drawn, both—angered her further. Each one wounded her as though carved into her soul by the Goddess herself.

Ailyssa stomped across the room and snatched the rag off the shelf. She shook it out, sending a puff of dust whirling through the air, but stopped before putting it to its use. It had been so long since she'd touched the rough material, an age since she cleansed the wall of its accusing marks.

The cloth dangled from her fingers as she held it out, hesitating a hand's breadth from the stone wall, arm quivering. She inhaled a hard breath through her nose, forced it back out, her teeth clamped tight behind her lips. Never had she erased the sacred lines marking the moon's passing before her blood came and told her to do so. But neither had she stopped inscribing the lines before the time to stop had come, until now. Her trembling hand moved toward the wall.

The knock on the door startled her, and the restoring cloth fell from her hand.

With a surprised gasp, Ailyssa plucked the square off the floor and fumbled it back into its spot on the shelf, folded just so beside the nub of chalk she'd worn down to almost nothing since her last bleed. When it was back in place, she wiped her fingers on the front of her smock and waved her hand in the air to disperse the chalk dust floating around her head.

He told.

The thought stabbed her heart. She'd begged him not to tell anyone they hadn't coupled, though it truly didn't matter if he did or not.

What difference would it make if he didn't? A few days? The lack of time she had remaining didn't cause her nearly as much pain as the possibility of her son's betrayal.

Ailyssa's fingers touched the handle, but she didn't pull it open immediately. She took an instant to compose herself, smoothing her smock and rubbing her hand along the gray stubble on her head. A swallow of bitter saliva was the most she could do to convert the anger and hurt in her belly to something else.

N'th Adesi Re probably meant her smile to calm and comfort her friend before she spoke any words. She held her hands tucked into the sleeves of her red trimmed-with-white Matron's smock and, when Ailyssa said nothing in greeting nor invited her in, Adesi tilted her head to one side.

"Are you all right, N'th Ailyssa Ra?"

Hearing the Matron speak the falsely earned title stung Ailyssa as surely as if a fire wasp flew into the room and planted its business end into her heart. The inexplicable rage filling her dissolved, leaving behind an emptiness that threatened to suck itself full of despair.

"Forgive me, N'th Adesi Re. Please, come in." The Matron entered the room as Ailyssa stepped aside.

"Leave the door open, Mother."

"Of course."

The Matron had never given her such an instruction before; the women of the order considered privacy of high value. They gathered for prayer, meals, exercise, and ritual, but the rest of the time they spent in private studies and communing with the Goddess, living their lives behind closed doors. A door left ajar was highly unusual, and Ailyssa suppressed a shiver at the implication of having done so.

Adesi strode to the center of the room and stopped, Ailyssa a pace behind her. She didn't need to see the Matron's eyes to know her gaze lay upon the marking wall. The woman silently counted the chalk marks every time she entered the room, calculating how many there were and how many there should be. Perspiration sprang to Ailyssa's hands, so she rubbed her fingertips together, loathing the wetness on her skin.

"Hmm," the Matron breathed. "You have stopped counting."

Ailyssa gazed at her feet as N'th Adesi Re turned her scrutiny from the stone wall to her friend. Silence hung between them, palpable and weighty. It filled the gap as though water had been poured into the room and, though Ailyssa searched for the ability to speak words, they eluded her, the silence choking her.

"Ailyssa?"

She raised her head to the Matron, whose calming smile had waned. Her lips lay flat and concerned upon her face.

"I have, N'th Adesi Re."

"Why have you stopped? Have you given up?"

Ailyssa inhaled through her nose, a sob teetering on its edge. "My blood has not come."

She wanted to divert her gaze from the Matron's more than she'd ever wanted to do anything in her life. More than she wanted to carry a child, more than she wanted to bleed anew. If she could just look away, she wouldn't care if she ever flowed again. The Matron put a hand on her forearm, her expression brightening.

"Perhaps you are seeded, Mother. Have you felt any signs?"

Ailyssa shook her head and a tear drew a wet path down her cheek.

"There is still time," Adesi said, nodding but not sounding convinced herself. "I have heard of—"

He didn't tell her. I've given myself away.

"No, Matron. I cannot be with child."

Ailyssa closed her eyes, quashing her urge to cry. When she opened them, N'th Adesi Re had tilted her head to the side again, questioning without speaking words. She wondered if she remained quiet long enough, would Adesi ask the question or simply let the silence go on until the Goddess summoned them to their next lives?

But she couldn't stand the hush. The Goddess considered the keeping of truth to oneself no better than a lie. Ailyssa had been lying long enough.

"We...we didn't couple."

"What?" Adesi's eyes went wide. "But why not, Ailyssa? The man was fertile. He was your last chance."

"He was..." Ailyssa hesitated, her eyes flickering away from the Matron's gaze to the wall behind her, the scratches of her life, the chalk marks condemning her. The words about to pass her lips would make those lines of condemnation seem pale. "He was my son."

N'th Adesi Re's hand dropped from Ailyssa's arm, her face became stony. The eyes Ailyssa had come to know as the caring eyes of a friend filled with aversion, as if she'd forced the Matron to eat a distasteful bit of food.

"Heretic," she spat. "No Mother has a son."

Ailyssa's chest tightened around her heart and lungs, forcing rapid blood through her veins, constricting her breath. She shook her head and a mewling sound akin to the cry of a distressed kitten slipped from her throat. Her hand reached out, fingers clawing for the front of the Matron's smock, but N'th Adesi Re stepped away, avoiding her touch like it carried disease.

"Your flow has ceased. You carry no child and neither you nor your Daughter have honored the Goddess, and now you utter the word 'son.'"

She shook her head, more tears spilling down her cheeks.

"You have birthed boys, too, Adesi," she said, her words choked. "You must wonder where they are, who they've become. Surely you have missed them, grieved them."

"Never."

The word fell to the floor like a stone spit from her mouth. She glared, her lips pursed, but didn't move. Ailyssa imagined what the Matron must be thinking: she'd come to offer her friend encouragement and goodwill and received sacrilege in return, words spoken against the sacred Goddess.

But how can a woman bring a child into the world and then forget him?

She parted her lips to say so, but the Matron raised her hand and slapped her hard across the cheek. Ailyssa's head jerked with the impact and she raised her own hand, touching the stinging flesh, and stared aghast at her friend.

"Adesi—"

"My name is N'th Adesi Re, Ailyssa," the Matron said. "And you will be stripped of your titles and expelled from the order."

She swept past Ailyssa toward the door, her red trimmed-with-white smock whirling around her. In desperation, Ailyssa caught her by the sleeve, stopping her and spinning her back.

"You can't," she shouted, tears flowing hard. "I've lived my whole life for the Goddess. You can't."

Adesi brushed her aside and approached the counting wall, arm raised and finger extended. The pad of her fingertip touched the circle drawn around a rut carved thirty-two before the last.

"You betrayed the Goddess the day you drew this," she said. "It is no wonder you have failed to mother a child for her honor since."

Ailyssa shook her head, but the Matron continued, forcing one last sliver of despair into her heart.

"On this day, the Goddess struck you barren and cast you out. The order should have done the same."

She strode for the door again, jarring Ailyssa with her shoulder and knocking her to the bed as she passed.

"No."

Ailyssa reached out stretching her fingers toward N'th Adesi Re, her one-time friend, but the Matron did not pause or hesitate. She went through the door, slamming it behind her, the impact making the shelf on the wall shudder. The cleansing cloth fell to the floor in a puff of chalk dust.

The woman once known as N'th Ailyssa Ra, now known only as Ailyssa, a woman who'd spent her entire life in service of the Goddess, collapsed on the bed in a heap of tears and sobs. In all the time she'd inscribed scars on the wall to mark the passage of sunrises and seasons, she'd never set foot outside the order's compound, and now she'd be cast out to live the rest of her days alone. No attendants or sisters, no fellow Mothers or Matrons.

And no Goddess.

Ailyssa buried her face in the pillow and prayed for the Goddess to grant her one last request: she wished for her life to come to an end.

XVII - Teryk - Procession

THE PROCESSION OF MERCHANTS rumbled along the inter-locking bricks of the promenade. Horse's hooves struck occasional sparks, wooden wheels clattered, boot heels clicked. At each cross street, another half dozen men leading pack animals or driving wagons, bearing stuffed-full packs or accompanied by man servants carrying their loads, joined the parade.

A thrill coursed through Teryk's veins. It had been near three full turns of the moon since he last set foot in the inner city, though he'd been here many times before. He recognized the Barzunian Fountain as they passed, its gold-leafed statue of Barzun the Bountiful bearing witness over Merchants' Square. The cleaners had already set to work scrubbing the day's bird droppings from poor Barzun's brow and, by morning, he'd be clean and sparkling, ready for another round of pigeon shit to find its way onto his head.

The column of men, wagons, donkeys, and horses made their way along the Promenade, passing the Avenue of Kings with its colorful banners dangling slack in the windless evening, then Duchess Way lined with shops selling the baubles and face paints any self-respecting noblewoman considered embarrassing to be caught without.

Teryk filled his lungs with the clean, fresh air. The scent of baked goods and roast meat hung in the air, wafting out of the food shops and taverns along Ellora Way, the bakeries finishing for the day and disposing of their leftovers, the public houses getting set to bustle through the night. Being in the inner city lifted his spirits—he hardly believed he'd made it this far.

Sneaking out of Draekfarren castle had been harrowing, but not so difficult as the prince thought it might be. As he'd made his way out, disguised amongst a group of cleaners moving from their duties within the castle to other chores in the city, he'd sensed every eye upon him. With each step, he expected someone to stop him and ask questions, or perhaps feel Trenan's—or worse, his father's—hand on his shoulder, but he didn't. He'd slipped through the gate with the troop of cleaners and disposed of the cleaning smock he'd used to blend in the instant he passed beyond sight of the gate.

Now, wearing a crimson waistcoat embroidered with gold thread and edged with gold piping, a white cotton shirt with flared sleeves, and purple britches he thought made him resemble a dandy more than a peddler, he blended in with the merchants. A silver gazelle-head clasp held a deeper red cloak in place around his neck, the cape's hood ready to be pulled up to conceal his identity when they approached Merchant Gate.

Hidden beneath the folds of his cloak, the stolen crown sword bumped reassuringly against his leg, its touch lending him confidence. The mute euphoria of his initial success helped him ignore the guilt he held over deceiving his sister, though the thought of disobeying their father didn't bother him in the least. He only lamented that Trenan might be blamed, but he'd decided he didn't care what happened to the crotchety old armorer.

Teryk shifted the sword on his hip and glanced at the man beside him, saw the merchant's black cape hid any weapon he might be carrying. A niggling worry wormed into the back of his mind, so the prince wended his way through the column, inspecting each merchant and man servant for what weapons they carried and how ornamented they were.

He eyed a dark-skinned southerner, a satchel of fragrant spices thrown over his shoulder and a broad grin on his face, but the sash around his waist was empty. A hawk-nosed man with a scar on his cheek sat on a bench at the front of a cart, urging his beleaguered-look-ing pony as it pulled his wagon laden with the vegetables he hadn't sold at today's market. The closest thing to a weapon he carried was a short, leather switch he used to encourage the poor beast.

Man after man he surveyed and found each one of them without sword or dagger, axe or spear. Not even a whip amongst them. Finally, it occurred to the prince: merchants were not permitted to carry weapons into the inner city for any reason other than sale. The prince rubbed his palm on the sword's grip, worried it wouldn't be the distinctiveness of the blade that might reveal him, but the mere fact he carried a weapon at all.

Teryk's stomach jumped with the realization. If he attempted to exit the gate as the only man carrying a sword, he'd surely be stopped. They'd ask questions at the very least; more likely, he'd be arrested. The prospect of arrest didn't cause him distress; no matter what, he was the prince and he wouldn't spend a moment in the brig, but they'd inform his father and end his adventure before it began.

His eyes darted from man to man, handcart to wagon. Somewhere amongst this assortment of goods and wares, he needed to find a place to secret the crown sword until they exited through the gate.

Teryk jogged forward, pushed his way between a tall, wide man wearing a turban wrapped around his head and his man servant pushing a handcart loaded with boxes containing intricate glass beads strung together in necklaces and bracelets. They grumbled at him, but he paid them no mind. He passed a wagon loaded with wood carvings, then a man lugging a sack with sharp angles pressing out from inside, distorting its shape.

Raising his head, Teryk saw the procession was approaching the gate. Two guards posted on either side, hands resting on their weapons, surveyed the line of merchants passing under the high marble arch. Guardhouses stood to both sides, more men within. A drop of sweat rolled down Teryk's temple.

He slowed his pace, falling back in the column to give himself an opportunity to think, to find somewhere to hide the blade. Each time it bumped against his thigh, it added to his building worry instead of offering comfort as it had moments before.

He considered tossing it over the side of the wagon loaded with carvings, but it might be easily noticed. Perhaps the wagon of produce—he could secret the blade beneath a sack of rutabagas. It'd be safe hidden amongst carrots and potatoes if they didn't search the wagon. They didn't appear to be stopping the merchants, but if one of the guards glimpsed the scabbard's tip poking out from under the vegetables, they'd have reason to search. Teryk would lose the sword and be responsible for an innocent man's incarceration.

I may have to leave it behind.

The prince sucked his bottom lip, eyes darting, searching for a hiding spot as the gate loomed. He fell back farther in the column, ready to concede the necessity of abandoning the crown sword. A shame—who knew what might happen to the precious weapon when an unsuspecting citizen wandering the inner-city streets found it. The thought of embarking on his journey to save the kingdom without a weapon didn't worry him—he'd purchase another blade once he reached the outer city. But ending whatever peril awaited with Godsbane in his hand had become part of the dream, a symbol of his ascension as successor to the throne.

Teryk unbuckled the sword belt, carefully keeping it hidden beneath his cloak as he sought somewhere to abandon it, when a glint of sunlight on steel caught his eye. The wagon rumbling along the Promenade behind him, second to last in the procession, belonged to a weapons merchant.

Relief flooded the prince's chest. He stepped aside and allowed the two horses pulling the cart to pass, then nodded at the man driving them—a tall, thin man, with legs so long his knees touched his chest as he sat on the bench with the reins in his hands. The man didn't return the prince's greeting, nor did the burly fellow sitting at his side.

The wagon passed, swords and daggers rattling against helms and chest plates in its bed. Teryk fell in behind, hurrying his pace to keep up. He peered left and right, saw no one watching, and reached over to place his sword gently in the wagon with the other weapons. Neither of the men driving the wagon noticed him and they kept their eyes on the avenue and gate ahead.

Even nestled amongst an array of finely-made weapons, Godsbane stood out. The intricate ornamentation of its grip, the majestic engraving noticeable on the blade that didn't fit inside the sheath; it was a weapon among weapons.

Teryk thanked the one God he'd decided to leave the jeweled scabbard in the armory.

He slowed, falling back from the weapon maker's wagon, glanced away to find the fellow driving the cart bringing up the rear glaring at him. Teryk smiled, shrugged, and the man looked away as though he intended to mind his own business. The prince pulled up the hood of his cloak to hide his face.

The column of merchants flowed through the gate with hardly a pause. Guards silently watched them go by, nudging each other on occasion and pointing to items that caught their attention. When the wagon hauling the wood carvings drew up to the gate, one of the guards halted the procession to haggle with the man over a toy wheeled horse with a long, red string tied around its neck.

Another jolt of worry shot through Teryk. What if they stopped the weapons seller? What if one of them spied the crown sword and wanted to purchase it? Would the merchant recognize it didn't belong amongst his wares and say something, or graciously accept whatever coin might be offered, then be on his way with a fuller purse?

Teryk licked his lips and stretched on his toes to peer over the edge of the wagon. To his relief, the cart's juddering had settled Godsbane in amongst the other swords; one had slid across it, hiding the two fingers of intricately scrolled blade protruding from the scabbard.

The last group of men before the weapon maker's wagon passed under the arch. The prince rubbed his thumb against the tips of his fingers, attempting to dry the perspiration springing up on his hands. To distract himself, he counted the steps bringing him closer to freedom from both the inner city and his worry.

A guard held up his hand, gesturing for the wagon to halt. The weapons merchant reined his horses to a stop. Teryk's heart jumped into his throat as the armored man strode up to the wagon and laid his palm on the edge by the driver's seat. The weapons seller doffed his hat.

"Good day, sir. How can I be of service?"

"I need me an axe," the guard said. "The head snapped off me last one."

"Obviously not purchased from me." The driver unfolded his ungainly legs and stepped down. He didn't require the use of the step. "Let's have a look what we have."

The merchant's burly companion remained in his seat, waiting while the other man took the guard to the back of the wagon to peruse his wares. He undid the latch and opened the back, swept his arm across the assortment of armaments with a grand gesture.

"Fellick and Ive have only the best weapons for sale, good sir. We acquire these items from the best smithies in the kingdom, take the time to ensure they use the purest steel."

The guard grunted and moved aside a spear and a buckler. Other items in the wagon shifted and Teryk drew a sharp breath through his nose as Godsbane slipped from under the pile of swords. The merchant must have heard the gasp because he spun toward him, a frown on his lips, but when the guard hefted a short-handled axe, its well-honed edge gleaming, he replaced the sour expression with a smile.

"This one might do." He stepped back and gave it a good swing, the angular head whistling through the air. "How much?"

"You are a man who knows fine weapons. That one—"

"Don't care 'bout its history. How much?"

The merchant rubbed his chin, assessing his customer. "Two and three."

"Two and three? Robbery. I'll give you two, and not a piece more."

"But sir, observe the workmanship, test the perfect balance. I can't let it go for less than two and two without feeling I've given away one of my children."

Teryk's gaze moved from the crown sword to the two men. Neither of them seemed to have noticed it, and the merchant's beefy companion continued staring straight ahead through the gates.

"Whatcha think, Urk," the man called out waving the axe over his head. "Two and two?"

The other guard shrugged.

"You won't find a weapon of this quality for a lower price anywhere else, sir. In fact, you likely won't even find one of this quality anyplace."

The guard studied the weapon as though considering his reflection in the polished steel. He hefted it again.

"Two and one. That's final."

The merchant rubbed his chin, scratched his cheek—gestures undoubtedly made for show. "Done!"

The guard's cheeks strained to contain a suppressed a grin. He obviously thought he'd gotten the best of the merchant, but the smile on the tall man's lips suggested the opposite might be the truth. The buyer fished the three coins out of a pouch on his belt—two coppers and one iron, as they'd negotiated—then returned to his post. Teryk let out his breath as the merchant slammed the wagon closed and shot the bolt, but the man hesitated, looking into the bed, before returning to his seat.

Did he see?

The tall fellow snapped the reins and his horses moved again, pulling his wagon of wares under the gate's high arch. Teryk followed close behind, cowl pulled up to hide his face, suddenly aware of a new problem: the lack of items he carried. He carried his pack slung over his shoulder, but if a guard searched it, he'd find it contained a change of clothes, a flint and steel, some twine, some coins, and a few days' rations. Not exactly a merchant's wares.

Teryk paced forward, staring at his feet and hoping for the guards to let him pass unharried. One of them cleared his throat and Teryk looked up to find the man who'd purchased the axe glaring at him. The prince nodded, the guard scowled.

A moment later, Teryk passed under the marble arch, his feet treading upon ground they'd never in his life touched. Outside the gate, the Promenade deteriorated from interlocking bricks to gravel, the wheels of the weapons merchant's wagon crunching through the loose pebbles.

They went by another pair of gatehouses, presumably manned by more guards, though Teryk saw none. Ahead, squat stone buildings lined the street, timber beams protruding from their sides at regular intervals to support their roofs. These were the barracks used to quarter the soldiers of the kingdom's army, he knew, though he'd never seen them. Simply knowing who lived within the buildings made their thick walls and dark windows appear more ominous.

Steel squawked against stone behind them, and Teryk glanced back over his shoulder to see the portcullis lowering into place. After that, the great wooden gates would swing closed, keeping the inner city in and, more importantly, the outer city out.

I did it.

A jolt of excitement energized his limbs.

I'm in the outer city.

Teryk hurried his pace, catching up to the weapons merchants' wagon. He reached over the side, wrapped his fingers around the crown sword.

"Oy! Whatcha think you're doin'?"

The voice startled the prince. Bitter saliva flooded his mouth as he raised his eyes to find the brawny man scowling at him.

"I...I'm..." He realized how lame and unlikely his true story sounded. He spit it out anyway. "I knew the guards would take my sword if I tried to bring it through. I stowed it in your wagon for safe keeping."

The tall man reined the horses in, bringing the wagon to a halt. Teryk held onto Godsbane, unsure if doing so was the best course of action, but the big man's glare froze him. He didn't move while the driver unfurled his legs again and climbed off his seat.

"I see you're interested in our wares," he said, drumming his fingers together.

"No, this sword is mine."

His teeth showing in what might be construed as either a grin or a snarl, the tall fellow cocked his head to one side. Behind him, the burly man descended from the bench, the wagon bouncing beneath his weight. Teryk swallowed hard.

"It doesn't appear to be yours, it appears to be ours. What do you think, Fellick?"

"It be in our wagon. Think that makes it ours."

A line of sweat formed between the prince's shoulder blades, sticking his shirt to his back. His gaze flickered from the thin man called Ive to the much larger Fellick, assessing them. Two against one, not good odds even if he thought he'd be able to free Godsbane from the scabbard before they fell upon him, which he didn't think he could. He peeked over his shoulder at the other wagon drawing up behind them—the man who'd seen him stow the sword.

The prince pointed with his free hand. "He saw. Ask him, he'll tell you." He donned a pleading look.

"What say you, Ebben?" Ive called. "Did you see such a thing?"

Ebben glanced between the three men. Teryk nodded at him, raised an expectant brow. The merchant coughed, spat, and snapped his reins, guiding his horse and wagon around the others stopped in the middle of the avenue without a word.

The wooden wheels rumbled past and Teryk considered imploring him to tell the pair of weapons sellers the truth, but he realized the man wouldn't get involved in another merchant's dispute. Minutes ago, the prince had hoped for the man to mind his business, now he hated him for doing so.

"It seems it's your word against ours," Ive said. "And since there's one of you and two of us..."

"But it's mine."

"Well, it can be." The tall merchant rubbed his chin, then spoke to his partner. "How much do you think, Fellick?"

"Four," the burly man said without moving his gaze from Teryk.

A wave of relief flooded through the prince. Four was a fair price for a sword, and a bargain to get him out of this situation with Godsbane in hand and his limbs still attached.

"Four it is," Ive said, nodding once. "Four gold."

Teryk nearly dropped the sword. "Four gold? Have you taken leave of your senses? Four gold buys a house and barn with a horse and wagon, not a sword."

"That be the price," Fellick said taking an ominous step toward him. "You want it or not?"

The prince's eyes flickered between the men. The cold sweat between his shoulder blades ran down his back into the crack of his ass and he shuffled from his left foot to his right, his pulse pounding in his temple.

"Fine," he whispered.

"Didn't hear ya." Fellick approached another pace.

"Fine. Four gold."

"We have a deal," Ive declared, clapping his hands as though the crack of his palms sealed the contract.

Teryk pulled the crown sword out of the wagon and moved to fasten the belt around his waist, but Fellick stopped him with a hand on his arm. The prince saw the muscles rippling in the man's forearm, the surly expression darkening his countenance, and understood the man's role in the partnership.

"Ya pay the coin before ya wear it."

With no point to defying the man, Teryk leaned the sword against the back of the wagon, unslung his pack and reached inside, his fingers groping for a secret pocket sewn in the front. It proved difficult to find without opening the pack, but he didn't want to reveal the hidden compartment and expose his cache to these two men. After a moment, he pulled his hand out, the four coins clutched between his fingers.

He held them up, the gold glittering in the waning light, and rubbed them together. Fellick tilted his head toward Ive.

"I'll take them," the tall man said.

Teryk extended his hand and dropped the coins into Ive's waiting palm. They clinked against one another and the merchant grinned.

"I do love that sound. A pleasure doing business with you."

Fellick took his hand off the prince's arm and backed away a step, granting silent permission for Teryk to retrieve his purchase. The prince wrapped his fingers around the scabbard and picked it up; Ive paused, eyeing the weapon before returning to his seat.

"That is an exquisite sword, isn't it?"

Teryk swung his cloak open and ushered the sword beneath. "It's mine. We struck a deal."

"Indeed, we did," he said and raised a brow.

For a moment, it seemed he might say more. Instead, he nodded once to his partner and the two men returned to their seats, the wagon groaning under Fellick's bulk as he climbed in. Ive carefully folded his legs into place and shook the reins. The horses set out with a jingle of harnesses and the crunch of hooves on gravel.

Ive's laugh wafted over his shoulder like a foul smell; Teryk's nostrils flared, his lips pressed into a bloodless white slash across his face. At least he had Godsbane back, even if it cost him.

"Perhaps we'll meet again," the lanky merchant tossed back as they drew away.

"If we do, it will be so I can remove your head for being a cheat," Teryk muttered, careful not to speak loud enough for Fellick and Ive to hear.

He stood in the middle of the road, glaring after the wagon rattling away as the sun sank toward the horizon. His hand shook with anger and disappointment with himself, but after a few moments to regain his composure, he realized his situation.

They left him with his purse considerably lighter, but a valuable lesson: trust no one. This wasn't Draekfarren castle anymore, nor the inner city. For the first time in his life, Teryk was in the outer city. His quest to become a hero had begun.

A shiver ran up his spine.

XVIII - Small God - Father Raven

*S*UNLIGHT GLEAMED ON FATHER Raven's midnight feathers; Thorn watched the huge bird hop across the clearing, felt the ground shudder with his power. Thorn stepped to his right, his skin color shifting with his background, and hefted his spear.

"I see you, little one," the bird said without looking at his stalker. "If you think to poke me with your pathetic stick, I'll peck out both your eyes."

Thorn laughed and allowed his skin to return to gray. "Thorn means you no harm, Father Raven. He has a deal for you."

The bird spun abruptly, flapped its wings once and leapt across the clearing to land in front of Thorn. The raven loomed over him, taller than two stormbirds stacked atop one another. No doubt Father Raven's size and powerful wings could carry him to the sky, given the chance.

"What deal do you have for me?" the raven squawked. "I don't need food, unless you're offering yourself. You do look tasty."

Thorn beamed. He knew the bird wouldn't eat him, he was merely trying to throw a playful scare into him, as when he threatened to peck his eyes. The bird might be large and strong, but they both understood his size and power were no match for one like Thorn.

"Thorn is too small to make a meal for Father Raven. Stringy and bitter. Blechh! Worms taste better than Thorn."

"Then why do you disturb my hunt?"

"A deal!"

Thorn bounded to the side, danced and whirled a circle around the huge bird. Father Raven watched, first with one eye, then the other. Thorn sensed his dubiousness, but once he'd listened to the proposition, his doubt would metamorphose to gratitude.

"Quit your prancing, little one. It will soon be time for my nap, so if you have a bargain to discuss, out with it before my interest wanes."

Thorn made one more circuit around the bird before skidding to a halt in front of him. The bird tilted its head, fixed the small gray man in the gaze of one black eye.

"Thorn can help you fly." He spoke it as though he told a secret, but the raven's reaction held no secrecy.

"Ha!" he guffawed. "I can already fly. You waste my time."

Father Raven made one short hop, but Thorn leapt up and grabbed a chest feather, tugging it and stopping him. The bird dislodged him with a firm shake.

"Don't pull my feathers."

Thorn ignored him. "How high can you fly, Father Raven?"

"To the tops of the trees," he said, his chest puffing with pride. "Higher than any other bird can fly."

"Hmm. Not so bad, I guess."

"Not so bad? What bird flies higher?"

"Thorn helped a stormbird fly higher not four sunrises past. Higher than the tops of the trees." He leaned in, held his hand up beside his mouth and lowered his voice. "Higher than the veil."

Father Raven's sooty eye glared at him. His beak opened and closed with a click. A moment passed and Thorn waited for the bird to agree to hear his proposition, waiting for the Father of Ravens to proclaim what an amazing feat Thorn had performed. He did neither.

"Impossible." Anger rumbled in its voice. Anger and a hint of interest. "No bird flies higher than Father Raven. How is this possible?"

Thorn jumped back and spread his arms, a wide smile on his lips. "Thorn did it."

The raven shook its head. "Your kind's magic keeps birds from flying higher, to keep us from crossing the veil and taking magic out where it doesn't belong."

"The stormbird crossed the veil."

Father Raven cocked his head, then tilted it back toward the bright sky hanging over his clearing. Thorn waited, patient. He'd dealt with the bird enough times in the past to know his pride. After a few seconds, the raven returned its dark gaze to Thorn.

"No one can release the binding."

"Thorn can. Thorn did."

"You did?"

He nodded.

"You'd do it for me?"

Thorn's grin spread wider.

Father Raven's head tilted. "And what do you ask in return?"

"Take Thorn with you."

Insects the raven normally would have snatched out of the air with his hungry beak buzzed around them as the two stared at each other, the bird's head canted to one side, the gray man's smile sparkling in the sun. Wind rustled the leaves, stirred the grass around Thorn's bare legs, tickling his thighs. He kept his gaze and his grin on the bird. After a long while, the bird finally spoke.

"We have an agreement."

Thorn whooped and danced, spun in circles until his head threatened to spill him to the ground. The raven watched with its unreadable face, its beak set in the same expression it always kept, its eyes staring one at Thorn the other at the sky. When the man's jubilation died away, the raven leaned in close, laid its beak on Thorn's shoulder, clicked it together once in his ear.

"Do not embarrass me, little one. I do not like to be embarrassed."

"Neither does Thorn."

The bird settled back. "What do we do?"

"Crouch, Father Raven. Thorn will ride on your back."

"No one rides on the back of the Father of Ravens," the bird snorted.

Thorn's smile sagged. "Thorn thought we struck a deal."

"Well, yes, but—"

"But...?"

The raven stared at him for a moment, then puffed up its feathers, shook them out, and settled on the ground as low as he could go. Thorn grabbed a handful of feathers and catapulted himself onto the bird's back.

"I told you not to pull my feathers."

Thorn laughed and shimmied himself into the spot where the bird's head met its back, gripping with his legs. He wiggled around until he found comfort, then closed his eyes.

"Do I fly now?" Father Raven asked.

"Sshhh. Thorn will say when it is time."

He leaned forward and extended his hand over the bird's head. Breaking the binds holding Father Raven close to the ground needed more energy than he'd expended for the stormbird. A bird as mighty as this one required powerful binding, and powerful magic to break them.

Thorn pictured the top of the forest, the sky beyond. He imagined touching the clouds with the tips of his fingers, looking down at towering trees reduced to splinters, vast pastures shrunken to patches of color. Wind moved his hair, sun warmed his skin, the scent of trees and grass, dirt and water fell away, replaced by fresh, clear, odorless air. While his mind conjured these things, his body directed its energy into the raven, passing his power to the bird. A portion of it he'd never get back, a cost he willingly paid for the chance to soar.

The Father of Ravens shuffled beneath him, feeling the power passed between them, and Thorn knew the time had come. He opened his eyes and lowered his hand, leaned forward to whisper in the bird's ear.

"Now."

Father Raven climbed to his feet and spread his wings. He hopped three times, then, with a powerful downstroke that flattened the grass in the clearing and momentarily stole the breath from Thorn's lungs, they took to the air.

Thorn held on to the feathers of the great bird's neck, tight enough to keep from slipping off, but not so tight as to cause his ride discomfort. He willed his skin black to match the raven's feathers lest eyes watched them from below.

Father Raven's mighty strokes powered them up into the air. He tilted his wings, steering their course, his body flexing beneath Thorn as each feather answered the bird's commands. They banked, circling the clearing. Thorn stretched his neck to peer down at where they'd stood a moment before and found they were already half the height of the tallest tree above it.

"Go higher," he shouted, the wind throwing his voice back over his shoulder, but the great bird heard his words and listened to his plea.

Father Raven's wide wings stroked them higher and higher. Thorn flexed his legs, gripping with his thighs and feet, and released his fingers from the neck feathers. He sat upright, the wind buffeting his chest, doing its best to rip him off the raven's back. A smile spread across his face; he laughed and laughed, the sound lost to the sky.

The raven's body flexed, flattening out their path, its wings holding firm as the feathers along the tip and trailing edge moved to keep them flying straight, gliding high above the ground.

"We are higher than the trees," Father Raven said, a joy in his voice Thorn had never heard from him before. "Higher than I've ever flown before."

"The stormbird flew higher. High enough to cross the veil."

"Then we shall fly higher still."

The raven stroked again, the movement threatening to unseat Thorn. He leaned in, wrapping his arms around the bird's neck, digging his fingers into its feathers as they angled toward the heavens, climbing, climbing.

Thorn peered past the bird's wing at the trees receding to the size of slivers beneath them, the clearing reduced to a spot of green. Amongst the forest, he spied the settlement he shared with the others, the single plume of smoke sketching a trail skyward from the fire at its center and dissipating long before reaching their altitude.

Father Raven leveled off again, cried out his joy to the sky.

"Ha, ha! None have flown higher than the Father of Ravens."

With an effort, Thorn straightened himself, but found the wind too much. He concentrated his energy, focusing on holding his seat, and the bird's feathers gripped him. When he sat upright, he saw the shimmering green of the veil fast approaching and realized they were soaring higher than its top.

"We should turn around, Father Raven," he yelled, struggling to make his voice rise above the howl of wind in his ears. The bird didn't respond.

They moved faster than he thought, closing the distance to the veil rapidly. If they didn't turn soon, they'd cross over to the other side.

Thorn gathered a handful of feathers in his fingers and tugged to get the bird's attention.

"Do not pull my feathers or I'll throw you off."

"Turn around, Father of Ravens, or we will cross the veil."

"Did you not say the stormbird crossed the veil, Thorn?"

"Yes, but—"

"Do you want him to be the only creature ever to view the veil's top? The other side? You and I could be the first in more generations than any can count to cross and come back."

Thorn opened his mouth, intending to protest. In his mind, he told Father Raven it was a dangerous idea, that they didn't know what might happen when they crossed to the other side. He doubted the bird would listen to reason and, so high in the sky, he could do nothing to stop him. Neither mattered, because his mind and mouth did not agree on the matter.

"Let's go!"

The raven took them higher, ensuring ample height to clear the top of the veil. They soared on his outstretched wings, cutting through the sky like a black knife slicing through lard. Unhindered, unfettered, unbound.

Thorn leaned forward again, not because he feared falling off, but because he wanted to see the top of the veil, to glimpse what none had seen before.

It surprised Thorn to find it no thicker than a blade of grass. The barrier holding back his kind, and the majesty of the beasts living behind the veil with them, was no more substantial than the stuff that provided sustenance for many of those animals.

It flashed past in an instant, and then they breathed the air on the other side.

The other side of the veil.

Thorn shifted to glance back over his shoulder and discover how the magical wall appeared from the other side, but it wasn't there. No shimmering green, no splinters of dancing lightning where animals or birds tested it. Nothing.

A spark of panic lit in Thorn's chest, bringing with it the certainty something was wrong. He squeezed his legs and sat upright. The wind grabbed him, tossed him backward toward the raven's wing, and he threw himself flat on the bird's back, heart pounding in his chest—the first time in his life he'd ever been afraid.

"Turn around," he screamed, battling the wind.

Father Raven didn't respond. Thorn dug his fingers in, tugged hard and yelled again. The feathers didn't grip him.

"Go back."

"Crawk!"

The bird call grating from the raven's beak froze the blood in Thorn's veins. As long as he'd known the Father of Ravens—all their lives—he'd never uttered a sound that wasn't a word.

"No time for jokes," he said. "You need to take Thorn home now."

"Crawk. Cluck. Cluck. Crawk."

Thorn clacked his teeth together over and over, making them chatter as though with cold. Somehow, crossing the veil had stolen the bird's ability to speak and left him unable to communicate with Father Raven.

What else has it taken?

He gripped the bird's neck tight, focusing his energy, concentrating on making him change their course to take them back. It had no effect. Thorn closed his eyes, pictured green fields, tall trees, soil under his soles and squeezing between his toes, thinking that if he recast the binding and return them to a safe altitude, he'd have a better chance to keep his wits and get them home safely.

Nothing happened.

Desperate, Thorn grabbed the raven's wing, manipulated the feathers in an attempt to force the bird to turn. It squawked, pecked at him over its shoulder, but he ducked away, his legs slipping from around its neck. He grabbed it, reseated himself, and tried the wing again.

The bird tilted its wings and banked, turning back the way they came, and Thorn took a relieved breath. Then the world lurched and the bird spun into a tight pirouette, spiraling down toward the ground.

It threw Thorn to the side, the force of the spin tossing him away from the bird's body. His grip slipped from its wing and he clasped tight with his feet, desperate to hold on as the ground spun and spun, still so far below him.

The spiral stopped abruptly, and the raven threw itself into a dive. Wind filled Thorn's face, pushing itself into his lungs, choking him. He struggled to close his mouth, his eyes, but the wind's power kept him from doing so, forcing him to watch the trees approach as they flew toward them at an incredible pace.

"Ahhhhhhhhhhh!"

His scream trailed out behind him, lost to the world, but too small to reach the heavens. Color drained from his skin as he diverted his energy to staying on the bird, though not convinced doing so was the best choice.

The bird lurched once more, pulling out of the dive and jerking back toward the sky. The move dislodged Thorn from his seat, sent him tumbling off Father Raven's back.

He rolled over and over, falling, nothing but air separating him from the trees rushing up at him from below.

Thorn closed his eyes.

XIX Danya - Betrayed

*C*ROUCHING HIDDEN IN THE cover provided by the wide trunk of a Bunyon tree, Danya shifted from one foot to the other, the soles of her bare feet squelching on the muddy ground beside the river. She looked up at the sky fading from afternoon cobalt to washed-out blue tinted pink by the sun disappearing behind the castle wall.

Water gurgled through the grate, and hearing its sound added to the anger churning in her gut. Teryk's lesson had ended and dinner had been eaten, though she didn't attend. Mother and father likely missed her at the meal, but her absence wasn't altogether unusual, especially during the warm seasons. And still she waited, every moment ticking past piling on to the surety her brother had lied and left her behind.

"Teryk," she said.

Danya had lost the guard assigned to her long before entering the gardens. He'd surely be searching for her, but she expected he'd continue searching on his own for a while before telling anyone he'd misplaced the princess. Doing so might prove worse for him than for her. If she hadn't checked in by bedtime, then he'd sacrifice his own well-being for hers, but she doubted he'd do it before.

She stared at the river, stewing. How long should she wait? How long before she deserved to name herself a fool?

Perhaps he lost his nerve.

Possible, but unlikely. His entire life, Teryk had been difficult to prod into something new, starting an adventure, but once he decided, the king's decree barely stood a chance of changing his mind. No, he'd gone, and he'd left her behind.

Danya stood, slung her pack over one shoulder, and slapped her hand against the trunk of the Bunyon tree. Leaves shuddered overhead and her palm stung with the impact. Neither changed the empty feeling of being abandoned pulsing in her gut.

Heedless of the noise she created, the princess stalked out of the tangle of trees and shrubs and into the north courtyard with its trimmed hedges and flowering bushes. The paths and lawns lay deserted at this time of day, but she didn't care if anyone noticed her, not even if the guard charged with keeping her from doing exactly the sort of thing she'd been planning found her. Indignation seethed within her as she stomped her bare feet on the flagstone path to knock the riverbank's mud from her soles. Dirty footprints followed her, each one fainter than the last, but she didn't look back, didn't return her longing gaze to the river, the grate, the promise of adventure beyond.

Instead, she stared straight ahead, brows drawn in a frown, determined to either find her brother or someone to help her stop him.

Danya found Trenan sitting on a hay bale at the edge of the practice arena, sword laid across his lap as he drew a whetstone along its edge. As a friend of the king and the most respected knight in the kingdom, a score of squires awaited the master swordsman's command to tend to his weapon, yet here he sat, a man with one arm fashioning a sharper edge than any but the armorer himself.

"Sir Trenan," Danya called, entering the practice facility. The knight tilted his head in greeting.

"Your highness," he said, returning to his sword. "To what do I owe the pleasure? Shall I light some torches so you can embarrass me?"

She ignored his barbs. Neither of them doubted he was tenfold the swordsman she was, but they both enjoyed the teasing.

"Not tonight, sir. Your embarrassment shall have to wait in favor of mine. I need your help."

Danya strode across the practice circle, loose straw and stray stones pressing against her bare feet. Trenan halted his nightly sharpening ritual and eyed her choice of shirt and breeches, the pack slung over her shoulder. He stowed the chunk of whetstone in a pocket on his belt then stood and sheathed his sword.

"The king and queen missed you at dinner," he said, one brow cocked. "And your brother. Where is your guard?"

"Teryk is gone."

She stared at the master swordsman, arms held firm at her sides to keep from fidgeting under his glare. He crossed the edge of the circle and strode toward her, stopping a pace away. Pink twilight gleamed in his narrowed eyes.

"Gone? What do you mean gone? Gone where?"

Despite her attempt to hold his gaze, she found herself peering at her dirt-streaked feet, a piece of dry straw sticking up between her toes.

"Danya?"

"He's left Draekfarren castle," she said, stomach tightening.

"What?"

"And the inner city." The princess looked up. Trenan's eyes were wide, alarmed.

"Why, Danya? Why has he done this?"

"The scroll. After everyone was asleep, we crept back to the great hall and found it unburned."

"I don't understand." He shook his head. "It was naught but blank parchment."

"No, Trenan. Something happened to it. We discovered words secreted on it, ancient words. A prophecy. Teryk thought it spoke of him."

The sword master's lips pressed into a tight, white line across his face, holding in rage the princess had rarely seen and harbored no desire to experience now. His gaze flickered away, as though searching for words to say amongst the practice dummies and bales of hay. Trenan drew a heavy breath, exhaled through his nose.

"I must tell the king."

Panic jumped in Danya's chest; open defiance of her father's wishes never ended well, and Teryk wouldn't be punished alone. Likely neither of them would see daylight for many turns of the moon to come.

Trenan turned to leave and Danya grasped his arm.

"You can't tell father."

"I have to."

He shrugged off her hold and marched across the practice ring, de-termination in his steps. Danya swallowed hard, dreading the thought of speaking the words perched on her tongue. Trenan had been a part of her life since her birth, there to support and comfort her more often than either of her parents who were often consumed by their royal duties. She loved him like the uncle he practically was and didn't want to hurt him.

"Trenan, stop," she said. He did, facing her. "If you tell the king, then I will have to, as well."

His forehead wrinkled. "Tell the king what?"

She crossed the ring, doing him the service of getting close enough to lower her voice and ensure no one nearby heard.

"I've seen the way you gaze at the queen when father isn't watch-ing," she said. The master swordsman stiffened almost imperceptibly. "And the way she looks at you."

Anger flared in his eyes and he leaned toward the princess. It took every bit of her effort not to back away.

"Ridiculous," he said, the word forced between clenched teeth. "You may be the princess, but you have no right to make such alle-gations. I am the king's most faithful servant. I lost my arm for him. How dare you—"

"I saw you in the garden, Trenan."

Her words stopped him with his mouth hanging open. He snapped it shut and took a wobbling step back, shaken as though she'd run him through on her sword. His gaze darted away, searching again, then returned to hers.

"I—"

Danya laid the palm of her hand on his chest over his heart, concen-trating on softening the hated words as they came out of her mouth.

"I won't tell if you don't, Trenan." She tilted her lips on a false smile. "You'll go search for Teryk, and you'll take me with you."

Trenan hammered the heavy wooden door, the thick brass ring serving as its handle rattling. He lowered his fist, waiting; a cricket sawed out a verse of its twilight song behind him. When the door didn't open, he pounded again, the sound silencing the bug.

After a third hard knock that left his hand pulsing from the impacts, the door finally swung inward on a groaning hinge and a scrape of wood against stone. Trenan stepped back, frowning.

"Who the fuck's waking me up? What's so important?"

The armorer stepped into the doorway, a rumpled nightshirt hanging to his knobby knees, white hair sticking out at odd angles around his puckered face. He looked the master swordsman up and down, his expression remaining unchanged.

"Shourn."

"Sir Trenan. What brings you to my door? In need of a one-armed hauberk?"

Trenan bit back a growl. "Was the prince here today?"

"The prince?"

"Yes, the prince," Trenan snapped. "Don't play games, old man. I'm in no mood for it."

"So I see." Shourn rubbed his chin, fingertips grating in the white bristle of his whiskers. "What's it worth for you to know?"

Trenan's fingers entwined the front of the armorer's nightshirt before he had a chance to jump back. The old man's eyes widened.

"Was he here or not?"

A moment passed as the armorer's expression returned to its customary dispassionate set. Shourn raised a brow, considering whether another taunt of the knight might be in order, then thought better of it.

"Aye, he was."

"And?"

"Whelp asked me to sharpen a sword that didn't need sharpening. For anyone else, I wouldn't've done it." He scratched his chin again and added: "I wouldn't've sharpened yours."

Trenan ignored the slight. "Then he took his sword and left?"

"No. That's the odd thing. When I finished and went to give it to him, he was gone."

"Gone?"

"Yup."

The master swordsman relaxed his grip on the old man's shirt front, allowing him to lower his heels back to the ground. Trenan looked toward the yard, glanced up at the stars the heathens called the Small Gods as they shimmered in the sky above, then returned his attention to the armorer.

"Why would he leave his sword?"

Shourn pulled out of Trenan's grip, smoothed his wrinkled night-shirt with both hands, cleared his throat. His gaze dropped away.

"What is it, Shourn?"

The old man kicked at the ground with his bare foot, coughed, then raised his gaze back to the knight.

"The crown sword," he mumbled.

"What?"

"The crown sword, Trenan. Godsbane is gone."

Though she'd forbade him from coming to her, Trenan sat on the edge of a chair in the queen's meeting chamber. He waited alone in the room but, when she arrived, she'd be accompanied by an entourage: her attendants, escorts. To avoid the appearance of impropriety, they should stay while he spoke with her. But he couldn't relate what he needed to tell her without revealing far more than the appearance of impropriety.

Footsteps in the hall brought the master swordsman to his feet. A thin sheen of sweat formed on his palm that he wiped away on his breeches. Swinging a sword in the hot sun for half a day didn't make him perspire, but the mere thought of seeing Ishla brought moisture to his skin. His mouth filled with nervous saliva; he licked his lips and swallowed, but it filled again. It was always thus when he knew they'd steal a moment together, no matter the reason. It didn't happen often.

The footfalls drew closer and Trenan rested his hand on the hilt of his sword, the one thing in the world that never failed to calm his nerves. He stood straighter, pulled back his shoulders, ignoring the phantom ache that plagued him despite what the surgeon said should be.

One of the queen's escorts entered first, a man named Cellin, who wore the red vest of the queen's guard over his mail shirt. His hand gripped the hilt of the sword dangling at his hip, and he scanned the room before his eyes fell on Trenan. They held each other's gazes for a few seconds before he stepped aside and the queen swept into the chamber.

As ever, she was the most beautiful woman Trenan's eyes ever beheld, with her wide orange skirt blooming out around her and sequins shimmering on her lace bodice. Despite the desire seeing her stirred within his chest, Trenan's face remained deliberately impassive. He bowed at the waist, his own hand never leaving his sword's grip.

"My queen."

"Sir Trenan," she said, her voice sweet music to his ears. "How unusual to have the king's trusted friend seek an audience with the queen."

"It is, m'lady. But I have words that require your ear."

He straightened to find the queen's two ever-present attendants and another escort had entered the chamber. The second guard, a burly man named Dansil who was thick through the chest and almost as thick in the head, favored an axe and served more purpose for instilling fear than he did confidence. Trenan had advised the king against naming him a queen's guard. Dansil's appointment topped a short list of the times his majesty had not heeded the master swordsman's advice.

"My ears are here, Sir Trenan. I've brought both of them, as a matter of fact." The two attendants tittered dutifully. The guards remained stone-faced.

Trenan's gaze flickered between them, then back to the queen. All of them watched him closely; his expression remained neutral in response.

"This is a matter for the queen's ears alone."

A shadow crossed her brow and a look entered her eyes for him alone to see: admonishment and longing folded together. It left as quickly as it came, her face returning to its royal mien. She nodded curtly.

"As you wish." She raised a hand and wiggled her fingers. "The rest of you wait outside."

They each bowed and exited, Cellin pausing with his hand on the door handle.

"We'll be right outside the door, my queen."

"Of course."

The door closed behind him and the queen's facade vanished; anger flickered in her eyes.

"Trenan," she whispered. "We cannot do this. What if the king—"

"I am not here for us, Ishla. I am here because of your children."

She parted her lips. Memories of their softness flashed through his mind. How long had it been since his own lips touched them? He forced the thought from his head.

"Has something happened to Teryk and Danya?"

Trenan's stomach clenched at what he must tell her. He didn't want to cause the queen distress, never wanted to chance hurting her.

"They're fine," he said, daring to touch her arm. "It's just that..."

"What?"

"Teryk has left Draekfarren. Perhaps the inner city, too."

She shook her head disbelieving. "Why would he leave?"

"He's got a head start, so there's not much time to explain. It's the scroll they found—it contained ancient gibberish he thought a prophecy naming him the kingdom's savior. He set out to fulfill it."

Color drained from the queen's face and her gaze trailed away, looking at nothing. For an instant, Trenan thought her knees might give out and leave her to slip to the floor in a swoon. Not with him in the room; he'd catch her.

"I have to tell the king," she said, her voice whispery and distant. "I have to tell Erral."

"You can't, Ishla."

She glanced toward the door. "I have to tell my husband."

Trenan squeezed her arm, pulled her to him. She gasped, her eyes wide and distressed.

"We can't tell him," he said.

"But my son..."

The sword master shook his head. "Danya suspects."

Her expression took on a bewildered aspect. "Suspects what?"

"Us. She wants to go with me to find Teryk and threatens to tell the king her suspicions if I don't let her."

The queen shook her head, dropped her gaze to Trenan's grip on her arm. He released her, his heart hammering in his chest. Did she blame him? Did she hold him responsible?

"They're my children, Trenan. I can't let anything happen to them. The king must know, even it means the end of us."

"Precisely what it means. If the knows he truth, my life will become forfeit, Ishla, and perhaps yours, too." He rubbed her arm and she flinched. "I can't let that happen."

Her eyes searched his face, melting his insides to jelly. There was so much power and strength in her, yet he'd shaken her with the words he spoke. He'd understand if she never forgave him, because he may never be able to forgive himself for making her feel this way.

"Can you find him? Can you bring him back?"

"Yes. But I will have to take Danya."

The queen's lips pressed tight together, forcing the blood from them and turning them as pale as her cheeks. Her gaze flickered away again and, for a moment, he thought he'd lost her to her thoughts, but she came back to him.

"Trenan, Teryk..."

Her voice trailed off and the muscles in the master swordsman's body tensed, waiting for her to speak. His heartbeat quickened, sweat came back to his palm and his stomach ached for her to complete her sentence, but she didn't. Resolve returned to her face, a steely nerve like she presented to her subjects and the court.

"Bring back my son, Trenan. Keep my daughter safe."

"Of course, my queen. But what of the king?"

"I'll handle Erral. Concern yourself with bringing both of my children back unharmed."

He bowed at the waist, the turmoil caused by what he thought she'd say splintering, becoming anger, determination. Disappointment.

When he straightened, she stepped up to him and laid her hand on his chest, leaned in and touched her lips to his. The kiss lingered, but the passion their infrequent embraces usually held was absent, stolen when the news Trenan spoke numbed his lips and turned the queen's cold.

They separated and the queen stepped aside. The master swordsman needed no further prompting. He strode by her, yanked the door open and pushed past the attendants and escorts, carried over the threshold by purposeful steps. Dansil grunted as he passed, but Trenan paid him only the attention the man was worth: none.

He swept down the hallway, his one hand gripping the hilt of his sword, his face chiseled determination as, inside, his guts swirled.

"Foolish boy," he muttered and went to find Danya where he'd left her.

XX - Horace - Fallin' From the Sky

THE TASTY ODORS WAFTIN' outta the window made ol' Horace's stomach gurgle in the manner o' somethin' what possessed its own life. He flattened himself against the wall, worried his damn belly might give him away. Nothin' happened, so he thought it might be all right and crept forward a step, cursin' inside his own head for gettin' himself into the predicament. His clan weren't no thieves, but here he found himself, thievin'.

He stood on his toes and peeked in through the window. A pot hung o'er the cook fire, brewin' the stew what were makin' his gut complain 'bout not bein' fed, but it weren't no bowl o' stew he wanted. A few chunks o' meat and potatoes might satisfy his hunger a short while, but the pig leg layin' on the counter be what he wanted to liberate for his own. That'd quiet his belly for a while.

With not a soul in sight, Horace rolled the piece o' wood he'd brought from the tavern's very own woodpile right up under the window. He pushed it o'er with a quiet *thud* so it'd keep from scootin' away while he stood upon it, then climbed up.

The counter holdin' up the pig's leg he desired were pushed up against the far wall, farthest from the window. Horace let out a breath and struggled himself up onto the sill. He hung there, bent o'er at the waist like one o' them sailors what likes a man to poke him in the porthole, the lintel cuttin' into his gut and makin' it growl some more. The stewy aroma set his mouth waterin'.

Horace teetered back and forth, hopin' no one'd come in and find him, mostly 'cause he'd be embarrassed bein' found caught up on a window. He leaned in, slipped o'er the window's edge, and tumbled to the floor in a tangle pretzel made outta arms and legs.

"Damn it," he muttered, forgettin' his situation, then snapped his mouth shut. Cursin'd have to be done in his head.

He rolled onto his knees and waited, mouth waterin', gut grumblin', to find out if anyone'd heard him. The door stayed shut; the galley remained empty but for him, a pig's leg, and a heavenly smellin' pot o' stew.

Horace clambered to his feet, back achin', and touched the scrape on his belly. No blood from it, and there weren't no time for pissin' and moanin' though—the barkeep or the server might come strollin' through the door and find him, then he'd either be locked up in the town hoosegow or sent back to try and catch his own food. Horace'd proven himself a poor hunter more'n once already.

He tip-toed across the floor toward the counter, eyes dartin' to the door and back, to the door and back. A fly buzzed 'round the pig's leg, landin' to take a bite outta Horace's dinner, then circlin' before landin' again and eatin' some more. Horace snarled at the big fucker and grabbed the leg by the bone stickin' outta the end, givin' it a shake and sendin' the insect buzzin' into the air.

The former sailor crept back across the kitchen, wishin' he'd brought a sack for carryin' the leg, but he forgot his lack o' plannin' before gettin' halfway back to the window because his belly took o'er from his brain in tellin' his legs what to do. Without intendin' to, he steered a course towards the stew pot stew danglin' o'er the cook fire.

Horace beheld the bubblin' goodness and licked his lips, then sucked back the spittle what wanted to escape his mouth. Meat-and-vegetable-scented steam washed o'er his cheeks, crawled up his nose and into his brain. His belly growled even louder'n before, the rumble stretchin' on near forever. He put his hand on his gut and peeked toward the door.

It stayed shut, a mute burble of conversation sneakin' through the crack underneath.

The handle o' the wooden spoon stickin' out from the stew pot's edge whispered to Horace, tellin' him he had time to take one little taste. Just enough to quiet his belly until he got a fire lit and the pig's leg cooked.

Don't be an ol' fool, Horace.

His brain knew the best thing to do, but the rest o' him didn't so much agree with what it had to say.

Horace swapped the chunk o' pig from his right hand to his left, wiped his hog-smelly palm on his leg, and grasped the wooden spoon in his fingers. He gave the stew a stir, releasin' more o' the growl-bringin', saliva-inducin' smells into the air. His belly growled again as he leaned in, sniffed deep, then scooped a spoonful o' stew.

A chunk o' meat burned his lip on the way in, but he didn't stop puttin' the spoon into his mouth. If it set him afire, his belly wouldn't've let him cease jammin' food in his gob. He'd barely swallowed before scoopin' another spoonful up, then another. Stew squirted out between his lips, runnin' down his chin and catchin' in the stubble what were on its way to bein' a beard. His stomach gurgled delight.

With the fourth scoop o' stew sittin' on his tongue, Horace's brain detected footsteps and the door bangin' open; it attempted tellin' him he should do somethin', but his achin' belly still held dominion o'er his actions. It took a woman's angry words for his body to let his head do what it were meant for.

"What are you doin'?" the voice yelled, startlin' Horace.

He dropped the spoon but kept holdin' onto the pig leg. The ol' sailor stumbled back a step, eyes wide and starin' at the tavern wench standin' in the doorway. Her shoulders was wide for a woman, her belly bigger'n what Horace liked to see. Hair stuck out from under the cap on her head and her cheeks was redder'n the wine stain on her dull white apron.

"Hungry," Horace said through a mouthful. A half-chewed potato chunk flew outta his mouth and plunked on the floor between him and the woman.

"Herrin," she bellowed o'er her shoulder without takin' her eyes from ol' Horace.

He didn't know who this Herrin'd be, but he didn't s'pose he wanted to meet him, neither.

The wooden spoon skittered across the floor as Horace kicked it in his haste to reach the window before this Herrin feller made an appearance. The woman yelled again, but he didn't bother payin' her no mind. So long as she weren't chasin' him or throwin' shit at him, Horace'd find more important things to be concerned for.

He heaved the pig leg out the window and draped his leg o'er the sill before sneakin' a peek back to see what the woman were up to and whether Herrin'd arrived or not. The woman'd gone to the same counter where the pig'd been and picked up a cleaver. She waved it toward Horace, but didn't come no closer. Then Herrin showed up in the doorway, and he turned out to be a big bastard wearin' a floppy mustache and an angry countenance.

Horace didn't wait no longer. He pushed himself out the window, landin' beside the pig leg with a breathy whoof from outta his lungs and a crack he knew'd cause him some pain later, but he had no time for concern. The ol' sailor snatched the pig leg up, holdin' it by the knobby bone, and bolted for the forest, Herrin and the fat woman both yellin' at him to come back.

He didn't.

Horace followed a long and windin' road back to the flat place amongst the trees he called his camp, confusin' himself along the way and almost missin' it. By the time he got there, the pain in his chest made it clear what the crack'd been 'bout. Each gulp o' air he took, the rib made sure he knew.

With the bone protestin' his ev'ry move, it took Horace longer than it ever had to get the fire lit. Collectin' wood hurt, pilin' wood hurt, makin' a spark outta two rocks hurt even more. Finally, a flame caught in the brown grass he'd wadded at the bottom o' the fire pit he'd dug the day before. He bent o'er, which hurt, and blew out his air to encourage the spark, which hurt most of all.

A while later, the fire smoked and crackled with ev'ry juicy drop from the pig leg hangin' on the makeshift spit he'd skewered it with. His belly weren't growlin' as bad as before since it'd been stuffed with four scoops o' stew to calm it, which he were happy for, but his achin' gut makin' him pause and near gettin' him caught upset him some.

"Fuck me dead. I could be rottin' in the brig right now," he said glarin' at his belly as if it were a child what needed admonishin'.

He hated livin' out in the woods, though not so much as he despised floatin' atop the sea, but it turned out it weren't far behind. Maybe he'd be good at livin' in a farmhouse, or runnin' a tavern like Krin's or the one from which he'd just pilfered, but he didn't dare show his face in town. Any town. After what he did to Dunal—the cousin of a skipper's wife—he weren't sure if the law mightn't be after him to remove his head from his neck, a place his head quite liked to find itself.

With a grunt what sent a shock o' pain through his chest, Horace stood from the log upon which he sat and rotated the pig leg a quarter spin. The fat 'round the edge'd cooked to golden and he licked his lips. Not only did he believe the meat'd be flavorful on his tongue, but he'd also have enough to last him a couple sunrises.

Horace stared into the fire, watchin' drips o' fat sizzle on the wood and contemplatin' his situation. He couldn't stay too long—he risked bein' caught if he o'er-stayed in one place, but he didn't know where he were. Fallin' off a ship and floatin' in the sea for an indeterminate time can leave a man disoriented, as it did with Horace, makin' it impossible to know if he were closer to sunrise or sunset, or somewhere in the middle.

If he were too far toward sunrise and went that way, he might end up at the Horseshoe, the city where his trip began. If the wrong people saw him returnin' on foot rather'n on the deck o' the *Devil*, there'd be hell to pay. Especially if they knew the *Devil's* fate. No one liked deserters any more kindly'n murderers, and somehow, ol' Horace'd made himself into both. On the other side, if he were too far toward sunset and he kept goin', stumblin' into the Green might be in his future.

He'd prefer the law chopped his head offa his body.

Horace rotated the leg another quarter turn. It'd be done soon and, when it were, he'd eat until his belly bulged and fuck whether he were near sunrise or sunset. Today, he were here with a blazin' fire, a stingin' rib, and a delicious smellin' chunk o' pig. Tomorrow, he might be dead, so he might as well enjoy it.

The ol' sailor tilted his head up toward the clear blue sky peekin' between the treetops. High overhead, a dark shape whisked past; a bird, but it streaked by too quick for Horace to identify. He liked birds. Gulls was the one thing he'd miss 'bout plyin' the sea.

He kept his eyes pointin' skyward in case it came back and was glad for doin' it, because he saw a speck droppin' through the air, somethin' the bird'd let go of. One thing Horace knew 'bout birds: they don't carry nothin' for pleasure. Likely whatever it dropped'd be food of a sort, and Horace needed ev'ry scrap. He glanced at the pig leg, ensurin' it weren't burnin', then struggled himself away from the fire for a better look.

The speck in the sky were gettin' bigger. Judgin' somethin' up in the air weren't the same as peerin' at a thing across the sea—which practice had made Horace better'n average at doin'—but it seemed to him like whatever the bird dropped were headin' right for his camp.

Horace watched it growin' bigger and bigger, hardly believin' his eyes while it plunged toward him. It twisted and turned through the air, sproutin' arms and legs and a head as it neared, turnin' out a man, he thought, maybe a child.

"Fuck me dead," Horace whispered when the speck with arms and legs and a head hit the treetops' first layer o' branches.

Wood cracked, leaves scattered, and the bird's dropped item bounced from branch to branch, tumblin' and gruntin' as each impact with a piece o' tree slowed it, redirected it improbably and inexorably toward Horace.

He saw a flash of gray, eyes wide with fear, a mouth opened in a scream, and the trees' slowin' effect gave him time to realize whatever the bird'd dropped were alive before it hit him.

Seein' the thing mesmerized him, and ol' Horace forgot he should try to get outta the way until it were too late. He twisted away, but the gray thing with arms and legs and a head smacked him hard in the shoulder, caught him upside the head, too, and set his ear ringin' as if someone'd sounded the ships bell right inside his noggin.

Horace tumbled back onto the pile o' wood he'd collected to keep his fire burnin' until sleepin' time, and a log he were particularly proud o' findin' caught him in his injured rib and knocked ev'ry bit o' air outta his lungs. His vision doubled, blurrin' the branches and leaves hangin' o'er his head and the sky peekin' through above them into one ugly, pain-tinted smear.

He lay on that uncomfortable woodpile for a time, blinkin' and gaspin', tears streamin' down his cheeks. After survivin' near thirty-five turns o' the seasons aboard ships, after bein' thrown into the sea and near ate by the God o' the Deep, after ev'rythin' what'd happened durin' a life o' happenin's, ol' Horace were gonna be done in by somethin' what a bird dropped on him.

Weren't no regrets in his head, mind you, 'cept he wished he'd got the chance to eat that pig leg, because it sure did set his mouth to waterin'.

Gradually, Horace's chest loosened up and, though the pain from his tortured rib remained, he drew breath into his lungs again. Air shuddered into his chest, tormentin' him and makin' him wish to stop one of the pain or the breathin', but neither wanted to quit.

He lay on the woodpile until his breath came more easy and the pain...well, the pain stayed and didn't act like it intended leavin' any time soon, but his head cleared enough to hear the sizzle o' fat drippin' on fire, smell the smoky aroma of his pig leg burnin'.

"Shit."

He pushed himself up on his elbow, the pile o' wood shiftin' under him and sendin' him to the ground on his ass and makin' him notice the pains in his back and shoulder, his neck and head. The ringin' in his ear'd dissipated, but ev'rythin' else hurt and his pig were burnt.

"Damn bird," he muttered, his words remindin' him 'bout the one thing he forgot: the whatever-it-were the bird dropped on him.

Horace raised his head, holdin' his breath both to keep his rib from tearin' out his chest and because that's what he did when somethin' scared him enough he might shit in his breeches.

The gray man stood less'n five wide paves away. He were small as a child, but not a child. A broad nose and wide-set eyes dominated his face; he had two arms and two legs like a man, and a cock swung between his legs same as Horace's would if he were the one standin' naked in the middle o' the forest. As the ol' sailor gaped, the small man's flesh shifted from gray, to green, to brown, then back to gray again, like colored waves washin' across him. Seein' it made Horace realize what he gazed upon.

"No," he muttered. He pushed with his feet, tryin' to get away, the heels of his boots diggin' into the ground and kickin' up dust.

The thing stared at him, took a wobblin' step toward him. If it were a man, Horace woulda guessed his expression fearful and confused, but since it weren't, the ol' sailor lacked the certainty it weren't hungry and loathin', or lusty and desirous.

"Stay away from me," Horace said, his voice scrapin' the inside of his throat raw. "I know what you be."

The thing's skin went green, brown, blue, gray. It tilted its head like an animal doin' its best to understand him.

"How'd you get outta the Green? You're one o' them Small Gods."

The thing's expression changed, becomin' an emotion easy to recognize. Its skin went a light shade of red, the ridge o' skin above its eyes where a man woulda had brows wrinkled down toward its flat nose. Long fingers curled into fists. Anger looks the same on ev'ryone.

"Small Gods?" the gray man said in a voice pitched high, but not so high as a woman's, and speakin' the language what Horace did. It stomped toward him a step, its small foot sendin' dust swirlin' into the air. "The Small Gods are useless pricks of light meant to decorate the sky at night and scare idiots and imbeciles.

"Thorn is not a Small God. Thorn is one of *the* Gods."

For the first time in his life, Horace were so scared, he shat in his breeches.

XXI Teryk - Rescue and Retribution

THE STENCH OF VEGETABLES well past their prime wafted to Teryk. His nostrils flared and he wrinkled his nose, realizing worse smells hid beneath the stink of rotten tomatoes and wilted lettuce, things he didn't want to identify.

Other than interlocking patterns of brick replaced by loose gravel, the first stretch of the outer city hadn't been much different from the inner city. Orderly rows of squat stone buildings housing the militia lined the avenues for two blocks. Once past them, the gravel became dirt and everything else changed, too.

Buildings in disrepair. Garbage strewn across the streets. Drunk men shouting obscenities. Women offering themselves for coin.

Teryk walked along the street, heels grinding in the dirt or clicking on the odd stone or chunk of broken paving stone left over from a time when the streets here matched those of the inner city. Weeds grew wherever they pleased and more than once the prince caught sight of a cat or dog with knobby ribs protruding beneath their grimy fur.

His mouth hung open as he stared at the unexpected sights. On occasion, he'd heard stories of the outer city's crime and prostitution, but he'd refused to believe them—surely a kingdom as peaceful and prosperous as Northward wouldn't allow its subjects to sink so low. Whenever he imagined the outer city, he pictured the pristine walks and tidy avenues of the inner city, the merchants and shops replaced by warehouses, artisans, and smithies. Now he saw for himself.

The sun had sunk below the horizon, leaving him wandering the shadowy streets. No oil lamps hung invitingly outside the doors lining the avenue; the only light offering illumination shone through the thin cracks around the closed shutters covering the windows of the buildings.

Ahead, noise spilled out of a slouching, single-story structure Teryk assumed to be a tavern. Loud voices sang a lilting tune, the words slurred and the air close by tinged with the aroma of potent grain alcohol. Part of him wanted to go inside, discover how the people who'd one day be his subjects lived their lives, but he decided his time was better served traveling across the city, finding a place to acquire a horse for his journey.

He strode past the public house and down the block to a cross street. On the corner, a woman leaning against the railing outside a building with a red door called to him.

"Hey, fella. Lookin' for a fuck?"

Teryk glanced sideways at her stringy, unwashed hair, her legs no thicker than the prince's forearm; she looked like the human version of the stray animals he'd seen earlier. He hurried his step to get past.

"Whatsa matter? Gotta problem gettin' hard? I can fix that."

He rounded the corner onto a darker street. No lanterns or torches seeped through cracks around window shutters, no harlots lolled on porches, no drunken song leaked from doorways, but the fetor remained. Teryk raised his hand to cover his nose and mouth and block the stench. It was stronger than anywhere else he'd been in the outer city and a few paces down the deserted street showed him why.

Moonlight peeked between the buildings, illuminating the refuse cluttered in the short, dead end alleys between the broken-down hovels. The prince took a step toward one but stopped a few paces away, the unbearable stink preventing him from getting any closer. He squinted, trying to penetrate the darkness and find out what caused the god-awful smell, but a noise farther down the street caught his attention and he abandoned his effort.

A vague shape moved in the shadows and shoes shuffled in dirt. A woman's choked cry spilled down the street, then cut short. Teryk's brow furrowed and he laid his hand on Godsbane's pommel.

"Hey there." He moved toward the shape, then realized the darkness concealed two people, not one. "Are you in need of help?"

"Mind yer business," a man growled.

The prince heard the woman again, too, her voice muffled as though the man held his hand over her mouth. Teryk continued toward them, their silhouettes coming into sharper focus against a cracked gray stone wall at their backs. The man appeared to be standing behind the woman, one arm wrapped around her waist, the other on her face.

"Let her go," the prince said and pulled the first few inches of the crown sword from the scabbard, making sure the edge scraped hard enough against the leather for the man to take notice.

"Fuck off."

The woman mumbled again, the man cried out.

"Bitch!'

"Help me!"

Teryk bared his steel and jumped forward, moonlight glinting on Godsbane's sharp edge. The man pushed the woman aside, retaining a grip on her arm, and drew his own blade, a weapon which paled in comparison to the crown sword.

"Let the woman go."

"I thought I told ye to mind yer business, whelp."

The prince gritted his teeth and felt the heat of blood burning in his cheeks. He wanted to tell this miscreant his name, inform him he'd referred to the prince—the firstborn of the king and next in line for the throne—as a whelp, but he bit back his retort. If he exposed his identity to anyone, his undertaking would come to an end without ever getting started. With the words aching in his mouth, he took up the stance Trenan had conditioned into him since his first lesson in swordplay.

"Unhand her," the prince grated between his clenched teeth.

"You want her?" the man said. "Well, here ye go."

He shoved the woman at Teryk, then followed close behind, jabbing the point of his sword toward the prince's gut. The woman hit Teryk's shoulder and spun him sideways enough for the attacker's thrust to go wide of its target. The prince stumbled with the impact, but the woman grabbed his arm, keeping him on his feet.

Teryk righted himself and ushered her behind him, then faced the man.

"Is that the best you've got?"

The woman's attacker growled deep in his throat and sprang forward again, swiping left to right at chest height. Teryk shuffled back, his feet scraping in the dirt and fractured pavers without crossing, the way Trenan had taught him. After so many lessons, the master swordsman might finally be proud of his student.

The prince launched his own attack, swinging Godsbane down over his head. His opponent brushed the blow aside with his blade, then flicked its tip against Teryk's thigh opening a shallow nick.

"Oh." Teryk glanced at the white flesh of his leg showing through the slice in his purple breeches, but the flash of moonlight on skin disappeared as the hole in his pant leg filled with blood.

"Is that the best ye got, kitten?"

The man waggled his sword at the prince, taunting him, and Teryk knew he shouldn't let it anger him. Trenan always preached that a calm head prevails in a hard fight.

'He who loses his temper loses his head.'

Trenan had repeated the mantra over and over until the prince became sick of hearing his trainer's voice. In that moment, with blood trickling down the inside of his thigh and his attacker advancing again, Teryk wished Trenan was beside him, shouting encouragement. Danya, too.

The man swung his weapon and Teryk jumped back, deflecting the swipe with Godsbane's edge. A clang of steel rang along the street and sparks flew into the darkness.

"Quite a sword ye got there, boy."

"I'm not a boy."

"We'll see about that."

The miscreant lunged and the prince jerked away. His feet tangled with the woman's standing behind him, throwing them both off balance. She fell, Teryk waved his arms trying to keep his feet, the tip of the crown sword flailing in the air, finding a space in the basket guard of the other man's weapon. The prince toppled over the fallen woman, his momentum wrenching the sword from his surprised attacker's hand.

Teryk scrambled to his feet and leaped the space between him and the man, preventing him from retrieving his sword. Godsbane's tip brushed the crook's throat.

"Leave it," Teryk said trying to sound menacing.

The man froze, open hand reaching for the weapon, his eyes rolling up toward the prince. Neither of them moved. Teryk heard the woman clamber to her feet behind him; she pressed herself close enough to his back, her breath whistled in his ear.

"It's time you be on your way." Teryk rotated the sword so the flat of the blade touched the man under his chin, then used it to prompt him to stand.

"You don't wanna—"

"No words, sir. You have been bested by a boy. A whelp. A kitten. Take your leave before I release the bear."

The man giggled, but firmer pressure from Godsbane convinced him of his poor choice. He raised his hands, palms out in surrender, and backed away. After he'd gone four paces, he spun and bolted into the darkness.

"You're so very brave," the woman said into his ear.

The thrill of the fight had ignited a spark in his belly, cleared his head of the ugliness he'd experienced so far in the outer city. His chest puffed up, swollen with the pride of victory, and he faced her, ready to accept her appreciation. Moonlight fell across the street, revealing her face to him for the first time.

She appeared older than his mother, with one empty eye socket criss-crossed by a shiny pink scar. Her smile revealed a gap between her front teeth—the cause of her whistling breath. Teryk's own grin faded as she laid a hand on his chest.

"So brave," she repeated.

"It was...uh...it was nothing."

"No, you risked yerself to save me from that bastard. You deserves a reward."

She stretched up on her toes, closed her eye and puckered her lips. The empty eye socket didn't close along with its partner, the lid having been either cut away or grown over by scarring. Teryk grimaced and leaned back, stepped away.

"Your appreciation is more than enough, young lady."

She opened her eye, put her fingers to her lips, and giggled.

"That fellow was right. What an impressive sword you got. Look at the size of it."

Teryk felt the warmth of embarrassment rise in his cheeks, her suggestive words sending discomfort through his limbs. He held the sword up to feign ignorance of her intent, and the engraved blade caught the moonlight.

"Beautiful," she whispered.

The prince decided flashing the crown sword in public might not be the best of ideas. He grasped the top of his scabbard and inserted the sword's tip, sliding it in until it thumped against the bottom, an inch of steel protruding from the top.

"Oho," the woman said, giggling again. "It looks like it's too big to fit."

Teryk cleared his throat. "I must be on my way."

"No," she cried reaching out to ensnare him in her arms. He backed away a step and bowed shallowly at the waist.

"Will you be all right getting home on your own?"

"I will, good sir. And thanks be to you again for your brave rescue."

Teryk nodded and strode away, tempted to look back over his shoulder to ensure she didn't follow him. No sound of footsteps hurried after him, no shuffle of skirts. When he reached the next corner, he stole a peek back at the woman standing in the avenue, still watching him, and he raised a hand to her. She returned the gesture, then scurried away.

The prince continued along the street, relieved she hadn't pursued him, pleased he'd been able to help. Most of all, pleased with himself for besting the first man he'd ever faced who wasn't employed by his father. Judging by the quality of the basket-hilted sword the man had wielded, he took his swordplay seriously, and Teryk beat him.

He stood straighter as he walked, the stench assaulting his nostrils seeming less offensive. If the rest of his journey went as well, he'd find himself the savior of the kingdom in no time.

But where do I start?

His first goal was to reach the city's outer boundary, where he'd acquire a horse. Despite the exorbitant price the criminals Fellick and Ive charged him to buy back his own sword, he still had a number of coins hidden in the secret pocket in his pack, including five more gold—half a gold should be more than enough to purchase an excellent steed.

Once he sat with a horse between his legs, he was undecided how he'd proceed. From what he recollected, the scroll made the man from across the sea his first priority. If such a man existed, he didn't expect to locate him in the outer city. But where, then? The prophecy also talked of Small Gods; perhaps the answer lay with them.

Teryk stopped in the middle of the street and looked up at the stars twinkling in the night sky. Stories told by the followers of the Goddess said she'd banished the Small Gods to the heavens long ago, forcing them to spend eternity watching the world but never participating. The prince thought the Goddess-followers' fables ridiculous. And how could a bunch of pinpricks of light flickering in the sky lead him to a man from across the sea?

No, stars weren't the answer, but he'd heard tell of other Small Gods. Legends spoke of magical creatures who walked the land before man, a race that hid themselves in the no-man's-land superstitious folk called the Green at the sunset end of the kingdom. Teryk didn't believe in those Small Gods any more than he believed the stars were once alive, but it gave him a place to start. In his heart, he knew wherever he went, he'd find himself in the right place. The prophecy said so.

He unshouldered his pack, the coins hidden within jingling quietly, and opened the front pocket. His thumb and forefinger slid inside and he fished out the folded sheet of paper, its blue tint washed out to off-white in the moon's dim glow. The temptation to unfold it, to read the words he'd written on it as Danya recited them from the scroll, nearly overtook him, but he resisted. Better to not linger in the middle of the street in the outer city—likely not the safest place to be, judging by what he'd seen. He stowed the paper back in the pocket and moved to replace the pack on his back when a voice stopped him.

"Ye may as well leave that off, whelp. Yer gonna be givin' it t'us, anyways."

Indignant anger ignited in Teryk's chest before he looked up to find the man he'd recently fought blocking the street in front of him. He held a dagger in one hand, a smoking torch in the other. Two of the three men with him held bare steel in their hands, the third wielded a stout club.

"Do I need to teach you another lesson?" Teryk slipped one of the pack's straps over his shoulder and edged his hand toward Godsbane's grip.

"Teach me a lesson? If it weren't fer that worthless whore, you'd be bleedin' in the street a couple of blocks from here."

"Watch your mouth when you speak of a lady."

The four men laughed and the sound of it sent a shiver along the prince's spine. He could dispose of one of them, he knew, likely two, but four? His eyes scanned the street for anything to give him an advantage, and his gaze fell upon a door to his left, a sliver of flickering light shining through the crack beneath. Perhaps someone within might help.

Teryk sprang for the door, his hand grasping the hilt of his sword, wrestling it from the scabbard. The four men jumped toward him together, a mass of arms and legs and sharp edges coming for him, shouting.

The prince hammered on the wooden door, rattling it against the lintel. He spun toward the men, back pressed to the wood, but the man he'd fought before swung his fist, caught him in the chin. Teryk's knees buckled and he slid down the door until his ass hit the ground.

Head spinning, agonizing pain spreading out from his jaw, the prince raised Godsbane defensively only to have the sword wrenched from his grip.

"I'll be takin' that."

Hands grabbed him by the front of his cloak, jerked him to his feet. Teryk raised his fists, but a punch to the gut doubled him over. Someone yanked his pack. He clutched the strap, desperate to keep it, but another fist contacting the side of his head made his grip loosen. The pack slipped off his shoulder.

Bent at the waist, Teryk directed his eyes upward and watched the man he'd fought hand the torch to one of the others and tear open the flap. He plunged his hand in and ripped out the prince's clothes, his rations, scattering them across the dirt street. When he'd pulled everything out, he flipped it upside down and shook it. The coins stowed in the hidden pocket jingled.

"I knew there'd be somethin'. You ain't dressed like a man who ain't got no money."

"Let—" Teryk coughed, gasped, found his breath. "Let me go and your lives will be spared."

The men laughed again. "You'll spare us, will you?"

"Let you live. I'm the—"

The man holding the torch kicked the prince in the belly, knocking the air out of him and cutting his words short. Teryk crumpled, his knee catching the corner of a broken cobblestone and shooting pain along his leg.

"Let's see what else you got in here."

The man with the pack jerked the front pocket open sending the button fastening it closed bouncing along the street. He reached in and pulled out the blue paper, held it up.

"What have we here?" He unfolded it, gazed at the words scrawled across it

"Read it," one of the others urged.

"I can't read. Can any of you?"

One man shrugged as if he didn't know anything about this thing called reading, the other two shook their heads. The man holding the scroll peered over its edge at Teryk.

"Well, if we can't read it, I s'pose we don't need it."

He stretched his arm out, extending the corner of the paper toward the torch.

"No."

The choked word died in the prince's throat. He reached his hand out, leaned forward, desperate to stop them from burning the prophecy, but flame flickered at the corner of the sheet, spread along the edge.

"No."

"Make him quit wheezin', will ya?"

The heavy club smashed into his face, crunching his nose and firing stars before his eyes. Teryk fell onto his side, bashing his shoulder on the hard ground. The man let go of the paper and, through the pain, the prince watched it flutter through the night air, a trail of light following in his doubled vision. The transcription settled on the cobblestones in front of Teryk, the light of the fire showing him the words before consuming them.

Firstborn child of the rightful king.

Coins jangled on the street as the man tore his pack in two, exposing the secret pocket. One of the other men gathered the money and they threw the ruined satchel aside.

"Get his clothes."

Rough hands tossed him around, yanking his cloak from his back, his coat, his shirt and pantaloons, leaving him in his underclothes. Teryk lashed out at one of the men, poked him in the eye. He kicked another weakly, missing the groin he aimed for and catching him in the thigh. For his efforts, he received a fist gripping a sword hilt to the nose and pain exploded through his head. He clutched his nose with both hands, felt sticky blood on his fingers.

After they stripped him, the men dropped him back to the street. A boot hit him painfully in the gut, the club bludgeoned him in the spine. Teryk threw his arms over his head, pulled his knees up to his chest. The urge to beg for his life replaced any thought of using his name to scare them off, but the punches and kicks kept him from filling his lungs to plead for mercy.

A boot struck his head, dazing him and blurring his vision. Steely fingers grabbed his balls and squeezed; rank breath leaning near his ear whispered words about teaching him a lesson. When the fingers released him, more kicks hammered his legs, his arms, his back, before relenting.

Teryk lay with his face hidden behind his hands, expecting the onslaught to resume. When it didn't, he spread his fingers and opened his eyes, saw the once blue-tinted paper lying on the street in a sheet of ash. A gust of wind picked it up, twirled it in the air, and blew it across the dirt in a thousand pieces.

The prince reached a quaking hand out for it, as though he might grab the myriad bits and puzzle them back together. A boot stomped on his fingers, crunching them against a stone. Teryk screamed and the man who he'd first fought knelt in front of him.

The criminal grabbed the prince by the hair, tilted his head back to direct his eyes toward his attackers. Teryk couldn't focus. The man's face appeared no more than a smear in the dark, the sound of coins jingling in his palm an indistinct rattle. He let the prince's head drop, his cheek banging the street and shooting pain along his spine, then he pushed him by the shoulder, rolling Teryk onto his back.

The man loomed over him and, through the haze of agony, Teryk recognized Godsbane in his hand. He held the weapon in both hands, the tip pointed toward the ground, and plunged it into the prince's belly.

Teryk always imagined being stabbed would be excruciating, but with the other pains plaguing his body, he didn't notice the blade sliding into him. He'd been dealt a killing blow and not noticed it happening. The thought struck the prince as funny. He laughed, he coughed. Blood sprayed from his lips.

The man yanked the crownsword out of Teryk and kicked him in the head; the prince's laughing and coughing ceased and darkness stole the world.

—⁓—

I'm sorry, Danya.

Darkness. Light.

Trenan, a sword hanging from his shoulder where an arm once was before Teryk was born but where none should be now.

The king; pointing, laughing.

Darkness. Light.

Teryk's lids fluttered, but they weighed too much for him to hold them open. He glimpsed a snatch of dirty cobblestone, a shard of burnt paper, a hint of shadow before they slipped shut.

Pain coursed through him as though it replaced the blood in his veins. He cried out, the mournful sound echoing in his head, but not a whisper passed his lips. Ragged breaths scraped his throat, burned his lungs.

Please let it end.

A shiver ran along his back, shaking his spine and spreading more pain. How did he let this happen? How did the fate that brought him the scroll and showed him his destiny allow it?

I'm sorry I lied, Danya.

He'd lost Godsbane and the writings from the scroll were reduced to ash. No one knew where to find him. The king and queen might not even realize he'd left the castle.

Blood seeped out of him, snaked along the ground and drained into a crack between two scuffed and broken cobblestones. He couldn't feel the precious fluid leaving him, but he knew it did, from so many wounds, so much of it.

The burden of his failure pressed down on him, squeezing his heart until it hurt along with the places he'd been punched and kicked, clubbed and stabbed, compressing it until the injury done his soul outweighed all others.

If he retained the ability to weep, he'd have done so, but not over losing his life. He'd weep for the kingdom because his failure left its populace vulnerable to an evil none of them knew, not even Teryk or Danya who'd read the scroll.

I'm so sorry, sister.

Darkness. Light. Darkness. Light.

Fingers pried his lids wide and a face swam into view, though he didn't know if it was real or a product of his reeling, grieving mind. Gap-toothed, one-eyed. Pink flesh glistened. Breath whistled.

Words floated through the buzzing in the prince's ears.

"...clothes..."

"...alive..."

Pain in his gut as someone pressed on his belly.

Trenan. I failed you, Trenan.

"...helped me..."

The face hovered over him, lips moving, words being spoken, but he didn't hear any more. His ears didn't care for the sounds the one-eyed woman made with her lips. His eyes didn't want to look at the too-pink skin by her blank eye, or the space between her teeth.

He wanted to be with his sister, see his mother, Trenan. He wanted the pain to stop.

He wanted to sleep.

Light. Darkness. Light. Darkness.

Teryk's lids slipped closed. The fragments of words quieted. The pieces of visions vanished. The burden on his soul lifted.

The pain disappeared.

XXII - Ailyssa - Cast Out

*T*HE WHITE EDGE OF N'th Adesi Re's red smock brushed the floor, swaying side to side as she walked, collecting dust. A leaf that must have found its way in stuck to the sole of someone's sandal caught under the hem and dragged along for a while, its soft green surface scraping the stone, wearing away. Walking behind the Matron, Ailyssa watched the wayward leaf until it worked itself free and they left it lying in the middle of the hall.

By itself. Alone.

The gentle slap of their sandals reverberated along the hall, heard by no one but themselves, at least no one else who could be seen. Ailyssa remembered a time not long after her first bleed when the halls had been cleared for a Matron to escort a Mother after her reckoning. Sylla, her name was, and once she'd been called N'th Sylla Ra. Ailyssa hadn't seen her make the dreaded walk, but she'd leaned her ear against the door to listen to their sandaled feet tread the hard, cold stone. Those footfalls echoed in her head for seasons after, but she never expected her own feet to produce the same sounds for the same reason. Three births and three deaths, two other children born dead before their time were Sylla's crime against the Goddess. Not even a son did she bring forth to aid other Mothers in producing Daughters.

At least I did that.

As she thought of the expelled Mother again for the first time in so long, she realized Sylla must have scored her wall with as many scratches as did Ailyssa when she walked the empty halls. The occasion of Sylla's walk was the only instance in recent memory of a Mother banished from the order. Until now.

"N'th Adesi Re?" Ailyssa's voice rang along the hall beside their footsteps, harsh in the quiet.

"Yes?"

"What ever became of N'th Sylla Ra?"

"Sylla? I do not know this name," she said, though her tone and her noticeable exclusion of the woman's titles suggested the opposite.

They came to the end of the hall and stopped in front of the gray-painted Mother's door. More times than she cared to count, Ailyssa had strode through this portal with the other Mothers—at least twice a day since the birth of her first son. Before it opened, she pictured the exercise yard on the other side, the prayer gardens beyond. The courtyard past the gardens, she was less certain of, with its ramparts and great iron portcullis.

What lay outside the gates, she hoped she'd only ever view from the seat of a Matron's carriage, a wish never to be.

N'th Adesi Re faced Ailyssa, her mouth titled in what one might consider a comforting smile if one used imagination.

"Ready?"

Ailyssa blinked, hardly believing she'd asked. Ready to what? How did she expect her to answer? Did she want her to say she was ready to relinquish the only life she'd ever known? To leave behind her friends? To be forsaken by the Goddess who gave her life and to whom she'd given hers?

Hesitant, she nodded. "Yes."

Adesi pulled the door open and sunlight streamed in, hurting Ailyssa's eyes, but she quickly grew accustomed to the light. She wanted to be happy for the sunshine and warmth of the air but, today of all days, she suspected it might be the Goddess taunting her, punishing her in so many tiny ways.

The Matron led her across the threshold and into the sunlight. The exercise yard lay empty like the hallway. A breeze stirred a dust devil into being, whirled it around the open space, danced it toward the sky until it faded and disappeared. Ailyssa took a step and wobbled, reached out and grasped the back of Adesi's smock to steady herself.

"Let me help," the Matron said and took her by the arm.

Their feet crunched on dirt and crushed rock as they crossed the yard. Before they reached the midpoint, Ailyssa detected the scent of the prayer gardens carried on the breeze: honeysuckle and rose, lilac, wisteria, and sweet alyssum. As a small girl, she'd pretended she'd been named after sweet alyssum.

"Whhhhere..." Ailyssa didn't mean to drag out the word, her mouth had done so on its own. She stopped and swallowed to refocus. "Where will I go, N'th Adesi Re?"

Adesi squeezed her arm. "I cannot say because I do not know."

"Can I come and vvvisit?"

They'd reached the edge of the prayer gardens and the Matron stopped, turned Ailyssa by the shoulders to face her. For a second, her countenance became a blur lost in the sun. Ailyssa blinked and the Matron's face returned, her expression tinged with sadness, regret, and compassion that dug a pinprick of hope into Ailyssa's heart.

"No, N'th Ailyssa. You will not be permitted into this or any other temple of the Goddess."

"N'th Ailyssa Ra," she corrected.

"Not anymore." Adesi took her arm again and led her into the garden. "And you will be N'th no more once you pass through the gates."

She quickened their pace, hurrying her charge through the deserted gardens. Ailyssa's eyes darted from flower bed to flower bed, the pinks and whites, blues and yellows blending into indistinct smears of color. Her sandal snagged on an errant rock and she stumbled, might have fallen if not for the Matron's fingers digging into the flesh of her upper arm. Righted, she blinked hard to clear the tears she thought the cause of her blurred vision, but the world remained hazy around her.

"Adesi, what's wrong with me?"

"Nothing, child. Just a little something to help you relax while you travel. We are almost there. Come."

Ailyssa dug her feet in, halting the Matron's efforts to continue. Her vision doubled, her thoughts tumbled through her head, dancing just outside her grasp.

"Ailyssa," the Matron snapped, pulling hard on her arm, dragging her along.

Ailyssa leaned back, tears of frustration and anger distorting N'th Adesi Re's face into a leering, monstrous visage. Another time, she'd have been scared, but too many other things frightened her about her life already for an illusion to add to her fears. Instead, one thought swam out of the murk twisting in her mind and found its way to her lips.

"Mmmy sons. Wwwhhhere are my sons?"

N'th Adesi Re's hands grasped her shoulders, shook her harder than a woman of the Matron's age should have had the strength for. Ailyssa's teeth rattled, her head spun sending nausea into her gut.

"You have no sons," Adesi yelled, her breath warm on Ailyssa's face. "They ceased to be the day they left your womb."

"No! I sssaaawww him. He's...he's...he..."

Ailyssa's legs refused to support her any longer. She sagged in Adesi's grip and her weight proved too much for the Matron. She floated to the ground, landed more gently than she should have, and realized Adesi had the good sense to at least lower if she couldn't catch her, to prevent the cobblestones from injuring her.

Her head touched the path and she lay staring at a green smudge of moss struggling for space between two of the walk's stones. Adesi spoke words likely meant either for comfort or condemnation, but Ailyssa's ears were beyond hearing, her mind beyond comprehending.

"Wwwwhere'ssss my other sssssssonnn...?"

In a haze, she felt hands upon her, more than just Adesi's, and the ground fell away beneath her. The scents of the gardenia and jasmine growing at the center of the prayer gardens found her nose, struggled their way into her mind the way the moss forced its way between the cobblestones. As the hands bore her to an unknown destination, she wondered if she'd ever smell them again, but then their aromas faded, her head settled, and the day that might have been beautiful but wasn't blissfully disappeared.

The world faded in and out, carrying with it the rattle of wagon boards, the nickering of horses, indistinct voices. Ailyssa neither saw nor felt anything during the snatches of time the vague and distant sounds reached her ears. They came to her as though through an impenetrable fog, a dream, then disappeared again.

The rushing of water *wooshed* around inside her head, came into focus, and this time remained for more than an instant. Ailyssa concentrated on it, filled with the sense of floating above it, hovering, hearing, but observing in no other way. Unease stirred inside her, the first time she recalled anything but the sounds since...since...?

Finally, something else came to her. An odor. It took time for her muddled mind to discern it, identify it. First, she needed to understand if she truly detected a scent, then she set to recognizing it.

Bread. Someone is baking bread.

Someone.

Water flowing. Bread baking.

She sniffed deeply, heard the air entering her nostrils amongst the gurgle and tumble of running liquid, inhaled the aroma of bread and earth, the scent of water touching warm rocks.

A tickle on the tip of her nose. An ache in her upper arm. Her stomach growled. Her head thrummed.

They poisoned me. Drugged me. How long...?

The rest of the world around her returned all at once, inundating her senses, taxing them. She pressed her eyelids closed tight lest adding vision might prove too much for her addled mind. Her breath flowed in and out of her chest, and she concentrated on this. Fill her lungs, empty her lungs, fill them, empty them, fill, empty.

After a time, the sounds and smells, tickles and pains and itches faded to a bearable level, a background of noise that didn't demand her attention and her body chose to ignore.

A foot twitched. An elbow bent. Ailyssa's fingers touched her cheek, her nails scratching her flesh lightly, startling her. It tingled, itched, faded to the background with the noises. Satisfied her mind had recovered enough, she forced her eyelids open,

Nothing.

Ailyssa pushed herself up to a sitting position, aware she heard no creak of wagon boards or nickering horses, and her stomach lurched with the movement, threatened to empty itself. Her throat spasmed. Once, twice. She leaned to the side, resting on an elbow, as her body worked to expel everything it found.

Bitter-tasting bile filled her mouth. She spat it out, gagged, heaved, spat.

Ragged breaths rattled along her raw throat and Ailyssa wiped her forearm across her lips, her sleeve's fabric softer than she expected. She spat again, clearing the vile fluid from her tongue, and her breathing eased, allowing her to return her attention to the last of her senses.

Slowly, she returned to sitting, careful not to set her stomach on its side again. She slid her eyelids closed, inhaled through her nose, and filled her lungs in the hope of calming her mind.

Please let me see, Goddess. Please—

Memory flashed in Ailyssa's mind, cutting the silent prayer short. Marks on a stone wall, a garden for prayer, an emptiness in her heart. Adesi had told her the Goddess would no longer listen for her prayers. She'd failed to honor the giver-of-life and, in return, the Mothers and Matrons, the Goddess herself, cast her out.

Eyes still closed, hoping time might heal her sight, Ailyssa ran her hand along her sleeve, her leg. Her fingers told her she no longer wore the thick, durable smock of the Order, but a cotton shirt and roughspun skirt. They'd stripped her titles, they'd stripped her of her faith, and they'd stripped her of her robes. With a sigh, she let her hands fall into her lap. Her shoulders sagged and her head dipped forward.

She sat that way for a short time, despair pressing on her and flattening her spirit, until she thought of the life yet remaining in her. If this was the life the Goddess meant for her, then this was the life she'd live and make the best of.

"I will see," she said, raising her head.

A bird twittered overhead, perched on a branch of rustling leaves. A corner of Ailyssa's mouth curved upward. Surely this was an answer, confirmation that all she needed was a positive attitude and everything would sort itself. The start of a new life; an opportunity to be whatever she wanted to be.

Ailyssa sucked at her bottom lip, preparing herself to open her eyes and view her surroundings, ignoring the lack of light glowing through her closed lids. Her hearing and touch had come back gradually, and so it would be with her sight: dim at first, then blurred, then returning.

"This is how it shall be."

She cracked one eyelid open, but saw nothing, so closed it again.

"I have to open them further," she said aloud. The bird above her chirped encouragement.

She opened both eyes fully, hope bursting in her chest, then disappearing.

Darkness. Black.

She blinked, waved a hand in front of her face, the wind of the movement brushing her cheeks and fluttering her lashes.

Nothing.

Despair flooded into Ailyssa's chest unhindered, sapping energy from her limbs, constricting her heart, clogging her throat. She tilted her head back and sobbed toward the sky. Overhead, a startled bird's wings beat the air, fleeing the sound and the anguish she hurled into the world.

The woman Ailyssa, formerly N'th Alyssa Ra, once a Mother of the Order of the Goddess, put her face in her hands and wept.

XXIII Trenan - Search

*T*HE NOISE WITHIN THE tavern was near loud enough to make a man's ears bleed. People shouted, flagons clanked, coins jingled, boots shuffled and danced. Oily smoke from the lanterns hanging at intervals around the room swirled together with the cloud of stinking, stagnant fumes exhaled by the patrons' sweetweed pipes, the concoction stinging Trenan's eyes.

A battle is a more enjoyable place.

But they hadn't entered the public house for enjoyment. The master swordsman contemplated the cup of mead on the table in front of him, but the knots in his stomach kept him from imbibing, no matter how parched he might be. He raised his eyes to study the princess sitting across from him as she scanned the crowd, searching for a sign of her brother. They'd both already realized he wasn't in the tavern; she searched anyway, ever the devoted sister. Devoted enough that, in order to protect the prince, she continued to threaten Trenan with allegations that might cost him his life, but she forgot her threats may also be exacerbating the danger her brother was in.

If Trenan told the king, he'd send a phalanx of armored men sweeping through the outer city, turning over every stone until they found Teryk. What happened after his recovery surely wouldn't be enjoyable for the prince and princess, but they'd both be alive, and sometimes you just needed to accept the lumps you deserved.

The irony of the thought struck the master swordsman as he found himself still seated in a noisy outer city tavern trying to avoid the lumps he likely deserved.

"We should talk to more people," Danya said, peering across the table at him. Her eyes darted away and back every time someone passed by close to them.

Trenan set his elbow on the table and leaned in to better make himself heard.

"Let me tell them we search for the prince, your grace."

"Don't call me that."

He shook his head. "Danya. Someone will remember if they saw the prince, but they may not remember a blond man-child approaching the twentieth day of his birth."

"No. He won't tell anyone who he is," she said with absolute surety.

"Perhaps he was recognized."

"And he's disguised."

Frustration sent bitter saliva across Trenan's tongue. He leaned against the back of the chair, rubbed his aching shoulder, and ground his teeth to keep from saying angry words to the princess he might later regret. He suspected the time to say such things may be fast approaching.

"We have to do something," he grated.

"You can ask—"

"We've asked," Trenan snapped. He stood abruptly, sending his chair tumbling backward into the man standing behind him. The man turned, a snarl on his lips, but thought better of his actions when he saw the threatening expression on Trenan's countenance. "We must do more than describe a young man who's one among thousands. We need to tell them for whom we search."

Danya stood, her own expression clearly stating that Trenan's sneer didn't frighten her.

"If you do, I'll tell father."

To the master swordsman, it felt as though his chest squeezed tight around his heart, choking it. He didn't care what might happen to him if the king knew the truth, but he couldn't allow whatever consequences his knowing would mean for Ishla. Clearly, they didn't concern the princess. He grasped the edge of the table and leaned toward her, lowering his voice.

"Someone is going to die because of you."

Her eyes widened briefly before narrowing again.

"No, someone will be saved because of me."

She disappeared into the crowd. Trenan considered going after her, but doing so would likely ensure an argument and slow them further in their quest to find the prince.

She is confident like her mother, and reckless like her father. A dangerous combination.

He pulled the chair back to the table, legs scraping the wooden floor, and sat, heaved a smoke-filled breath. He rubbed his eyes with his thumb and finger, pinched the bridge of his nose. Caring for children wasn't how he'd imagined his life, but one long-ago heroic battle ended his warrior dreams, saving the king, losing him his arm, and ending him up here.

Not a day went by he didn't regret it.

Without that one action, his life would be so different. He'd have his arm, the command of an army, and nothing standing between him and the woman he loved. If only he'd...

"No," he murmured and moved his hand away from his face.

If he'd chosen differently and not stepped in front of the king and saved the regent's life, he'd have been unable to live with himself. But the agony of inaction would have outweighed the torture of a love that could not be, the ever-present ache in an arm that no longer existed.

So he told himself every day.

Trenan ruminated over the cup of mead as the warm bodies crowded into the stinking hole of a tavern moved around him. A man's hip jostled the table, knocking over the master swordsman's drink; he slid his chair back to keep the liquid from dripping on his boots and bumped into someone else.

"Watch it," the man snapped, pushing Trenan.

The master swordsman pivoted to respond, but the angry words caught in his throat at the sight of Godsbane's hilt jutting from an ill-fitting scabbard at the man's hip. Trenan jumped up and grabbed the man's arm, sending the chair tumbling to the floor in a clatter of wood. He spun the fellow around to face him.

"Where did you get that?" he asked, nodding toward the sword.

The man sneered. "Fuck off." He spat and turned away.

Trenan put his hand on the fellow's shoulder and he responded by aiming his fist at the master swordsman's head, but Trenan expected it. He ducked under the wild swing and shoved the man back a step, giving enough separation between them to free his steel.

The sword Trenan had once wielded with his right hand sung from its scabbard, but in the tight quarters of the packed tavern, his elbow smacked another man in the head, slowing him. By the time he trained the point on the possessor of the crown sword, Godsbane was in the man's hand.

"There doesn't need to be trouble," Trenan said. "Tell me where you got the sword."

The man grinned. "It's been in my family for generations. Belonged to me great grandpap."

Trenan lowered his brows. A hush fell over the crowd around them, but the sounds of drinking and carousing continued emanating from the rest of the tavern, so he raised his voice more than he wanted to be heard.

"Do you not know what blade you hold in your hand?"

The man shrugged and glanced at the inscription running along the length of the steel, but his eyes flickered back to Trenan immediately. "A nice one."

"One that's never belonged to your grandpap or anyone else low-born. It's only seen the outside of Draekfarren castle to protect the kingdom in times of need, wielded by only one hand."

The man barked a sharp, disbelieving laugh, but then his gaze traveled the sword's length again, hovered on the gold-braided hilt.

"Well, fuck me with a javelin." His mouth twisted into a grin and his eyes returned to Trenan. "Seems someone'd probably pay dearly for this sword."

"Someone is going to pay dearly if you don't tell my where you got it."

"Found it."

"Where?" Trenan demanded. He took a half-step toward the fellow and two men, one on each side of him, drew their steel. His gaze strayed to each for an instant, then returned to the grinning thief.

"Why should I tell you?"

To Trenan, the world slowed and sprang to greater clarity. He inhaled a steady breath through his nose, ignoring the scent of sweetweed, old thresh, and spilled ale. The air filled his lungs, fortified him, then his sword flickered and the sword bearer to the man's right yelped, his weapon falling to the floor. He grasped his injured hand, blood flowing between his fingers.

"I'll ask once more. Where did you get the sword?"

The man holding the crown sword glanced at his friend grasping his wound. His grin became a scowl as he faced Trenan.

"We took it off a pompous ass too full of himself to know how to use it. Left him naked and dead in the street."

Trenan's gut knotted, his throat closed. "Where?"

"Fuck yerself."

The man lunged, swiping Godsbane at Trenan's chest. The master swordsman's blade jumped in defense, its edge catching the arm of a tavern wench standing too close to him. She screamed, but he didn't allow the distraction of her voice or the hitch in his swing to stop him.

His blade slammed against Godsbane and the crowd around them erupted into panicked screams.

As was the case in any fight, even when sparring and training, Trenan's vision narrowed to include only his opponent and prospective adversaries. The man holding the crown sword drew back to attack anew, the man to his left lunged, the one on his right let go of his wounded hand and plucked a stout club from where it hung at his belt. Behind them, a fourth man unsheathed his steel and waited his go.

Dimly, somewhere in the back of his mind fogged by the fight and grief at the news of the prince, Trenan remembered Danya was amongst the crowd. He imagined he heard Ishla's voice pleading him to bring her children home safe.

Stay out of this, girl. Keep yourself in one piece.

Trenan's blade flashed, knocking the attacking man's sword away before slashing the other's dagger hand and returning to parry Godsbane's swipe. Before any of them recovered, he returned to the offense.

The man with the injured hands got the tip of the master swordsman's blade in the throat, felling him. Trenan twisted his wrist to pull the tip free and blood spattered the face of an innocent man standing beside him. The fellow shrieked, dropped his tankard of ale with a thud and a splash, and rushed from the fight, but the fourth man ran him through.

The edge of Trenan's blade slashed Godsbane's wielder across the chest, opening a shallow wound, then cut deep into the shoulder of the other man's sword arm. Another shriek, another spray of blood.

The master swordsman ducked and the crown sword whispered past his ear. His own steel came up between the legs of the man with the injured shoulder and relieved him of the responsibilities of being a man.

Trenan straightened, parried a blow from Godsbane, and the flat of his blade slapped hard against the wielder's face, spattering it with the blood of his companion's balls. The fellow jumped back, swung wildly. The master swordsman caught the attack, jostled the blade, and relieved the man of it with a flick of his wrist. He moved forward, tip of his sword to the man's throat. As he closed, he realized he'd lost track of the fourth man.

Damn me.

"Where?" Trenan growled between grinding teeth.

The bandit's eyes flashed with anger and fear, but he said nothing. He swallowed hard, the man lump in his throat bobbing against Trenan's blade and opening a nick in his flesh. A drop of blood squeezed out and ran down the side of his neck.

"Where is the boy?"

The man shook his head. Trenan's sword flickered and the tip of the fellow's nose came off.

"Where is he?"

Blood dripped from the end of his nose and the man grinned. "In hell."

The point of the master swordsman's blade entered beneath the man's chin and only encountered mute resistance before it came out of the top of his head. He gurgled. Steel clattered behind Trenan and he spun around, defenseless with his sword embedded in his enemy.

The fourth man stood behind him, a shocked expression on his face and a sword protruding out of his chest. He coughed once, spraying bloody mist into the air, then his knees buckled. The sword slid smoothly out as he collapsed leaving Danya looming over him, blood on her blade.

Trenan nodded his thanks, then yanked his weapon from the man's head with a dull pop and let him fall. He slid his blade back into its scabbard, disgusted with himself for doing so without cleaning the dead fellow's brains off it first, and retrieved the crown sword from where it lay on the floor.

The last time Trenan's fingers touched Godsbane's hilt, they'd been the fingers of his right hand. The weapon's weight and balance were perfect, sitting in his grip as if the master smith who made it cast the sword for him. He hefted it, resisted the urge to swing it. With his eyes upon it, he became aware of the hush in the room.

Trenan looked up. Fear twisted lips and shone in eyes around him and the princess, but he saw anger amongst them, too, a desire for vengeance passing between some of them. He spoke to Danya without taking his gaze from these few.

"It's time to go."

The princess nodded, her own eyes darting from face to face amongst the throng surrounding them. She stepped over the man she'd killed as coolly as if she'd done it dozens of times before, moving toward the master swordsman, and the crowd pressed closer behind her.

"Hold on to me," Trenan commanded and headed for the door.

With the crown sword held out before him, the horde gathered between them and the exit parted. As they passed, a murmur handed from one mouth to the next, following them as their footsteps carried them away from the bodies of the four dead men.

"Careful," he whispered over his shoulder to the princess gripping his sword belt with one hand. She didn't reply.

The muscles in Trenan's legs tensed and bunched as the palpable tension in the air bathed his skin and battered his armor. His heart wanted to ache over the news he'd have to bring to Ishla, but every second they remained in the tavern, the possibility for worse news grew, and the likelihood it would need to be brought by someone other than himself. Having his heart carved from his chest seemed to Trenan a poor solution to stop its pain.

Somewhere in the crowded room, a steel blade scraped a leather sheath. The master swordsman didn't pause, but pointed Godsbane in the direction of the sound. The door was only a few strides away; if the tavern's patrons were going to seek to punish Trenan and the princess for slaying their friends, they'd do it now.

He heard Danya suck a hard breath through her lips and hold it while he concentrated on maintaining short, regular bursts of air to his lungs. If they were attacked, lungs struggling for air or a light head would do him no good. He'd remind the princess of her forgotten lesson later.

The last of the crowd moved aside, leaving the door clear. Trenan gestured with his shoulder for Danya to move past him and exit the tavern ahead of him. As she did, the master swordsman faced the dozens of sets of eyes glaring at him and backed the last few paces to the exit.

Outside the tavern, the night was still warm, but the air was cooler than within, and free of the oily smell of lamps, the cloying scent of sweetweed. Trenan took a second to fill his lungs with fresh air before ushering the princess along the avenue at a jog that set his armor rattling. He didn't expect the tavern denizens to stay put. A fighting man needed to be ready for the worst, so he assumed the entire crowd, their courage bolstered by numbers, might come boiling through the door seeking retribution.

Down the avenue, they took a right turn, Trenan heading them toward the gate to the inner city and the militia quartered around it. Invoke the king's name, raise some swords for protection, then back behind safe walls. The law wouldn't care about the dead men when the master swordsman revealed they'd been slain in protecting the princess.

And they killed the prince.

The ache he'd been keeping from his heart grabbed hold. He thought of Ishla, her command to bring her children back unharmed, of how she'd react. The king might have his head removed from his body for letting this happen to the prince, but it seemed small punishment in comparison to how the queen's sorrow would shred his insides.

Trenan slowed and stopped, listening. Danya halted beside him, her heavy breathing loud in his ears, competing with the hammering of his own blood through his veins. Crickets sang, the wind stirred, but no footsteps followed them. Realizing this proved ineffective for removing the weight from his chest. If the princess wasn't with him and in need of his protection, he'd have welcomed a sword wielding throng falling on him to administer retribution. He imagined it so much simpler and easier to bear than what lay ahead.

Danya glanced along the street, then back to Trenan. Her flushed cheeks gleamed in the moonlight and, even wearing shirt and trousers instead of her customary dress, she resembled her mother enough to send another lance of regret through the master swordsman.

A smile crossed her face. "They're too frightened to follow us."

Her expression and her words reminded Trenan she hadn't been close to hear when the man wielding the crown sword told him they'd slain her brother. Trenan held Godsbane up for her to see.

"Do you know what this is?"

"Of course," she said. "Godsbane. The sword of the realm."

"Do you understand how it comes to be in the outer city?"

Her bottom lip moved like a response lurked on the surface of her tongue behind it, but refused to come out. The smile disappeared from her mouth, one corner twitching downward. Wetness shimmered in her eyes. Not for the first time, Trenan wished he possessed a second arm to put on her shoulder and offer comfort and support, but whenever someone he cared for needed solace, his one and only hand always seemed to hold a sword.

"Teryk stole the sword before he left Draekfarren," he said, his tone gentle. "It came to the outer city with him."

"And the brigands took it from him."

Trenan nodded. A moment of silence passed, Danya's eyes sweeping the chipped cobblestones and scattered pebbles as though she might find words written upon them to help her make sense of things, to deny the reality of what she must suspect.

"Did they," she said finally, her voice so quiet the crickets' song nearly overpowered her words. "Did they kill him?"

A knot clawed its way into Trenan's throat as she raised her gaze to his, and he swallowed in an attempt to keep it down. Her nose, her eyes, so like Ishla's. And her pain. The master swordsman found himself without words, so he nodded once and awaited her tears.

None came.

Danya tilted her head back, lifting her gaze toward the night sky. Her shoulders rose and fell with a deep breath and when she looked back to Trenan, her eyes were clear and penetrating, anger and sadness burning within but their intent unreadable.

"I'll escort you to the gate, your grace, and find someone to take you home. I'll stay here until I...until I recover your brother's body."

She stared at him without responding and he thought she didn't understand.

"Danya?"

"No."

"I have to be sure the brigand told the truth. If he did, Teryk must be brought back for a proper burial. Your mother..." His words trailed away.

"I'm not going back."

Trenan's mouth fell open. "What? Of course you are."

"No. You find my brother's body. You take it back. I'll carry on what he began and honor his name."

The master swordsman's brows dipped, a frown crossing his countenance. "Princess, you can't—"

"Do not tell me what to do," she snapped, her eyes flashing.

Trenan shook his head. Her mother's eyes, her nose...and her spirit. Neither of them needed to speak any more words for him to know she'd resist his commands. He'd have to reason with her, for the queen's sake.

"But you told me the prophecy was about Teryk."

"The firstborn child of the rightful king." She considered the sword in her hand. He followed her gaze to the blood smeared along the steel, earned when she saved his life. A chill ran along Trenan's spine. "If Teryk is dead..."

She let the words lay between them, the rest of the words unspoken but their meaning plain. The master swordsman adjusted his grip on Godsbane's hilt, uneasy.

"And the scroll burned." Trenan's mind mulled through all she'd told him and a spark of hope that he might yet persuade her glimmered to life. "You should at least come with me to find your brother's body. He had the transcription and you'll need it."

Danya slid the blood-smeared blade into its scabbard and put her hand on his shoulder the way he'd wanted to do for her. A jolt of phantom pain jarred his non-existent arm.

"I see what you're trying to do, Trenan, and I thank you for it, but I cannot let Teryk's death be for naught."

"But the transcription."

"I read the scroll to my brother for him to transcribe, but there was no need for him to do so." She took her hand from the master swordsman's shoulder and tapped the side of her head. "I memorized it."

Trenan's heart sank. She was leaving and he could do nothing to stop her short of knocking her over the head and carrying her back to Draekfarren. He bounced the crown sword in his hand, gauging its weight, but couldn't bring himself to strike a woman who didn't deserve it, let alone the princess. The daughter of the woman he loved.

The woman he'd have to tell he let her daughter go.

"At least tell me where you will go."

Danya tilted her head back, contemplating the stars shimmering in the sky overhead. "The scroll spoke of Small Gods. I don't know where to find them, but that's where I'll start."

Her gaze dropped back to his again, tears shining at the edges. A corner of her mouth quivered as though it might lift into a smile, but it stalled and fell back. Trenan wanted to convince her not to go, to comfort her, say something, but the way of sword and axe were his to command, not the intricacies of words. Ishla was the only woman he'd ever found words for, and the only woman to whom he'd never be able to speak them.

"I'll find you," he said. "After I've found your brother, I'll come for you."

She nodded, and then he watched her walk away, shoulders slumped, boot heels scuffing the dirt of the deserted street. An urge to follow and protect the last child of the woman he loved pulled him, but a lifetime of ingrained training and loyalty to the king prevented him. He needed to find the body of the kingdom's heir, return it for burial. Erral would expect it of him, and he had to put the king's wishes first, despite how strongly his own thoughts pushed him toward what he considered best for the queen.

Trenan raised his hand, stared at the sword it held. He ground his back teeth, despising the feeling of being torn. His life had been built around quick, decisive thinking. His life and his losses.

He gripped the hilt tight in his hand and stalked away, determined to find the prince's corpse quickly so he'd be able to catch up to the princes and spare the queen additional pain.

———

Danya held in her sorrow as she left Trenan behind. Her brother—her closest friend—gone. Their lives had been spent in near-constant company with each other. Laughing and playing, adventuring, learning.

But he'd never learned his true limitations, or the art of care.

She wanted to blame the master swordsman. He'd lied to the prince, led him to believe his skills were greater than what they truly were, but Danya understood Trenan was merely another puppet of the king, following orders, doing what his regent expected of him. No, the responsibility for her brother's death lay on their father's shoulders, though he'd never accept the blame for it. Ultimately, it would be the guard assigned to watch her brother who'd pay, and likely Trenan because he'd known the prince left. And Danya was at fault for whatever punishment awaited the master swordsman.

I could have stopped him. I should have.

Tears blurred her vision and she fought to hold them back. She stumbled around a corner, leaned against a wall to collect herself, but felt exposed standing in the open. Eight paces farther along the street, she found the opening to a short, dark alley. The stench was overpowering, but the knotted sob choking her throat kept if from her lungs.

Danya leaned with her back against the wall, let her knees give way and slid along the stone to sit on the ground, her head in her hands. Small Gods, a man from across the sea, the seed of life, her brother dead. None of it made any sense and his death was her fault.

She sobbed into her hands, smothering the sound with her palms. Frustration and despair leaked down her cheeks, her shoulders trembled.

I should have gone back with Trenan.

The thought made her picture the castle—her home, so empty without her brother in it, exploring it at her side, adventuring with her. She thought of swimming in the river, playing hide-and-go-find in the gardens, sparring in the practice ring. The certainty of her mother's sorrow squeezed her heart, then the image of her father's face, his responsibility, hardened it.

The princess dragged her sleeve across her face, wiping the tears off her cheeks. She drew a shuddering breath, nostrils flaring as the stink of the garbage-filled lane assaulted her, pushing her to her feet.

"You didn't die for nothing, Teryk," she said aloud and strode out of the alley.

Her jaw set and determined, she swallowed the last of her tears. She had no use for sorrow; grief couldn't bring her brother back to life. She'd cried her tears and sobbed her sobs.

Should Small Gods rise, man will fall.

The ominous line made her shudder, but Danya didn't know where to find a Small God, or a man from across the sea. Her brother had set out to find them, determined to save the kingdom, and now he was dead, so it fell to her to continue his task. But she couldn't begin to guess where to search for this creature of fable, or a man who couldn't exist.

A lock with no key. Living statue. Seed of life.

None of it made sense. Not a line gave a clue how to save man from the rise of the Small Gods.

A barren Mother.

The priestesses of the Goddess were called Mother. Could the scroll refer to one of them?

Danya stepped out of the stinking alley, straightened her doublet and adjusted her sword. 'Mother' might refer to any woman who'd given birth, perhaps even her own, but there were Goddess temples in the city, and it gave her a place to start. Small Gods and men from across the sea were shadows to chase; a Goddess Mother could be found.

She set out along the avenue, picking her way between potholes in the pock-marked street, unsure which way to head, but knowing she had to go. The night wind stirred her hair and she gripped her sword's hilt, ready should she need to draw it. As her boots carried her along a bridge over the swirling river she paused at its apex and stared down into the dark water.

At first, she saw nothing but the whirlpools and eddies caused by the current flowing around submerged rocks. A chunk of wood bobbed past, destined to catch against the grate separating the outer city from the inner, then a piece of fabric floated by. She watched it drift into the distance, then another caught her attention, followed by another.

A hand floated past, its fingers curled into claws, and Danya gasped. She took a step back from the edge of the bridge, one hand held to her mouth, but curiosity forced her back to the brink. She leaned on the rail, looked over the edge.

An arm. A leg. A head floated by, turning over and over, its shriveled face glaring up at her before rolling over into the water, then tumbling again to cast its dead gaze upon her once more. Other bodies drifted past, carried on the current, their exposed flesh hacked, burned, stripped.

Danya wanted to run from the bridge, but her legs refused to take her. She wanted to close her eyes or look away, but her head wouldn't do that which she asked of it. Instead, she leaned farther over the precipice, teetering above the water as the moon's light reflected on its surface.

The body of a child bobbed past.

Finally, the princess pried her fingers from the bridge's railing, covered her face, rubbed her knuckles hard in her eyes. She sucked a deep breath through her nose, inhaling the scent of the water, and it turned her stomach queasy.

After a moment, she took her hands away and gazed down at the water, ready to view more atrocities. She saw only a log.

"A vision," she whispered.

The night wind rose again, touching her face and whistling by her ear, whispering in response:

Should Small Gods rise, man will fall.

With a shudder, Danya forced her feet to carry her from the bridge and went into the dangerous city, determined to find the Goddess.

XXIV - The Sculptor

*T*HE FIRST BEAD OF sweat formed as Vesisdenperos molded the middle finger of the right hand. The droplet rolled down his temple, along his cheek. When it reached the angle of his jaw, he stopped sculpting, took the vial from the ground by his knee, and caught the drop in the glass container. He put the stopper in the top, then set it carefully back on the ground.

The finger grew to fingers, the fingers into a hand, the hand led to an arm. The clay whispered and sang under Vesisdenperos' expert touch, each knuckle rendered exactly so, each vein and ridge of muscle in the forearm proportionate to his vision of the overall size.

As his work progressed, the master sculptor stopped more often to collect his perspiration in the vial. When he'd filled it to the top, he uncorked another.

The right shoulder came into being, and he directed his attention to sculpting the side of the prone figure, recalling his plan: eight handspans from armpit to waist. Clay collected beneath his nails, clogged the lines in his fingertips. Vesisdenperos hummed.

Waist, hip, thigh.

Each detail exact, meticulously measured and depicted.

Knee, calf, foot.

Not once did he have to flatten the clay and begin a section again, such was the sculptor's skill. Since the time he gained control of his hands, he'd trained for this. A thousand hundred replicas he'd made to get him here, miscues and wrong placements long ago worked from his fingers, banished from his abilities. Every day of his life he'd knelt in a cave like this one, molding the clay, humming, whispering words. Always the same figure, always the same dimensions, never in this cave.

Until now.

He completed the inside of the right leg and paused. He leaned back, raised his arm to wipe sweat off his brow, nearly forgetting himself, but stopped and used the vial. A deep breath inhaled through his nose brought the tang of his own perspiration, the grittiness of the clay, a hint of beeswax wafting from the tapers burning around him. He removed his shirt, the back of it soaked due to his efforts and the sticky heat gathering in the cave. An unseen hand attached to an unseen arm took the damp chemise from his grasp and disappeared back into the shadows.

Vesisdenperos flexed his hands. The ache was beginning, but his dexterous fingers were yet a long way from the twisted, knotted things they'd be when he completed his work. He rested his hand on the sculpture's thigh, leaned forward to examine the clay awaiting his fingers to mold next—one of the most important places, where a mistake likely meant failure.

One of the areas of power.

He rubbed his palms together sending flakes of dry clay spinning through the air in a cloud. After waiting for it to settle, he set to work.

The sculptor formed the scrotum first, setting one testicle lower than the other, shaping it as though the figure stood rather than lay prone, getting the dangle just right. With that task complete, he moved on to the next: the penis. Erect, of course, and large enough to do justice to a creature of such power.

Vesisdenperos' own cock stirred as he formed and molded, smoothed and stroked. It neither surprised him nor gave him pause when it did for it was always so, even in practice. He'd have been more concerned if his manhood didn't stiffen when given the honor of laying his hands on the magnificent specimen.

The construction of the genitals took as long as the arm and leg combined. The veins needed to bulge the right way, the tip shaped in the perfect manner, the ridges straight and true. He formed it lying against what would become the figure's belly, as though contained behind breeches, and its tip extended beyond the spot earmarked for the navel.

More than once, the sculptor stopped and peered into his own loincloth, observing, inspecting, comparing. Another man might have judged himself inadequate when surveying his own worm next to this python, but not the sculptor. The sculpture's python was his creation, as the Father had created the sculptor's worm.

The power center complete, Vesisdenperos leaned back on his haunches and extended his arms to the side. More unseen hands wiped his chest and back with soft, absorbent cloths, the fabric to be wrung out and the salty water collected, but that wasn't the sculptor's job.

He returned to his work, forming the left leg from its inside. His throat hummed, his lips parting occasionally to whisper words the meaning of which he didn't know, but which he'd learned by rote. The leg came into being, kneecap positioned in the exact right spot, toes splayed, muscles contoured.

The sculptor's fingers worked as though each one possessed its own mind, manipulating the clay into a ridge of hip bone, rippled stomach, slabbed pectorals. He leaned in close to do the detailed work of the nipples, pausing to collect his sweat, careful to ensure none of it dropped onto his creation. Not yet.

The torso complete, Vesisdenperos built the left arm. This time, he rendered the hand with the palm facing upward, laboring over the lines, making sure each one matched his, but for two. The line representing strength he made deeper, longer. The life line began farther down the palm, ended sooner. To create the whirls and loops at the tips of the figure's fingers, he pressed his own fingertips into them, the only way to make them identical.

When he completed the arm, he stood, stretched. Twilight muted the glow outside the cave, making it indiscernible from the early dawn light that shone through the opening when he began his work. He nodded to himself, pleased things were progressing exactly as expected. The sculptor allowed a smile to creep onto his lips.

Movements whispered in the shadows around him; the priests were beginning their roles, expecting to complete theirs the same time he finished his. No more time for rest.

Vesisdenperos knelt at the top of the headless clay body, closed his eyes, pictured the face his hands were about to create. He imagined the wide-set eyes, the aquiline nose. High-set bones, full lips. He'd sculpt no hair on head or cheeks, nor any part of the body.

Ears made for hearing. Nostrils formed for breathing. A face never meant to smile.

The sculptor bent to his work, the humming in his throat louder, the words more frequent. Next to the genitals, this was the most crucial part, but his hands moved with the grace and knowledge of practice beyond practice. He knew this face better than his own. Every curve, every hollow, every line honored him in his dreams each night, implanting themselves in his mind until his fingers lost the ability to make any other nose, any other eyes.

Vesisdenperos smoothed the final line from the figure's forehead and leaned back. A sigh shushed through the shadows as the others completed their tasks, as personal and alone as the sculptor's, equally important. Without them, he spent his life to create the most detailed, lifelike statue ever seen. With their contribution, it became so much more.

Together, they created a god.

The sculptor pushed himself to his feet, knees creaking after being folded beneath him, feet aching from toes curled in concentration. His back complained, his head throbbed. In a short while, his fingers would curl into claws, but not before he'd finished.

A hooded figure stepped from the shadows. In his right hand, the man held an ewer, the vessel formed of the clay found in this very cave, designed and molded by the sculptor's hands, fired in his kiln. Vesisdenperos nodded and took the pitcher in both hands, gripping as tightly as his aching hands allowed. Only a few moments remained before they'd become useless, but he needed but a few moments.

He faced the sculpture and the hooded man disappeared into the shadows. Vesisdenperos tilted the ewer, splashing the model's brow with perspiration of his own brow, dampening its chest with sweat of his own chest, moistening its arms with sweat of his own arms. He doused it head to toe, emptying the jug.

Finished, he stepped back and a robed and hooded figure took the pitcher. Another replaced it with a bowl, born of the clay from this very cave, shaped by the sculptor's hands, hardened in his oven. He gazed at light reflecting in the pearlescent white liquid it held. Semen of the twelve priests, plus his own—the first deposited before the sun rose, before the work began.

Vesisdenperos held the bowl in his cramping fingers, extended his arms. The shadows lining the walls of the cave hummed as the priests took up their chant. Words vibrated the clay beneath his feet, the air thrummed with their intonations of power spoken in a language dead before the Goddess banished the Small Gods to the sky.

And I will help them return again.

Vesisdenperos' chest swelled with pride. He inhaled deeply, the musky scent of the bowl's contents invigorating him, making him forget the painful cramps warping his fingers. He tipped the bowl, allowing a thick and stringy stream of viscous fluid to flow over the edge. It spattered the statue's scrotum, drenched its erect cock.

The clay absorbed it hungrily.

The last drop fell and the sculptor turned the bowl upright. A thrill shivered through him, shaking his hands. He bobbled the bowl but kept from dropping it. The hooded figure—the same man or perhaps another—relieved him of the vessel, untangling his gnarled fingers to pry it away.

With his shriveling hand emptied, the sculptor allowed his arms to fall to his side. His fingers were curling and he knew from experience that they'd soon become claws, not opening again until the sun returned, but he'd not see the sunrise marking the new day. This morning, he'd watched the sun creep over the horizon cloaked in hues of purple that became pink and then faded away. He'd drank in its rays, inhaled its warmth, knowing it to be the final time, and he experienced no hesitation at what he must do, no regret.

Another hooded man slid out of the shadows, a black shape born of darkness, and the sculptor wondered if the priests were truly with him in the cave, or if they appeared from where once there was naught but air. This man held a long, curved dagger. Light cast by the flickering tapers danced on its blade, winking and shining as Vesisdenperos watched him approach.

Apprehension fluttered in his belly. His eyes flickered to the clay statue on the ground at his feet.

What if it wasn't as perfect as it needed to be? What if his fingers betrayed him?

His gaze crawled over the prone shape, reassessing every detail. The eyes appeared the same size, one arm a reflection of the other, each leg the same length as its twin.

The power center.

Had he sculpted the genitalia correctly? Had he created manhood worthy of a god?

A splinter of doubt crept into the sculptor's mind and sweat sprang to his brow. His eyes scanned the ground near his feet, searching for a vial to capture the droplets before they escaped, then he remembered that task was complete. His breath shortened, his heart beat faster. He swiped the inside of his mouth with his tongue, attempting to prompt saliva to return, give him something to use to wet his parched lips.

The hooded man touched his shoulder.

Vesisdenperos jumped, startled. He dragged his gaze to the priest, squinting into the blank spot beneath the hood and saw not even a reflection of the light. It appeared as though night had gathered beneath the robe, night with no face but with the hand of a man to hold the dagger.

Something about the lack of face—no eyes to see him, no mouth to speak—siphoned the panic from the sculptor's chest, relieved the ache in his belly. He looked back to the figure at his feet and now saw the perfection of every finger, every joint, every muscle. With a breathy sigh, he expelled the last of it and let peace enter his body.

The priest gestured with the knife, flicking its tip once, and Vesisdenperos nodded. He reached out with both arms, wrists facing the ceiling of the cave, his fingers and hands bunched into painful knots he refused to acknowledge. He wouldn't allow the pain of the work to usurp the glory of the accomplishment.

Chanted words droned back to life, their cadence drifting through the dank cave like wisps of smoke from the guttering tapers. The hooded man holding the knife stepped toward Vesisdenperos, grasped one of the sculptor's forearms with his free hand. His fingers were cold as death, the air whispering from the black hole where his face should be stank of rotted things.

"I am ready," the sculptor murmured, though he didn't need to.

The dagger's pointed tip dug into his left wrist. Pain raced up his arm, his hand spasmed, but the priest gripped him tighter as he drew the knife up toward his elbow. Blood welled up and flowed over the sides of his forearm, a trickle at first, then quickening as the hooded man increased the size of the cut. Droplets of Vesisdenperos' life spilled over and fell on the clay statue's chest.

When the priest withdrew the knife, the sculptor rotated his arm and the blood flowed free. It pattered and splashed, but its wetness didn't mar the surface of the clay chest, it disappeared into it.

The hooded man grasped Vesisdenperos' other arm, inserted the tip, made the cut, then stepped behind him. The sculptor watched his blood spill, feeding the mud man, his life force sucked into the heart of its clay chest. A smile dawned across his face, slow and sure the way the sun had found its way over the horizon that morn. The last sunrise he'd ever see. The last smile he'd ever smile.

A pinpoint of regret pricked the sculptor's heart. All that time and practice, years spent on his knees, alone with the clay. He'd completed that for which he'd been given life and now, without him to see it, his art would live on to change the world.

The flesh of Vesisdenperos' cheeks prickled and the cave grew hazy around him, the dark creeping out of the priests' hoods to steal the light. His knees shook as though they'd give way, but the priest he'd forgotten stood behind him encircled his chest with an arm. Gratitude for the man keeping him from falling, perhaps ruining his creation, flowed through the sculptor, and he opened his mouth to say so, but the touch of a cool metal edge against his throat stopped him.

The priest sliced his throat with one quick swipe. It stung, and the coppery scent of blood filled Vesisdenperos' nose. He gagged, gurgled. The hooded man let him go and his knees buckled. In vain, he attempted to redirect his path and avoid falling on the statue, but he possessed no strength, what wasn't up by the hard work of the day having been freed from him by the dagger's sharp edge.

Vesisdenperos fell upon the clay man's chest, his life's blood flowing straight out of his wrists and throat onto the figure. His breath burbled in his throat, the calming scent of the clay filled his head. The regret he'd experienced earlier returned, but not for the lack of seeing a sunrise this time; he regretted he wouldn't live to see the product of all that practice, all that work. He'd never see why he'd spent day after day hunched over a pile of clay, putting aches in his back and working his fingers until they couldn't clutch or feel.

A rumble beneath him.

With great effort, the sculptor opened eyelids he hadn't realized had slipped shut. He gazed at the underside of the statue's chin, the slope of the top of its chest. The tip of its nose showed beyond the chin and, if he concentrated his focus, he thought he saw the lobes of its ears.

The rumble beneath him again, a sound in his ear. Vesisdenperos' breath caught on the slice in his throat, choking him with blood flowing out of his arteries. The rumble came again, again. Two together, then a brief pause. Two more, a pause.

And the rumble became a heartbeat.

The cave went dark to Vesisdenperos' eyes, as though all the tapers blew out at once, but he realized it was his life extinguishing, not the light. His mind wandered from the beating in the statue's chest as a sculpted arm fell across his shoulders, the scent of his own perspiration and his own blood on clay wafted into his nostrils. A single line from the prophecy the Fatherhood held so dear came to him in his last moment, lending him satisfaction as his life slipped away.

The End of Book 1

The Books of the Smalls Gods continue in The Darkness Comes, available at your favorite book store

Also By Bruce Blake

Curse of the Unnamed epic fantasy:

The Book of Shadow
Shadow Scarred
A Shadow Upon the Land
In the Shadow of the Dragon - coming July, 2023

Khirro's Journey epic fantasy:

Blood of the King
Spirit of the King
Heart of the King

The Books of the Small Gods epic fantasy:

When Shadows Fall
The Darkness Comes
And Night Descends
When Ravens Call
The Twilight Fades
And Kingdoms End

The **Icarus Fell** urban fantasy series:

On Unfaithful Wings
All Who Wander Are Lost

Secrets of the Hanged Man

Blood of the King (Khirro's Journey Book 1)

A kingdom torn by war. A curse whispered by dying lips. A hero born against his will.
With a vial of the king's blood in one hand, and a sword of legend in the other, one soldier sets out on an odyssey that will change his life... or end it.

Forced into the army, Khirro never wanted to fight. And with the monarch dead, any hope for the kingdom's survival hangs by a slender thread. But when the king's shaman charges Khirro with a curse, he's compelled to undertake a journey to the haunted land in search of the outlaw necromancer. And if he fails... the very walls of the fortress itself will fall to the blood-crazed undead.

Can Khirro complete his quest in time to save his realm from a brutal end?

"Blood of the King is a masterpiece. It is as close to perfection as I would consider a book to be."- Ella Medler, author of *Blood is Heavier*
"Blake has a knack for bringing you into the story"
"Mr. Blake's writing is masterful and clear, he draws you into his story and when it's finished you feel like you're leaving an old friend."

The Book of Shadow (Curse of the Unnamed Book1)

Llyris Fildarae is an outcast tainted by a sliver of magic in a world terrified of the supernatural. Loathed and distrusted, she uses her ability to control a magical Unnamed to survive.

Caedric Carpera is desperate to save his son from a deadly illness. He enlists Llyris to locate a lost tome containing secrets capable of healing him, but its location is a mystery that's already claimed lives. Thrust into a hostile world, Llyris and her companions risk everything to find the relic and return before the child's sickness prevails.

But who is the enigmatic old man who appeared out of nowhere to set them on this dangerous expedition? And what does he really want?

Only a perilous mission to an untamed land can save the boy and reveal the truth.
Except some truths are too shocking to be exposed.

"Bruce Blake has written a hell of a book and I am eagerly awaiting the sequel!"
"I'm usually a chapter per night type, but I couldn't put this book down."

On Unfaithful Wings (Icarus Fell #1)

To some, death is the end; to others, a beginning. To Icarus Fell, it should have been a relief from a life gone seriously awry.
But death had other plans.
Icarus doesn't believe that the man awaiting him when he wakes up in a cheap motel room is really the archangel Michael, or that God's right hand wants him to help souls on their way to Heaven. Icarus doesn't believe there's a Heaven, so why should they want his help?
But the man claiming to be the archangel tempts him with an offer he can't ignore--harvest enough souls and get back the life he wished he'd had.
It seems Icarus has nothing to lose, until he botches a harvest and the soul that went to Hell instead of Heaven comes back to make him pay by threatening to take away the life he hoped to win back.
To save the wife and son he already lost once, Icarus will have to become the man he never was. Somehow, he will have to learn to believe.

"The next book in this series cannot come out soon enough for this reader. Not just my favorite Kindle book of the year, but one of my favorite books ever."

"I loved this book."

"Bruce Blake's On Unfaithful Wings is a great urban fantasy novel. I love good character development in a story's protagonist and Blake nails it with Icarus Fell. I found myself rooting for him from the get-go and laughing out loud at some of his observations."

"On Unfaithful Wings was an impressive first novel. All of the characters were interesting and engaging, but in particular the main character and his struggle to reconcile with his new identity/job. This is one of those stories that stays with me long after I read it and I'll be on the lookout for more from this author."

"This is just, simply, amazing. Icarus is one of the best characters I've ever "met", chock full of virtues and faults and doubts and worries and a simple HUMANNESS that comes through so clearly, I almost expect to run into him around the next corner."

"Icarus Fell is a flawed man but a wonderful character. From the moment I started reading On Unfaithful Wings I was pulled along by this interesting character and wanting to know what would happen next."

About the Author

Bruce Blake lives on Vancouver Island in British Columbia, Canada. When pressing issues like shovelling snow and building igloos don't take up his spare time, Bruce can be found taking the dog sled to the nearest coffee shop to work on his short stories and novels.

Actually, Victoria, B.C. is only a couple hours north of Seattle, Wash., where more rain is seen than snow. Since snow isn't really a pressing issue, Bruce spends more time trying to remember to leave the "u" out of words like "colour" and "neighbour" than he does shovelling.

Bruce has been writing since grade school but it wasn't until the mid-2000's he set his sights on becoming a full-time writer. Since then, his first short story, "Another Man's Shoes" was published in the Winter 2008 edition of *Cemetery Moon*, another short, "Yardwork",was made into a podcast in Oct., 2011 by *Pseudopod*. Since then, he has concentrated on writing novels, publishing the **Khirro's Journey** trilogy (*Blood of the King, Spirit of the King*, and *Heart of the King*), three books in the ongoing **Icarus Fell** urban fantasy series (*On Unfaithful Wings, All Who Wander are Lost*, and *Secrets of the Hanged Man*), and the **Books of the Small Gods** series (*When Shadows Fall, The Darkness Comes, And Night Descends, When Ravens Call, The Twilight Fades*, and *And Kingdoms End*). *The Book of Shadow* is the first book in the **Curse of the Unnamed** series, to be followed by

Shadow Scarred, *A Shadow Upon the Land*, and *In the Shadow of the Dragon*.

Bruce has many more projects simmering on the back burner, so stay tuned.

Find Bruce online at www.bruceblake.net for free stories, signed copies, and to keep up to date on new releases